PARKING VIOLATIONS

Clifford broke from behind the gray Toyota where he had been concealed, and pointed the gun at Captain Jack Zodiac, and pulled the trigger.

The first thought that came to him, when nothing happened, was that Mom-n-Pop had sold him a defective weapon, a piece of junk for five and a half million dollars, and were laughing at him right now behind his back.

The captain turned around and saw him, and sized up the situation immediately. In less time than it takes to blink he had his blaster out, and a purple beam made the Toyota beside Clifford burst into flame and sizzling fragments.

Clifford was thrown by the blast into the grille of another car, possibly a Chrysler, but didn't lose hold of his gun.

The captain, down on one knee, followed Clifford with the blaster, so that Clifford was just barely able to dive under a nearby Porsche before the Chrysler followed the Toyota's fate with a deafening roar.

"A good thing," Clifford thought, thinking of his Audi, "I didn't park here."

CAPTAIN JACK ZODIAC

ZODIAC

Michael Kandel

BANTAM BOOKS

NEW YORK · TORONTO · LONDON · SYDNEY · AUCKLAND

For Rose

CAPTAIN JACK ZODIAC

A Bantam Spectra Book / April 1992

ISBN 0-553-29367-2

Published simultaneously in the United States and Canada

*Bantam Books are published by Bantam Books, a division of Bantam
Doubleday Dell Publishing Group, Inc. Its trademark, consisting of
the words "Bantam Books" and the portrayal of a rooster, is
Registered in U.S. Patent and Trademark Office and in other
countries. Marca Registrada. Bantam Books, 666 Fifth Avenue, New
York, New York 10103.*

PRINTED IN THE UNITED STATES OF AMERICA

RAD   0 9 8 7 6 5 4 3 2 1

There was laughter in Antarctica.

—JAMES MORROW
*This Is the Way the
World Ends*

Who told the little kid about sticking pins
into us?

—CHARLES SIMIC
The World Doesn't End

CAPTAIN JACK
ZODIAC

1

The bombs started falling a little after two in the morning. The sky turned an acid white; it hurt your eyes like a mercury vapor lamp. And the ground rumbled and rumbled, an earthquake that kept on going. Clifford's first thought was, he'd better change his name. With Koussevitzky, people would probably lynch him. Tear him limb from limb, snarling Goddam Commie Russki Koussevitzky. Suburbanites were not tolerant in time of war. The red-blooded American flag. How about . . . Kay? Clifford Kay. Nicer rhythm to it; a cleaner, brighter name. Better for business, too. Music and lyrics by Clifford Kay.

Clifford was in fact part Russian, and in fact related to the famous (or once-famous) conductor. Second cousin to Sergey Koussevitzky's grandson, Harry, who lived in Seattle now and did the books for a men's clothing chain. But Harry Koussevitzky and Clifford hadn't seen each other in more than twenty years, and anyway, there wasn't much Russian in Clifford, not if you went by the chromosomes. He was one-thirty-second Russian. No, less, because the Russian was patrilineal and the Y's, as everyone knew, contributed less hereditary material than the bigger, matrilineal-mitochondrial X's. But try explaining the fine points of genetics to a mob frothing at the mouth and gnashing its teeth for vengeance against the goddam Commie Russkis and chanting: String the Red son of a bitch up.

The overwhelming majority of Clifford's chromosomes were Slovak. His mother had been all Slovak, his father at least half Slovak. True, the only Slovak that Clifford knew was how to say hello and good-bye, and the names of some dishes, and a few earthy peasant proverbs like *Ne rushay hono ta budet smerditi,* which he probably didn't even pronounce right. You could see his earthy Slovak origins in the fact that he preferred beer to vodka, preferred ordinary Black Label to the expensive yuppie Stoli from the country that was now attacking our God Bless America and its fruited plain

Still in pajamas, Clifford put on his hat, an old pair of sunglasses, and went outside. Why, you ask, the hat, if he was still in pajamas? The reason: he was growing a little thin on top and therefore feeling vulnerable there, slightly nude, as it were. And he had this image of radioactive particles drifting down. The thought of plutonium dust settling on the top of his head made him shudder. He squinted up at the sky and listened carefully to the rumble, trying to determine the direction of the catastrophe, but there didn't seem to be any one direction. His neighbor Bernie Rifkin called from across the street.

"What the fuck is *this?*" said Bernie in his hoarse bullhorn voice. He was standing in the middle of his lawn, shielding his eyes with cupped hands. In a bathrobe, hairy-legged. And no doubt in a fog of beer, because Bernie put away a couple of six-packs, easy, every night— and not Black Label, either, but the best, Beck's or St. Pauli Girl. At two in the morning, he wouldn't have had a chance to sleep it off.

At the house next to Bernie's stood Bob Petruzzo,

not in a bathrobe or pajamas but in boxer shorts: blue stripes. Totally unashamed of his pot, which stuck out like a wrinkled leather volleyball. He was squinting up at the sky, too. But he kept off his lawn, which had been giving him trouble lately, what with the chemicals and the greenhouse effect.

Clifford, not wanting to shout, walked over to Bernie.

"A nuclear strike on the city, is my guess," he said.

"Holy shit," said Bernie, scowling, because the light hurt. "So they finally did it, eh?"

"Looks like it."

"And where were the sirens? Did you hear any air-raid sirens? I sure as hell didn't. Fucking Essex County. What do we pay taxes for?"

"Yeah."

Clifford was thinking that it might not make any sense now trying to get back to sleep. His alarm was set for four, because even though Marsha lived in Elton Beach, only fifteen miles from Woodhaven, and even though tomorrow was Sunday morning—correction, to-day was Sunday morning—if he left as late as seven or even six, there would be gridlock, what with all the other people out there trying to avoid the inevitable gridlock at eight, because rush hour officially began at nine.

But with World War III now broken out, there was no telling what the traffic situation would be. People might stay at home and listen for evacuation instructions on their radios and TVs. Or they might all climb into their vans and campers and head south, to Aunt Edna's in Norfolk or Uncle Dave's chicken farm in Tuscaloosa, hoping to get the jump on everyone else.

"I suppose," said Bernie reluctantly, "that this is a job for Power Man."

"You might want to wait a day or two," Clifford suggested, "for things to sort themselves out. For the dust to settle. Anyway, most of the damage has been done, I'd say."

"You think?" Bernie clearly wasn't eager to get into his tight costume and go flying off to the rescue. He had been putting in a lot of overtime the past couple of weeks—he was a steam fitter at Burk Brothers, and they were renovating their plant on the river, up by Kimberley. He didn't have the energy these days, he didn't have the enthusiasm. "There might be looters . . ." he began.

The sky got twice as bright, blinding. Then there was a big gust of wind that tore leaves from the trees and a long spray of shingles, like playing cards, off the corner house on Washington and Pearl, which belonged to Mrs. Brady, who was living in Florida now with her daughter and crooked drugs lawyer son-in-law. Then, a thunderclap.

"Jesus!" they all said, jumping.

When they got back their vision and their hearing after a minute or two, the sky was dimmer and the rumbling more distant.

"Hey, Bob!" called Bernie. "Your aerial!"

Bob Petruzzo looked up: his TV antenna was at a forty-five-degree angle, and a piece of it dangled. "Shit," he muttered, and turned and ran back into his house, probably to get a ladder from the garage.

The sirens all went on, and Bernie nodded sarcastically: Way to go, Essex County officials.

Clifford wondered where his children were. Neither would be affected, he realized with a grim smile. As if they were on a different planet. Josh, chances were, actually was on a different planet. With the pills he got from those old bloodsucking spacesalts like Captain Jack

Zodiac. And Trish—poor Trish was adrift in a limbo beyond the reach of anything solid, anything real. When had he seen her last? Once, on a Saturday night at the mall, he thought he saw her: a wavering ghost before a shoe-store window. But that could have been another zombie. They all looked alike . . .

Thinking about Trish, Clifford got a lump in his throat, swallowed hard.

Bernie told him, lowering his voice, pulling him over by the elbow, that it might not be a bad idea if he changed his name. At least get rid of that "itzky" ending. "Not that I'm prejudiced. Hey. But a lot of people around here, they don't think." Maybe shorten the name to Kouss. Kooz.

"I was thinking of Kay," Clifford said.

"Super." And they shook hands, said "Hang in there" to each other, and went back into their houses.

It was almost three. Clifford turned off his alarm, took a shower, got dressed, had an English muffin for breakfast, and took out the garbage. The southern half of the sky was almost a normal night-dark now, but the northern half, especially at the bottom, glowed an aching neon-white. As for the rumbling, it had become so faint, you could have taken it for a departing storm. At the curb, Clifford noticed that his last garbage, the garbage he had put out Thursday night, hadn't been picked up. That meant the strike was on.

"Shit," he said.

2

He was nervous, it goes without saying. Having to face his first formal, official meeting with Marsha's father. They had met a couple of times before, but on the run only, in passing. A muttered hello, a nod, that was it. But this was a sit-down lunch with linen napkins. This was the Popping of the Question. Can I have your daughter's hand? The boxed ring ready in his pocket. It cost a million dollars, twice what he had planned to pay, but Marsha was an old-fashioned girl and wanted a diamond. A million dollars nowadays, he reminded himself, wasn't what it used to be. Even what it used to be five years ago. But it still seemed, Jesus, a lot.

Bumper to bumper on Newcomb Highway. At least the traffic was moving. Then, at the Harper Road intersection, a gridlock update on the radio, interrupting the war news. Fortunately Clifford, in the right lane, was able to turn off into a Park-n-Walk, and fortunately there was a spot there, and from this lot it was less than five miles to Marsha's. Not bad at all. Could have been a lot worse.

The humidity wasn't that bad, either, maybe because of the gusts of air from the bombed city, so he didn't have to stop so often at the roadside AC bars, which saved him a couple hundred dollars, which was great. The heat had been getting impossible, and this was only March, two weeks to go till spring. Some days, you had to duck in every few minutes, gasping and bug-eyed like a trout in the middle of the Sahara.

Clifford had seen one of those new AC helmets in a catalog recently, but the price, two and a half million, was outrageous. He wondered where people got the money to buy the things they did.

He arrived at Marsha's at five, sopping wet and dizzy from the air pollution but otherwise all right. He used his deodorant stick, reaching inside his shirt—left armpit, right armpit, button up shirt, smooth down tie—before knocking on the door.

Marsha opened, bleary-eyed, wearing an old, torn, counterpane housecoat. It took her a minute to focus and say, "Clifford."

"In person," said Clifford. "And I have the ring."

"But, Clifford. It's dark out. What time is it?"

"Five. Five-ten."

"You're five hours early."

"I'll go to a motel," Clifford said, his heart sinking.

"Don't be silly. Come in."

"Hope I didn't wake you up." Not the brightest remark.

Marsha said that she and her father had been up at two, because of the bombs, but after listening to the radio for fifteen minutes or so, they had gone back to sleep. Clifford could hear Mr. Feldman snoring from an upstairs bedroom. A good old-fashioned no-nonsense snore. The bear in its den. Would he give Clifford a hard time, or not?

Marsha had been married before. Twice before, actually. Her first husband was a pale, weedy, anonymous teenager, and the marriage didn't last more than a month or two. Marsha said it wasn't worth discussing. Her second husband was a well-known professor of anthropology who disappeared in the Philippines, on Mindanao, while searching for a tribe even more Adamic than the Tasaday. His name, coincidentally, was Philip, and his photograph, framed, stood centrally on the hutch in the Feldman dining room. Broad smile, big beard, crow's-feet at the corners of the eyes. Jovial, wise, weather-beaten Philip Hirsch. He had disappeared ten years ago—another coincidence, since it was ten years ago, almost exactly, that Clifford's wife, Jeannette, had walked out on him and Josh and Trish, saying she loved them but wanted something more out of life.

All Clifford Koussevitzky wanted out of life was to have a regular family, and a lot of grandchildren around his bed, dutifully wringing their hands, when he finally kicked off.

3

Bob Petruzzo had had a perfect lawn for years, the kind people called manicured or "an emerald carpet." While others suffered, in their lawns, brown patches, white patches, bare spots, thin spots, mushrooms, crabgrass at the edges, and so on, Bob displayed unbroken, flawless, thick, homogeneous green. You knew to the millimeter where Bob's lawn left off and his neighbor's—Maury Bergholz—began, and Maury was no slouch in the lawn-and-grounds department. Maury took pride in clipping his hedges and bushes into neat geometrical shapes. But Maury's lawn was nothing, nothing, compared to Bob's.

Bob knew all the secrets. When to water, how much, how long. When to put down the preemergent poisons, the right way to apply the 10-50-40 fertilizer, or the 30-60-10, or the 40-40-20, and exactly what those numbers meant. He knew how to stop grubs before they went into action. He knew which seed was best in full sun, in intermittent sun, in shade, in heavy shade, and he knew how to thatch, and knew all about the pH of soils, and the merits of lime in pellets as opposed to lime pulverized. In short, he may not have had that much upstairs, but he was an Einstein when it came to grass.

So imagine his shock when he looked down one day and saw dandelions. He blinked. His first thought was

9

that he was in someone else's yard. That, preoccupied, he must have wandered over to Maury Bergholz's. "Jeez, look at that. Maury didn't put down his broadleaf killer." Maybe Maury was having family problems, a nervous breakdown, or maybe it was Alzheimer's creeping up on him, even though Maury was only in his fifties, his early fifties. Everybody and his kid sister nowadays seemed to be coming down with Alzheimer's.

His second thought, when he realized that this was his lawn, all right, and no one else's, was: I'm hallucinating. But since he had never hallucinated in his life and didn't take drugs, only aspirin, and sometimes Fit when he had a bad cold, he proceeded to the third thought, the most solid, the most awful, and the most likely: Ron's Garden Center had sold him a defective forty-pound bag of Weed n' Feed. Bob Petruzzo experienced such a rush of anger, he nearly passed out.

Teeth clenched, he ran to his car and drove to Ron's Garden Center. He had to use all his self-control not to honk at the cars in front of him. Honking, fist waving, and gestures with the middle finger—something you did routinely ten, twenty years ago, when in a hot hurry to get from Woodhaven to Terryville—were unadvisable now, with people so near the boiling point and more than half of them carrying guns because of all the crime. During rush hour, a guy could get his head blown off for forgetting to signal a turn, or for no reason at all.

"It must be that new species of dandelion," Ron said after Bob, red-eyed, sputtering, choking, made his complaint.

"New species of dandelion?" Bob gasped. "I never heard of no new species of dandelion."

Ron nodded, grimaced. "It's very new. They discovered it maybe a week ago. Some kind of mutation. The greenhouse effect, all those ultraviolet rays getting through our atmosphere because the fluorocarbons are screwing up the ozone. It was on television last night, *Sixty Minutes.*"

Bob reeled at the prospect of his lawn being invaded by mutant dandelions.

"There isn't anything I can use?" he asked in a faint voice.

Ron took him over to the poison shelf. "Well, the biotech people have come up with an update. It's experimental, of course. You shouldn't let the children or your pets—"

Bob waved children and pets aside. To hell with children and pets. He grabbed the red plastic bottle with the warnings on it, quickly shelled out the hundred and thirty dollars it cost—highway robbery—and drove home, talking to himself.

On Orchard Street, the white Chevy he was tailgating opened fire, knocking out his left headlight and putting several nicks and one small hole in his windshield. A spray of broken glass in his face and lap. He backed off, but was careful not to brake too hard, because then he might be rear-ended by the car tailgating *him,* and that could start one of those battle royal shootouts that had become so common lately on the road.

If you survived the bullets, your insurance premiums, already astronomical, went completely out of sight.

But, the main thing, Bob wanted to get back to his lawn without incident and without delays. In his mind's eye those new dandelions were multiplying even now and choking out the grass he was so proud of, his top-grade Kentucky fescue. Its precious blades and roots, once choked out, took so much time to replace, to reinstate.

The teenagers Power Man had reduced to a pulp

one evening a month ago, for tearing up the lawn of the
corner house on Washington and Persimmon with the
wheels of their Jeep—some of the neighbors had tsked
and shaken their heads at that, but Bob Petruzzo still
chuckled when he thought of it. Right on, Power Man!
People didn't realize the work, the constant attention,
that went into a lawn. Those asshole scuzzball kids, not
a thought in their heads, just chugging beer and guffaw-
ing, got what they deserved. Bob felt no pity for them or
for their parents. If only there were more superheroes
like Power Man.

4

It was, curiously, through an antiperspirant and not because of radiation exposure, the usual method, that Bernie Rifkin acquired his superpowers. He had been more than half-asleep that morning in the bathroom, still hung over from Poker Night and the effects of a bad cold and a Fit. Consequently, groping in the medicine cabinet, he had taken not his Old Spice spray but the Arrid Extra-Dri stick that belonged to his son. When the stick wouldn't spray, he saw his mistake, but mumbled, "What the fuck," and used the stick, even though his son had conniptions when anybody touched his stuff. The chromium silicate contained in the stick triggered an allergic reaction; there could have been some synergy, too, between the silicate and the Fit. And the alcohol in Bernie's bloodstream, who knows, might also have had something to do with it. An hour later, on the train (he was commuting into the city then), he became dizzy, and his armpits ached. Somehow he got through the day, running a fever and with funny blotches on his face. He crawled into bed without supper. The next morning, he felt terrific.

Attempts by university scientists to duplicate these conditions—they mixed, in every possible combination, the ingredients of the antiperspirant, antihistamine, and the congeners found in the alcohol of St. Pauli Girl lager—were unsuccessful. Professor Hartwick of Adelphi, in an interview that appeared in the September issue of *Nature*, expressed the opinion that no one could acquire superpowers through an antiperspirant, an antiperspirant used in hundreds of thousands of American households and approved, moreover, by the FDA. There was nothing the least mutagenic about any of the chromium silicates in Arrid Extra-Dri. Mr. Rifkin, the professor opined, was an alien from another system, possibly from another galaxy altogether, who was, for reasons known only to himself or herself or itself, posing as a humble steam fitter in a lower middle-class East Coast suburb. When Bernie heard this, he was incensed. "My family may not have come over on the *Mayflower*," he told reporters, "but that don't make me an alien." He brought out his birth certificate, vaccination records, high-school diploma, and draft card, which were all photographed and appeared in major newspapers throughout the country. The stock price of Pfizer, the maker of Arrid antiperspirants and deodorants, shot up thirty points, a gain of almost fifty percent, despite the scientists' inconclusive data. And, for a couple of weeks, until the spotlight moved to the unrest in Burma, St. Pauli Girl was unavailable in the stores and selling on the black market for two hundred eighty dollars a bottle.

That second morning, anyway, the morning after the morning after Poker Night, Bernie Rifkin, feeling terrific, jumped out of bed, went through the ceiling as one might go through a cobweb, and found himself in the attic. Hearing his wife scream, he looked down through the ragged hole that was dribbling bits of sheetrock; and she, in bed, looked up at him, eyes wide.

"Bernie," she gasped, "what the *hell* are you doing?"

5

Mr. Feldman woke at six-thirty, went to the bathroom, and gargled. Clifford, sore from having dozed on the settee in the television room downstairs, was charmed. It had been ages since he heard anyone gargle. The sound brought back childhood memories: Uncle Ralph. Baggy pants, suspenders over one of those old-timey undershirts with straps instead of shoulders, and thick glasses that made his pale eyes look like the eyes of a giant fish staring at you in a municipal aquarium. The skin of Uncle Ralph's cheeks, he remembered, was almost painfully smooth and shiny, as if not only all the hair but the freckles and moles, too, had been scrubbed off with concentrated lemon-scented ammonia and steel wool. Uncle Ralph had a high voice, with a twang. A friendly comedy voice. Where was he now? Six feet under, probably, or else in an old-age home.

Mr. Feldman came down, wearing a worn terry-cloth bathrobe. He started, surprised at seeing Clifford on the settee. "Aren't you early?" he said.

Clifford got up, straightened his jacket, made an absurd little old-world bow, which he instantly regretted. "Trying to avoid the traffic," he explained.

"H'm," said Marsha's father. The h'm sounded like a humph, which Clifford thought meant: The impetuous lover, eh? We'll see, we'll see.

Marsha interposed with some cheerful hostess remarks having to do with coffee, and they adjourned to the kitchen. A small table and a yellow-tile floor covered with cracks and scratches. The Feldmans were clearly not well off. But, then, how could they be well off, with the inflation nowadays and the father retired and the daughter working only part-time because she was taking courses at Essex Community College, in anthropology, going for a degree in honor of her lost second husband, the famous author on primitive tribes?

They sat at the small table. Marsha poured.

The interrogation, which was supposed to have taken place over a fancy lunch—the chicken salad with herbs and capers was waiting, ready, in the refrigerator—began now, over coffee, even though Clifford was the only one dressed for the occasion. Mr. Feldman hadn't even combed his hair yet, and it stuck out in all directions.

MR. FELDMAN, *leaning forward and squinting:* I'm sorry, I don't believe I know your last name. Marsha may have mentioned it, but . . .

CLIFFORD: Koussevitzky.

MR. FELDMAN: Koussevitzky? You're Jewish?

MARSHA: Dad. That's not relevant.

MR. FELDMAN: Not relevant? H'm, yes. It's not relevant anymore. Forgive me. We are dying out.

CLIFFORD: I'm thinking of changing it, actually, to Kay, because of the war.

MR. FELDMAN: But you're not . . .

CLIFFORD: I'm Slovak. Catholic. I'd like to marry your daughter.

MR. FELDMAN: And you're not young, either, Mr. Koussevitzky. What are you, forty?

MARSHA: Come on, Dad. I'm no spring chicken myself.

CLIFFORD: Forty-four. I have two teenage children. My wife left me.

MR. FELDMAN: And mine died on me. It's not a bowl of cherries, marriage, is it?

MARSHA: Clifford has a nice house in Woodhaven. I'll be moving in with him.

CLIFFORD: You're welcome to visit anytime, er, Dad, and can stay as long as you like. We have a full-sized guest room. It used to be my daughter's.

MR. FELDMAN: Married? In college?

CLIFFORD: She's . . . Trish, well, is . . . she's a mall zombie.

MR. FELDMAN: Ah. One of them. I'm very sorry.

MARSHA: Maybe we could ask Mr. Nagel . . . Maybe he could reclaim her.

MR. FELDMAN: So what do you do for a living, Mr. Koussevitzky?

CLIFFORD: Call me Cliff.

MR. FELDMAN: What, I ask, do you do for a living, Mr. Koussevitzky? And don't Dad me, please. I'm not your dad.

MARSHA: Oh, Dad.

CLIFFORD: I'm a songwriter, sir. For the Upbeat label.

MR. FELDMAN: Upbeat label? What's that?

MARSHA: Dad, you know. "Brother Dolphin." "My Silver Lining." They're on the radio all the time.

MR. FELDMAN: So you're a songwriter? You write songs?

CLIFFORD: Yes.

MR. FELDMAN: And you make a lot of money doing this?

CLIFFORD: Not a lot. I'm on the staff, one of ten. It pays the rent.

MR. FELDMAN: You're renting? You don't own your house?

CLIFFORD: Just a figure of speech.

MARSHA: Clifford has paid off his mortgage, and he drives an Audi.

MR. FELDMAN: An Audi.

CLIFFORD: It's a used Audi. I bought it used.

MARSHA: Cliff, don't sell yourself short. You make good money.

CLIFFORD, *producing diamond ring:* Well, here's the ring.

MR. FELDMAN: I see you two have made up your mind . . .

CLIFFORD: Of course, we'd like your blessing. *Kneels on the kitchen floor, presents the boxed ring to Marsha.* Will you be my wife, Marsha?

MARSHA: Oh, Clifford. *Pleased.* You're so conventional.

MR. FELDMAN: My blessing you can have, Mr. Koussevitzky, for what it's worth . . .

CLIFFORD: I'm changing my name to Kay.

MR. FELDMAN: . . . and as far as I'm concerned, though I still try to keep the Sabbath and I eat matzo on Passover, you can bring up the children—if there are children, at your age—whatever way you like. Catholic, Jewish, nothing, it doesn't matter to me.

CLIFFORD: Thank you, Dad—Mr. Feldman. *Takes million-dollar ring from box, puts it on Marsha's finger.*

MR. FELDMAN: However . . .

CLIFFORD: However?

MR. FELDMAN: The religion matters, I am afraid, to someone else.

CLIFFORD: But if you, the father, don't object—

A sudden crash, coming from the refrigerator. A light bulb overhead explodes, making Marsha scream.

* * *

MARSHA: It's mother! *Opens refrigerator, groans, takes out tray. The chicken salad has been arranged in the shape of a grinning skull, noxious purple fumes spiraling up out of its eye sockets.*

MR. FELDMAN: Yes. Emma objects. She's always objecting, bless her heart. She threw a fit, you wouldn't believe what a fit, when Philip decided to wait to have children.

CLIFFORD: Philip?

MR. FELDMAN: Marsha's husband, the Pygmy expert. So many people nowadays put their careers first.

MARSHA: Damn! Damn!

CLIFFORD: Emma is . . . your wife?

MR. FELDMAN: Was.

MARSHA: I can't stand it. She's always interfering. Whenever I want something . . . whenever there's a chance for me . . .

MR. FELDMAN: They waited to have children, and then Philip's plane went down. Emma's probably giving him an earful down there. "I told you so, I told you so." Poor man. I feel for him.

CLIFFORD: Down there?

MARSHA: Call Mr. Nagel!

CLIFFORD: Who's Mr. Nagel?

MR. FELDMAN: Young man—well, you're not young, are you? But take my advice. *The burners on the stove all come on, hissing and shooting sparks.* Cool it with this marriage business. *Blood spurts out of one of the walls like a water fountain, narrowly missing Clifford.* You have money, a house, an Audi, you're comfortable. *Another light bulb explodes, and the fixture on the ceiling begins to rotate.* Why ask for trouble?

MARSHA, *tearing her hair:* I can't stand it. It's not fair, it's not right. I have my own life to live . . . I'm an adult, I'm over thirty.

CLIFFORD: I suppose I could convert . . .

MR. FELDMAN, *shaking his head:* She wouldn't accept it. Emma was always on the ultra side of Orthodox, and now that she's dead, she's even worse . . .

MARSHA: I don't want you to convert! Why should you? There's nothing wrong with Catholicism, it's a perfectly good religion. *Marches to the phone, dials angrily. Smoke comes out of the mouthpiece, but she blows it away and continues dialing.* Hello? Mr. Nagel?

Mr. Feldman shrugs, and his shrug suggests that Mr. Nagel has been called in before, more than once, but never with much success. Clifford sits, the empty jewelry box in his hands, and regards the leering skull-shaped chicken salad on the table in front of him as the lights dim and the scene ends.

6

He uttered a strangled cry when, on his hands and knees, he saw the blue chinch bugs. An almost iridescent blue. More than twice the size of ordinary chinch bugs, they were crawling in and out of the thickly woven turf. He uttered another strangled cry, and another. And whimpered and gibbered all the way to Ron's Garden Center, his white-knuckled hands clutching the steering wheel as if he were not in a car but on a roller coaster headed toward the Mouth of Hell.

The heat, because of the greenhouse effect, was certainly great enough to bring to mind the nether regions: a hundred and ten degrees, and no relief in sight, according to the meteorologists.

Ron nodded, not at all surprised by the chinch bugs. "It's the greenhouse effect," he said. "The damn ultraviolet does a number on the chemicals you put down. The xylenes. Turns them into mutagens. Breaks the carbon-phosphorus bonds. The cis/trans isomer ratio. 5-phenyl-methyl-3-furanyl-cyclopropane. 3-amino-1,3-triazole." He shook his head. "Can't use that stuff anymore, looks like."

"But . . . what can we do?" Bob Petruzzo asked from the pit of despair. He had no idea what a mutagen was, but it sounded serious.

Ron took him over to the poison shelf. "Giant blue

chinch bugs," he murmured, scratching his jaw. He hesitated, as if trying to decide. The black bottle with the red lettering? The green-and-yellow bottle with the purple lettering? Both bore the skull and crossbones and a hundred cautions in fine print. "It's all experimental, you understand. Just came in today. The companies won't take responsibility . . ."

More than three hundred and fifty dollars for the two poisons. Bob groaned, wrote a check, drove home with these latest biotech weapons of lawn defense in a brown paper bag—and that same afternoon, he was back at Ron's Garden Center. A new kind of grub, this time. And a new kind of ant. And something that looked like a new kind of crabgrass.

Bob's voice now was curiously flat. The left side of his face twitched, and a strange, evil light flickered in his eyes as he took out his checkbook and waited for Ron to ring up the purchase at the cash register.

"Goddam lawn," he said to himself, but absolutely everyone in the store could hear him. People shifted uncomfortably, looked away. "Eat me out of house and home," Bob went on. "Goddam lawn. I break my back. For what?"

The stuff from the black bottle with the red lettering and the stuff from the orange bottle with the dark-green lettering he applied using the hose, but the stuff from the green-and-yellow bottle with the purple lettering and the stuff from the gray bottle with the scarlet lettering had to be applied in more concentrated form, from a hand-held pump sprayer. The combined stink was awful, the worst Bob had ever smelled. Even with his face mask on, he gagged. And the sun beat down unmercifully. A hundred and fifteen degrees. The sweat poured off him. His eyes burned from the sweat and from the chemicals. His head pounded.

With every step, he cursed his lawn. He who for so many years—twenty years—had treated it with greater respect, solicitude, and affection than he had ever shown his wife and children. Or shown his ninety-year-old mother in the nursing home in Franklin.

The fumes from the chemicals formed a peculiar haze over the greensward. Perhaps this was because the humidity was so high that day, and the sun so fierce, and the ultraviolet so intense.

Also, had anyone listened carefully—over the continual noise of the traffic—he would have heard a peculiar bubbling, down where the roots of the grass were. A percolating that probably never would have taken place if it hadn't been for the greenhouse effect, and, who knows, maybe the radiation, too, from the bombed city . . .

"I ought to pour concrete over the whole goddam thing," said Bob Petruzzo, "and paint it green."

Hardly an original sentiment, but heresy, shocking heresy, in the mouth of one who had had no rival when it came to the creation of a suburban carpet of living emerald.

And, leaving, on his way to discard the empty bottles of experimental poison, he actually kicked it.

Kicked his own lawn.

As he fumbled with the garage door, the lawn, behind his back, stirred, or seemed to stir. But it may have been only a freak gust of air rippling through the grass. Except that a gust of air could not have accounted, surely, for the growl—it was definitely a growl—that then issued from the earth.

7

Joe Smith blinked. He saw a white ceiling. He was on his back, looking up. Someone came and bent over him—a mild face—and asked how he was feeling. "Am I in a hospital?" Joe thought. He tried to remember if there had been an accident. What was he doing last . . . ? A blank. He had been at the mall . . . and then what?

The nurse extended a hand, helped him sit up. Joe wiggled his toes, moved his fingers, swiveled his head a little. Broken bones? Restraining bandages? Pain? No, he seemed to be all right, in one piece.

"Don't stand yet," said the nurse. "You might get dizzy. It takes a few minutes to acclimate."

Joe was sitting on a gray table. One of those narrow padded tables, with sections, that doctors used for examinations. The nurse's hair was cut very short, like a man's. Perhaps she *was* a man. Joe couldn't tell for sure. The person was sort of in-between. Neuter.

What had happened after the mall? Where had he gone? Home?

"Would you like a Coke?" the nurse asked.

Joe nodded, said please. His voice sounded strange, as if it had an echo to it but not quite. Occasionally a connection on the telephone was like that. A very slight time lag, hardly noticeable, between saying a word and hearing it. Something out of sync.

Had he banged his head? Fallen? Been mugged? It was shameful, the number of people mugged these days. In malls, parking lots, broad daylight. Beefing up security didn't help. His cousin Ellie had had her pocketbook snatched walking out of Sears. The strap burst on her shoulder, left a bad welt. Too many homeless, desperate people out there, with everything costing ten times more than it did a year ago.

An ice-cold can of Coke, with a straw: wonderful. Nothing like a Coke to settle your stomach, to clear your head.

Now he remembered where he had gone after the mall. To lunch. It had been almost twelve.

What time was it now?

Joe noticed, sipping the Coke, that there was no clock on the wall. No clock on any wall. He frowned. Hospitals and doctors' offices always had clocks on walls.

The doctor came in, smiled, shook his hand. He held a clipboard but wasn't wearing a white smock. "I'm George," he said, introducing himself. A look at the clipboard. "And you are Joseph David Smith."

"Yes," said Joe.

"Height, five feet nine and a half inches. Weight, a hundred and fifty-two pounds. Brown eyes. Blood type, B positive. Appendectomy, age ten. Wisdom teeth pulled, age thirty. Married Leslie Karen Giambucci from Apalachicola, Florida, divorced uncontested, no issue. Embezzled twenty-five million eight hundred and seventy-three thousand dollars as purchasing agent at Burk Brothers—"

"That's a lie," said Joe, but, oddly, felt no surge of emotion at the accusation. Neither fear nor anger. He was probably not back to normal yet, from whatever it was that had happened to him. "That wasn't embezzling.

How do you know all this stuff anyway? Did I talk in my sleep? You're not a doctor, are you."

George smiled. "I am many things," he said. "A doctor, too, after a fashion. I should say, rather, after the fact." He winked at the nurse, as if that was terribly clever. But she—or he, if it was a he—did not return the wink, and actually seemed to disapprove of the joke. George cleared his throat with a businesslike "Hem," tapped the clipboard, and said, "You had a cholesterol problem. That's what did it."

"Did what?"

"You don't remember?" asked George.

"They often don't," said the nurse.

Joe closed his eyes, tried to think. After the mall, he had gone to lunch. To a Taco Bell, yes. Ordered—what did he order? A Mexican pizza? A super-burrito? A steak fajita? Junk food, sure, and chock-full of cholesterol. But with all the troubles and aggravation he had in life, damned if he was going to give that up, too. Going cold turkey on the cigarettes had been murder. Joe was not about to eat oat-bran muffins and waddle-march at six in the morning with the health nuts in the neighborhood, no thank you, swinging his arms as if he were swimming, looking like an asshole . . .

"What, I had a heart attack?" But he felt no pain, no tightness in his chest. He felt fine. Just a little funny.

Smiling, George shook his head. "It was a stroke. The buildup of fatty plaques in the arteries can also cause—"

"What are you talking about, a stroke? I don't have any paralysis." He wriggled his fingers and toes. They wriggled perfectly.

George shook his head again, and the nurse took Joe by the arm, to steady him, as George said: "Of course there's no paralysis. It was fatal. You were gone in under three minutes."

Joe looked at the doctor—and now remembered seeing, on the table in front of him, at the Taco Bell, the Mexican pizza, with only a few bites out of it. He remembered the curious way it dwindled. As if there had been a spotlight on it, and the light narrowed, contracted into a point at the center of the pizza, and then went out.

"Are you trying to tell me," Joe said, "that I'm dead?"

"Bingo," said George.

"And they have Coke in the afterlife? Give me a break. I mean, what a great franchise that would be. Think of the market: every generation since Adam. Things go better with Coke. Sure."

"He's skeptical," said George.

"They usually are," said the nurse.

Then the two of them, with a sigh, went through a routine they had obviously gone through hundreds of times before. Or thousands, or millions, or maybe billions of times. The doctor took Joe's right hand and pressed it against Joe's chest, over the heart. After a few moments of that, he told Joe to put two fingers to the side of his neck, where the carotid artery was. After a minute of that, he told Joe to press the two fingers to the wrist of his left hand. Meanwhile, the nurse held a pocket mirror to Joe's mouth; then to his eyes, so he could see his pupils. The doctor put a thermometer in Joe's mouth, under the tongue, took it out after three minutes, and showed him the reading.

But what really convinced Joe was the fact that he was not upset by any of this. He was completely calm, as if nothing in the world could possibly faze him anymore.

George lent him a pen, had him sign a couple of

forms, shook hands with him again, and the nurse ushered him down a hall and to an office area, where an impersonal woman with no breasts asked him to sign more forms and gave him a packet of papers.

"We recommend," she said, "during your period of adjustment, a support group for the deceased. The one nearest you is at the Holiday Inn on Wymbeck Road, off Exit 19 of the expressway. It meets Thursday evenings, eight-thirty."

"Wait a minute," said Joe. "I live only five minutes from there."

"Yes," she said. "It's the one nearest you."

"But I . . . Aren't I . . . ? I thought I was supposed to be . . ."

"You are, Mr. Smith," the lady said, gave him a brief, unseeing smile, the kind bank managers give you when the transaction is over, and then she took up the next packet of papers and tapped them on her desk edgewise, once, twice, three times, to straighten them.

Behind him, waiting, was someone else. The next deceased.

Joe, uncertainly, almost stumbling, made for the door. He glanced at the papers in his hand. An orientation kit. It included what looked like an application for a Social Security number. Outside the swinging glass doors were steps, a street, traffic. He blinked. He was in Maplehurst. Was this a joke? A dream? Had someone, maybe, slipped him—in the Mexican pizza—one of those polka-dot pills that whisked you to places not on any map?

But a closer look, as he walked, told him that he was not in Maplehurst—not quite. For one thing, the diner on the corner of Broadway and Teller Avenue. It was the old white flaking brick before they put on new vinyl siding five years ago. And the sign said RICK's, not NICK's.

For another thing, the houses on Teller Avenue had gray lawns, every one of them, not green lawns. But gray, here, seemed to be the proper color, because the lawns were all well maintained, even lush, and on most of them the sprinklers were going.

The traffic was worse than he had ever seen. But that made sense, in a way, if you considered the population: all those, that is, who had passed on, since the dawn of time.

Joe looked up at the sky. Instead of sun and clouds he saw earth, dark–brown earth with roots in it here and there. Directly overhead, high up, a worm slithered.

8

Oh yeah.
You gotta be
My silver lining.

These sure are rough times,
Scrapin' nickels and dimes,
The dollar it don't go far.
But with you at my side,
Baby, I can ride
To the moon in my getaway car.

Can't see the day
Through this damn ozone haze,
The sun it don't wanna shine.
But when you're near,
Baby, even landfill air
Smells like a forest of pine.

I see your bright face
After the rain.
I hear your sweet song
After the thunder.
I feel your soft love
After the storm
Of my pain.

Oh yeah.
You gotta be
My silver lining.

We got moral decline,
All kinds of crime,
People they don't seem to care.
But when you smile,
Baby, the bad guys go to jail
And they all get the 'lectric chair.

Society's ills,
Poppin' polka-dot pills,
And everyone fadin' with AIDS.
But when you take my hand,
Baby, I'm a thousand-piece band
In a Fourth-of-July parade.

I see your bright face
After the rain.
I hear your sweet song
After the thunder.
I feel your soft love
After the storm
Of my pain.
Oh yeah.
You gotta be
My silver lining.

9

He went through his son's old comic books for ideas. The name to use. The kind of costume to wear—the colors, chest logo, whether or not to have a cape. And what to do, if anything, about a secret identity. He consulted Cliff Koussevitzky, who—being in entertainment, sort of—knew better than most what the public would like. "I don't want to make a fool of myself," Bernie said.

He would be a crime fighter, of course. There was no question about that. All those years, taking the train into the city and reading, in the morning tabloid, as the train rattled from station to station, about this rape and that stabbing. The cabby, father of five, who was shot in the head by a sniper for no reason. The Irish cleaning woman who was planning to retire in a couple of weeks and go live with her widowed sister outside San Diego but instead was bludgeoned so badly by a crack-fiend on her way home from church that she was a vegetable now, on a respirator. And so on, a dozen such stories every day of the week. It made you sick in the stomach.

The police could do nothing, especially with all the rights-of-criminals crap that tied their hands and also now that there were so many women, for Chrissake, on the force. What could a woman do in an emergency, when bullets were flying and you had to get physical?

Clifford asked him which particular superpowers he had. "You could base your name on that. The Flash, for example. He's superfast."

Bernie counted on his fingers.

One, his strength. There seemed to be no limit to that. Lifting cars was nothing. He had tossed an old Chevy Nova into orbit the day before, because his brother-in-law decided to junk it and didn't want to go to the trouble. This feat hadn't even put Bernie out of breath. Hadn't even raised a sweat.

Two, he was invulnerable, like Superman. Mosquitoes, pins, broken glass couldn't get through his skin. Fire from a match didn't burn him. He had pressed his hand on the coil of an electric stove turned up all the way, as an experiment. It felt warm, that was all.

He could hold his breath for an hour, incidentally. Two hours, more, with no discomfort. He tried that in his bathtub. His wife had kittens.

Three, he could fly. He had been to Houston—it took him five minutes, without straining. The wind flapping in his hair. He went at night, because he didn't want to be seen yet, not without a costume. "People would think I was some kind of alien." There was a lot of resentment against aliens lately, after that tragic incident on the cruise ship in the Pacific, off the coast of Mexico, which claimed the lives of forty American Shriners.

He had been to the moon, too. Piece of cake. As easy as going for a walk around the block. He hadn't been able to time this flight, because the Van Allen belt screwed up the liquid-crystal display on his wristwatch. He wasn't sure whether it took him three hours twenty-two minutes or two hours thirty-three minutes to make if from doorstep to moon to doorstep.

Four, he could see through walls. He could see people in their bathrooms—several houses away, if he wanted. He could see them taking showers, taking craps. "Cliff," he said, pulling Clifford closer, with a confidential man-to-man leer, "you should've seen the knockers on this girl on Persimmon Street. Incredible!"

Finally, five, he could shoot particle beams from either hand.

"What are particle beams?" Clifford asked.

"I don't know all the physics, but it's sort of like lightning," Bernie explained. "Except that you can't hear or see anything. There's this blur in the air, that's all, and a little bit of a glow when it's dark. Ever go fishing out in the bay at night? In the summer, you get that glow in the water, sometimes, on and off. A couple of feet down. So faint, you have to look out of the corner of your eye to see it."

"Phosphorescence?"

"That's the word. But when a particle beam hits its target, kerblooey, fireworks!"

He had zapped one of those big blue iron mailboxes, to test the beam. From two blocks away, using only his left pinkie. The box exploded with a pop, as if there had been a bomb inside, and tiny confetti fell all over the place like a snowstorm for almost fifteen minutes.

"That's a federal offense, you know," Clifford said.

Bernie shrugged. "Ehh, it was probably nine-tenths junk mail. You know, we start getting Christmas catalogs now in August. Can you fucking believe that? It was a week before Labor Day. I remember the missus went out and the mailbox was stuffed with six of those suckers. L. L. Bean, Nieman Marcus, Eddie Bauer. And then, after that, it's every day."

"Well, let's see. Maybe you could call yourself Zapman."

Bernie shook his head, made a face. "Sounds like a joke. And too much like Batman."

"How about The Zap? You could have a Z on your chest."

Bernie thought about that, imagined people shouting, "Hey, there's The Zap! In the nick of time!" Or: "Hey, thanks, Zap. You saved the day, man."

"It's still too jokey," he said. "A superhero shouldn't sound like a detergent. Anyway, Zorro has a Z on his chest."

"No, I think he makes Z's on other people's chests, with his sword."

"Same difference."

Clifford couldn't think of a better name but said he would work on it.

Actually, it was Bernie himself who came up with "Power Man" a few days later. He was watching television, and there was an ad about a new flashlight with a revolutionary new battery system called a Power Pak. The announcer said, "Power Pak," making the P's pop, for emphasis. He said, "Power Pak," again, popping the P's again, and again, a third time, the same way, and Bernie, ensconced in the sofa and more than half into his St. Pauli stupor, repeated the words himself a couple of times, popping the P's, too. Pak made him think of Pac Man, and from that he went to Power Pac Man, or Power Pak Man, which didn't have a bad ring to it, but the name was too long; it had too many syllables or maybe the wrong rhythm. Power Man was better.

He went upstairs and asked his son.

"What do you think of Power Man?"

His son, who had his notebook open in bed, for homework, and was watching a different TV show, screwed up his mouth and squinted like a professional wine taster, then nodded slowly.

For the costume logo: a large, thick P, bright red, on a royal-blue background, and a circle of white stars around the P, ten of them, one for each of the Ten Commandments. The colors, of course, were those of the American flag.

No cape. A cape would flap too much; it would get in the way. Besides, Bernie had always felt that capes were old-fashioned and, when it came down to it, sissyish. Captain America didn't wear a cape. The Flash didn't wear a cape. Spiderman didn't wear a cape. Daredevil didn't wear a cape.

Bernie Rifkin wasn't going to be posing for the cameras, anyway. He was going to be wading in there and righting wrongs.

10

Lucy Hoff had it up to here with the garbage strike. All that stuff sitting on the curb, stinking and not being picked up, accumulating, attracting neighborhood dogs and cats, who tore open the plastic bags at night and scattered chicken bones, meat wrappings, eggshells, tea bags, not to mention used Kleenex and Kotex, yuck, all over the sidewalk and street. And those big ugly flies buzzing around, as if this were some place in the Deep South, for Chrissake, or a slum, and not a community where the cheapest house went for three hundred million.

And they were expecting sex company, too: the Humphreys, Bill and Barb; the Baxters, Dave and Mona; the Peppos, Art and Janice. Their guests, coming up the driveway, would all see the garbage, they couldn't miss it.

"You really should do something about the garbage," she said to Mark.

Mark looked at her slowly over his glasses, over the newspaper. It aggravated the hell out of her, how calm he always was, no matter what happened, so comfortable and confident in his armchair. Not one wrinkle of a frown on his face, as when they had that awful radon-in-the-basement scare, for example, last week. Sometimes Lucy suspected he was on Quells or Quiets, but she never caught him popping or sniffing anything, and they had been married almost seven years now, sharing a bathroom.

"What can we do?" he said mildly.

"It's piling up!" she exclaimed.

He nodded, as if to say: "Of course it's piling up. There's a garbage strike, remember?"

It drove her up a wall sometimes, how insufferably logical he was, like a computer giving you error messages at the bottom of the screen.

The Humphreys arrived, cheerful as always; but Barb blinked a lot, seemed flustered, under a cloud. It turned out, after they got their gin and tonics and sat on the patio together, with the beautiful view of the willow tree and the old-timey fence and the winding brook in dappled shadows, that her best friend Belle had just tested HIV positive and was a nervous wreck.

Barb sighed. Would they have to start talking about *that* again? The testing, the right to privacy, the notification of partners, and how long it took, and was there any hope.

"She never thought it would happen to her," said Barb, and took a big glug of her gin and tonic.

Lucy couldn't stand the way Barb got after a few drinks. Poetical-philosophical, with a lilt in her voice, as if she were some kind of deep thinker in an ashram on a mountaintop, when in fact she was one of the stupidest people Lucy knew.

The Peppos showed up, Art and Janice, with a friend of Janice's, Bill. Janice told everybody that Bill was recuperating from a messy divorce and needed lots of mothering. She and Barb started to coo over him. Bill was quite handsome, with a wonderful mane of thick black hair and an ascetic artist's face. Meanwhile Art and Mark got into their usual discussion of what the yen was doing and what the Fed should do, leaving Bill—Barb's Bill, not the gorgeous friend—out in left field, since he was an electrical engineer and didn't know diddly about Wall Street.

The Baxters didn't come until it was growing dark and Lucy told Mark they probably wouldn't come and he should go ahead and put the steaks on the grill, even though she knew they were coming. The Baxters were always two hours late; it didn't matter what the occasion was. At the Hammonds' wedding, they missed not only the ceremony but the reception, too. Dave and Mona were trying to prove something by always coming last. It aggravated the hell out of Lucy, but she tried not to show it, because Dave had clout at Shaw, where she worked, now that his brother was a vice president.

Family shouldn't count in business, but it did, it did. That was the way of the world, and you couldn't change it.

Mona complained about the heat. She had a headache all the time, she said, from the heat. "I'll move to Yellowknife," she said. "Or Barrow. Put my forehead on a piece of tundra. Jesus, won't it ever let up?" She drank her gin and tonic as if it were water.

Dave wanted to talk about the war. "Did you hear about the Russian paratroopers in Compton? It was on the radio coming over. Fantastic." Apparently, the paratroopers landed on Interstate 28 right in the middle of rush hour, and this after a tractor-trailer had jackknifed on the outbound ramp near Exit 40, a bad spot at any time of day. "The motorists—well, you know how they get. You know what commuters are like during rush hour, after a hard day. Animals. The Russians didn't have a chance, a prayer. And we outclassed them, too, in firepower, which tells you something, doesn't it, about our society. The N.R.A. lobby is too damn powerful, if you want my opinion."

"Did you know," said Janice suddenly, turning to the girls, "that Gloria's fucking her piano tuner?"

"Gloria?" said Barb.

"You're kidding," said Mona.

"How's your sister, by the way?" Art asked Lucy. "Still in California?"

Lucy didn't like to talk about Jeannette, the black sheep of the family, who was now active in a save-the-dolphins anti-oil-spill group that made its political statements through the assassination of public officials. Jeannette had been in jail twice already, the last time for killing someone in the Department of the Interior. Lord knows what would become of her.

They all had to hurry indoors after they ate, because Mark and Janice and Bill—Barb's Bill, not Janice's Bill—were getting bitten. It was that new kind of mosquito or black fly or whatever it was, which raised awful welts that itched like the devil for days.

This turned the conversation to Lyme disease, which Mark was an expert on, because he had had it. They talked about camping, Deet, and rheumatoid arthritis.

Bill—Janice's Bill, the gorgeous friend—told them how gin and tonics with kiwi fruit were a whole different thing from gin and tonics with lime, and they all had to try it. Janice, hand on his arm, said enough gin and tonic for him, because she wanted him nice and hard for fucking. This caused an embarrassed silence. Bill might have been a friend of Janice's, but he was a stranger to the rest of them, not in the group; there was no telling where he had been and what he had done, and with whom. That was the whole point, wasn't it, safety. That was the whole point of everyone getting doubly tested first. And swearing the oath about being exclusive. With witnesses and signatures. United we stand, divided we fall. Lucy was really put out. But it was hopeless. Janice could be so selfish, so willful; when she got something into her head, it was like talking to the wall.

To tell the truth, Lucy was probably a little envious, too. Bill looked so intelligent and full of soul. She wouldn't have minded having him herself, running her fingers through Mr. Beautiful's long black mane while he humped her, grunting.

No one else was in the mood to fuck, apparently. Except Barb's Bill, who always had a thing for Janice. But Janice was off him lately. The man, face it, was boring. So she didn't nod to him to come, too, when she led her Bill upstairs by the hand.

The conversation moved to Jeannette. Art, for some reason, was interested in her.

"How are her kids doing, the ones she abandoned?"

"The girl's a mall zombie," Lucy said with a sigh, "and the boy's a space cadet."

"And their father, he's still, what was it, a song-writer?"

"Children need a father, an authority figure," Mona put in, loopy. She would probably be snoring, head back, mouth open, in a few minutes.

"Did the father remarry?" Art asked.

"Not yet. He's thinking of it," said Lucy. "I still see him occasionally. A very old-fashioned type. An emotional dinosaur. He considers me family, his sister-in-law. I kind of like it. It's so quaint. It would be a better world, you know, if more of us were quaint." She was feeling the gin herself. Her lips were Novocaine numb.

Dave started in on his diet, his cholesterol level, but Barb said she was sick of hearing about triglycerides. She began to reminisce about Belle, who was going through hell now because she had just tested positive.

"I should probably get tested," Mark said, as if to himself.

"What are you talking about?" Lucy said. "You *were* tested." They had all been tested, doubly tested, certified clean, that was the whole point, wasn't it, but Janice had to go and bring a stranger into the group, even if he was mouth-watering gorgeous. Janice was willful, like a spoiled child. Her cake and eat it, too.

"Well, I heard from Edith," Mark said. Edith was his first wife, a bubblehead with enormous tits. "And she has it."

"But you're clean," Lucy insisted. *She* was clean, no retrovirus, even though both her first and third husbands, Sebastian and John, died of it last August. They had gone to John's funeral. Very touching. Half the people toothpicks, *sic transit*.

"You realize," said Mark, "that those tests are not a hundred percent."

Lucy didn't want to hear about it; she was sick of hearing about HIV and AZT, and T cells and Karposi's sarcoma. She shut him up with a kiss. She wanted to make love, because thinking of Janice and Mr. Male Beauty going at it upstairs in the waterbed made her antsy and romantic. She would do it, damn it, with her own husband if she had to. She pulled Mark down on the thick rug, which had been vacuumed and scented that morning for the purpose, and started taking off clothes. No one else joined in; they weren't in the mood. Dave and Art talked real estate, Bill sulked, Barb went on and on in a lilt about the meaning of it all, and Mona snored, head back, whistling on the exhales like an old woman. What a depressing evening. It took Lucy more than half an hour, even with the help of the sex Yoga trick and that new state-of-the-art vibrator they bought last Friday at The Sharper Image, to have her orgasm.

11

Mr. Nagel was a thin, short, bent man who carried a box of tools, like a plumber, and his eyes glittered. A rat's eyes, caught at night in your headlights. Introduced to Clifford, he smiled shyly.

"Pleased to meet you," he said, offering a bony hand covered with long black hairs.

Clifford liked the man instantly. How many people nowadays said, "Pleased to meet you"? Old-world manners. Was Mr. Nagel Jewish, too?

"No, German," said Mr. Nagel, apparently a little telepathic in addition to his other talents. "Nine-tenths German."

"I'm three-quarters Slovak," said Clifford, and they shook hands like Central European neighbors.

"Hello, Osborn," said Mr. Nagel, and shook Mr. Feldman's hand, too.

"Sorry to bother you at this hour, Ben," said Mr. Feldman. Seven in the morning, after all, Sunday.

"Would you like some coffee, Mr. Nagel?" asked Marsha. "Mother's driving me crazy."

"You're getting married?" guessed Mr. Nagel. "Congratulations." And he turned and said, "Congratulations," to Clifford, too, and shook his hand again. Clifford was charmed. This exorcist or ghost exterminator, despite his rodent looks, was obviously a decent, civilized individual.

43

A gentleman. His stringy frame reminded Clifford of the leather-skinned Portuguese construction workers he always saw at the Restaurante Martinho, a place in Terryville, off Route 9A, where he had supper a few times a week, because it was unpleasant eating alone, no human noises around you, except for a talk show on the radio, and that soon was harder on the ears than silence.

Mr. Nagel took a sip of coffee and got to work.

From his toolbox he pulled a white chicken and cut its throat with a razor, deftly, quickly, before the bird had time to squawk or beat its wings. He dribbled a circle of bright-red blood around the kitchen table, and around the tray of chicken salad in the shape of a skull. He did this with a bored expression, as if he had done it hundreds of times before. The salad subsided, with a sigh, to its normal form, and the purple fumes disappeared. Mr. Nagel stuck a Band-Aid on the chicken's neck and tossed it back into the toolbox, where it gave a stifled cluck-cluck, evidently not much the worse for wear.

Then Mr. Nagel lit a punk stick and took out a brace and bit, a small box of mothballs, and an adjustable wrench. A light bulb exploded in the living room, and the sound of gas hissing filled the house. Mr. Nagel looked worried, but his movements were slow and deliberate. With the brace and bit he made a two-inch-diameter hole in the wall, about six inches over the light switch; he filled the hole with mothballs, then inserted a kind of plug with a bolt head, which he tightened counterclockwise with the wrench.

"No Latin?" Clifford asked, curious.

Mr. Nagel smiled but didn't answer; he was in the middle of something difficult and had to concentrate. He gave the plug a few more turns, then took a tiny bottle of sky-blue paint and with a tiny brush carefully painted the number 6 on the bolt head.

Meanwhile, angry faces were appearing on the ceiling. Glaring down, they soundlessly cursed, sputtered, gnashed their fanged teeth. And the nineteenth-century ceramic shepherdess in the alcove in the hall crackled and spit flame.

Mr. Nagel, hurrying now, produced a pitch pipe, sounded a note on it—poot—and began to sing "Annie Laurie" in an awful falsetto. Immediately after the words "answer true," the plug flew from the wall with a loud pop, like a champagne cork, and hit him square in the forehead. He sat down hard on the floor, his eyes wide with surprise. On his forehead Clifford could see a backward sky-blue 6, since the paint was, of course, still wet. Around the stunned exorcist, mothballs bounced and rolled.

"Mrs. Feldman won't listen to reason," Mr. Nagel said in a hoarse whisper.

Mr. Feldman rolled his eyes, meaning: Did she ever?

"And she's gotten stronger," Mr. Nagel went on, half to himself. "Maybe she's been working out. Or has help now. I don't know." He shook his head. The reversed 6 sadly went from side to side.

"You can't do anything, then?" asked Marsha, anguish in her face. Clifford took her hand.

"The mothballs usually work, at least short-term," Mr. Nagel replied, still sitting on the kitchen floor.

"I told you, didn't I, this was a waste of time," Mr. Feldman finally said. "Why can't you two, Marsha, Clifford, live in sin like other people? Emma wouldn't object to that. Who gets married these days anyway? The divorce rate, it says in the papers, is eighty-six-point-three percent and going up."

They invited Mr. Nagel for breakfast, but he declined politely, saying he had to be at church at nine. He and the missus always tried to be out the door before eight, otherwise it was murder finding a parking place, even though their church was practically around the corner, and as far off the beaten path, moreover, as one could get in Elton Beach, being located as it was right next to the dog pound by the railroad tracks on Cedar Avenue five blocks south of Newcomb.

"A pleasure," said Mr. Nagel, shaking Clifford's hand a third time. "Good luck to you. Very sorry I couldn't be of assistance." And with a wave to Mr. Feldman and Marsha and a ratlike twitch of his face, he took his box of tools and left, closing the door decorously behind him.

12

The lunch, clearly, was off. The Question had been Popped and the million-dollar ring given, but even barring further disruptions from the beyond the three of them could hardly sit down to a chicken salad that moments before had been a sulfurous head of hell. Clifford wasn't at all hungry. Marsha, close to tears, said she had a migraine and wanted to be alone. She went upstairs, tight-lipped. Mr. Feldman looked at Clifford but apparently had nothing more to say. The subject had been exhausted. Two plus two equals four, young man or not-so-young man, too bad, but the mother says no, what can you do? Clifford nodded, feeling choked up, close to tears himself; he walked backward to the door. Slivers of glass, from the light bulbs, crunched and tinkled under his shoes. Mr. Feldman didn't even say, "Nice meeting you" or "Do come again."

It was sweltering outside, though the sun was still low in the sky. The day was going to be a killer, would probably set a new record, which seemed to be happening now almost every week. In less than a minute, Clifford was covered with sweat, and his heart was doing flip-flops. He started back to his car, but happened to look down a side street and see Mr. Nagel walking away, toolbox at his side.

On an impulse, Clifford followed the man, quick-

47

ened his pace, caught up with him, and said, panting, "Excuse me."

Mr. Nagel raised an eyebrow. "Yes?"

"I wonder if I could ask you some questions," said Clifford.

"Certainly," said Mr. Nagel. "But I am almost home and—"

"I know, you're on your way to church. I thought, perhaps, if you don't mind, I could join you at services. I'm a Christian, too. And then afterward we could talk a little . . ."

Mr. Nagel looked up at Clifford with a hesitant expression. "Actually—of course you're welcome—but our church is not exactly a Christian church. I don't know if you . . ."

"You're Muslim? Buddhist? That's fine with me. I respect all religions."

They stepped through the gate of a modest row house, and at the door Mr. Nagel introduced Clifford to Mrs. Nagel, who had her coat and hat on already and was holding her pocketbook. A large, ordinary bleached blonde with nothing of the rodent about her, she shook Clifford's hand cheerfully, said her name was Maureen, said that unlike her husband she didn't have any psychic powers, but Clifford would have to excuse them, whatever his business was, because they were on their way to church and hadn't missed a sabbat service in nine years. Nine years ago the toilet had backed up, in the middle of the night, Saturday night, when her in-laws were staying over and also Beth Ann, her overweight cousin from Maine. Beth Ann got the flu then, wouldn't you know it, Beth Ann's timing was always like that, and the runs, awful, and of course they didn't have anything like a bedpan in the house. Who has bedpans in the house? Unless you're an antique collector. They gave Beth Ann a mixing bowl, but that didn't work too well, the poor girl was so large.

"I didn't sleep a wink," said Mrs. Nagel. "I told Ben to go to church without me, but he stayed home instead like the angel he is and helped out. We've been married thirty-two years, isn't that incredible?"

There was a loud, long rumble in the direction of the city, and what sounded like the chatter of gunfire.

"We should get going, dear," said Mr. Nagel, looking at his watch.

"I know," she sighed. "The parking is dreadful. Brother Cain has proposed we expand the lot or go high-rise, but it's all so expensive nowadays, land, labor, and our congregation is not that big anymore, since the purge."

"I'm surprised you're wearing a coat," Clifford couldn't help remarking, "in this heat."

"I know," said Mrs. Nagel. "But I don't feel dressed, going to church without a coat. I guess I belong to the old school."

Clifford repeated his request to join them, if they didn't mind, at services, because he really had a serious problem—a personal problem—and he hoped that Mr. Nagel could help him, if they could talk later, just for fifteen minutes or so. It had to do with contacting the dead.

13

Captain Jack Zodiac held out a horny hand. The pill, nestled in the center of his palm, was a slender capsule, lemon-yellow—more precisely, a lemon-chiffon-sherbet yellow, with deep vermillion dots in it, dots so small, you almost couldn't see them. It looked expensive. Josh whistled. Bobby Bergholz hummed in admiration and said, "A lotta shit, man."

The captain nodded. "This'll take you outside the local cluster, no question."

Josh had never been that far. He wasn't sure about this. Only last week, he had got stranded somewhere in the Oort cloud and almost froze his butt off before the stuff wore off. Thinking about it still made him shudder. What did you do when there was no call box in sight and your oxygen was running low? What did you do when a seaweed tentacle came snaking out of an innocent-looking crater and wrapped itself around you fifty times before you could say, "Wha—"? The perils of space. Not everyone came back.

But, then, who cared? I mean, what was there to come back to anyway?

They were in an AC bar on Harper Road, across from Farmer Carver's pumpkin stand. Condensation trickled down the windows, and the refrigeration units growled like an old bulldog weight lifter, in a cartoon, going for a gold medal in his sleep. Every five minutes, the manager came around to collect his twenty dollars, except in the case of someone well off, who paid for a block of time up front, with a credit card: a whole half hour. But usually such types didn't come here in the first place; they had a private lift service from the Park-n-Walks if they were really rich, or they had those helmets from The Sharper Image, which made them look, the nerds, like walking purple Tootsie Pops.

The manager was the bouncer, too. He looked like Bluto except without the facial hair; even had tattoos—a string of bombs falling down his meaty biceps and forearms like a formation of geese. If you didn't fork over your twenty when he passed, and there was no waiting, out you went, out the door headfirst through the air (the door had a special electronic eye, to open quick and shut quick), and if you broke your nose or cracked your skull on the pavement, tough garbanzo beans, Jason, the sign SAYS NOT RESPONSIBLE FOR INJURIES SUSTAINED UPON EJECTION FROM THE PREMISES.

A dog-eat-dog world, as Captain Jack would say, and often did. Capitalism.

"How much?" asked Josh, making up his mind.

Captain Jack smiled his flinty smile, and the crow's-feet and countless other weather-beaten cracks and seams on his spacesalt's face deepened and doubled sardonically. The captain was always bad-mouthing capitalism, but he was one hell of a capitalist himself; could have held his own with the worst of the Wall Street sharks, or the best of them, depending on your point of view.

"How much?" asked Josh.

The captain pulled his faded blue captain's cap down over his eyes and said, "Seven hundred thousand."

"For one pill? Jesus," said Bobby Bergholz.

"I don't have that kind of money on me," said Josh, eyes fixed on the beautiful little capsule, lemon and vermillion, in the captain's rough hand.

"I'll trust you for it," said the captain. "Fly now, pay later."

Josh would have to break into a lot of houses to scrape together seven hundred thousand. It would have to be a house a day—a house a night—for two weeks at least, unless he got lucky. And it wasn't good to owe Captain Jack too long. He would start looking the other way when you said hi.

"Okay," said Josh.

"Wait!" said Bobby Bergholz. "Count me in."

The manager came around and took a twenty from each of them, without a "Thank you" or even a nod, and moved on. The AC bar was full already. This day was going to be a killer.

Captain Jack looked at Bobby Bergholz out of the corner of one of his skeptical squints. The kid wasn't too bright, was lousy at breaking into houses, especially now with all those latest computer-chip surveillance devices that phoned the police if you sneezed on the wrong frequency or let the door sniff an unentered fingerprint. The only real money Bobby had ever got was from ripping off his old man, and that ride was pretty much over, since the old man, who didn't have too much upstairs either, had finally caught on and put retinal locks on everything, even the Chivas Regal.

Bobby—let's face it—was a punk, and would probably end up in Franklin State, in a ward for crackfiends, where they kept you full of Quiets around the clock and sometimes veggied you permanently, with a shot of frog-green L-50 at two in the morning, to make sure. L-50 wasn't legal, but it made life easier for all concerned.

That had happened to Dave.

Josh gave a pursed-lip nod, which meant: All right, let the kid come, too, what the hell. If he can't pay it, I'll pay it, don't worry, you know I'm good for it. I mean, after all, come on, I've been doing this almost a year now.

Captain Jack adjusted his faded blue captain's cap, moved it a little to the right, and that meant: It's your funeral, Oscar, not mine. And he produced, from his captain's jacket pocket, a twin of the seven-hundred-thousand-dollar space pill, just as lovely and beckoning, and the boys each took one.

"Got your blasters? Your direction finders?" asked the captain.

To the back of the tongue, a hard swallow, no water necessary for them, and an implosion of air, foop, where they had been. No one even turned around, space cadets were so ordinary now, which tells you something, doesn't it, about our society.

14

He first suspected something was wrong when he heard a cough behind him, though no one was there, and turned and saw, on the grass, Fluffy's collar. It was unmistakably Fluffy's collar, the silver sequins arranged in the name FLUFFY, though the strap was torn at one end, was chewed at, and the buckle was surprisingly dull, like metal that has been in the sea for a couple of months. Or in an acid bath for an hour.

Bob Petruzzo had never cared much for the dog, had not missed it when it disappeared. It was his wife's thing; let her pay for ads in the paper if she wanted; let the kids make weepy faces at the dinner table when another day went by and still no one answered the ads. Kids and women liked to be sentimental about stupid little animals.

"Listen," he told his family, bothered by the memory of the cough and the chewed collar, "you all stay off the lawn for a while, okay? I put some chemicals down, poison."

Then, right after that, Princess disappeared.

"Princess, Princess," his wife called at the open door the next morning, holding a bowl of cat food in her hands, the gourmet Norwegian salmon loaf that was Princess's favorite. "God, I hope she wasn't hit by a car."

Bob didn't say anything, but looked out the window

at the grass, which seemed to throb evilly in the rays of the setting sun, as if *it* knew, chuckle, chuckle, what had happened to Princess. Bob rubbed his temples. His imagination was running away with him, filling his head with ridiculous science-fiction Venus flytraps and Audrey Twos and Threes. "I have lawn on the brain," he thought. And little wonder, after all the aggravation with the new mutant dandelions and giant blue chinch bugs and crabgrass that now had thorns that went right through your heavy-duty leather garden gloves, making scratches and punctures that itched like crazy, suppurated, and wouldn't heal without an antibiotic. Not to mention the endless running back and forth to Ron's Garden Center, and Ron churning out that scientific gibberish about the greenhouse effect. And the thermometer going up and up, and up.

Thank God for air conditioning.

Looking out the window, Bob saw that the grass needed cutting again; it was three, four inches too high. "Goddam lawn," he muttered. Hadn't he mowed Sunday, just two days ago? He hated mowing now, and not only because of the murderous heat. The grass was no longer beautiful, no longer a pride and pleasure to look upon. Time was, there was nothing he liked better: walking effortlessly, steadily, in overlapping crisscrosses through unbroken green, while before him the mower hummed with contentment as it made even neater what seemed already at the height of neatness. A model for others to marvel at, strive for, and envy. They would all ask themselves, "What's Petruzzo doing that I ain't doing?"

But now: uneven, discolored clumps here, there, everywhere. And places where the ground sank underfoot, almost as if you were in a bog, mud sucking at your shoes.

It was embarrassing now to be out there mowing.

People driving by would say to themselves, "Look, there's an asshole who needs a lawn service but he's too cheap."

So Bob got up extra early the next morning, Wednesday, to avoid both the heat and the mental remarks. He would do the mowing before he went to work, and if the noise bothered the neighbors, tough shit for them. He put up with squealing tires and blaring radios at two, three in the morning; why should he be at the receiving end all the time? Let other people get red in the face for a change.

Bob was in a foul mood.

Even though the dawn was barely glimmering and the sun wasn't up, the air was insufferably close. Bob took off his pants and shirt, went out in only his blue-striped boxer shorts. No one would see him, just a few truckers, who rumbled by, off and on, and they didn't look any better in their shorts than he did. They, too, had big pots, most of them. But this morning, surprisingly, there were an awful lot of cars, an unending stream, maybe because of the Russian invasion. The cars were practically bumper to bumper. People turned and looked at him.

Bob didn't care. "Fuck you," he said to no one in particular, to the world at large, and started up the mower.

In less than a minute the mower was sputtering, the blades jamming the way they did when you tried to mow and the grass was so thick that it wouldn't dry out even a few days after a rain. Grunting, bending over, Bob checked the blades, the gas, the oil; made sure the spark plug wasn't loose. No, the problem was the grass. The grass was not especially wet, but it was very coarse, he noticed, coarser than he had ever seen it, worse than quack grass. The cut pieces seemed to twitch angrily at him. He blinked. He started up the mower again. In less than a minute the blades were jamming again. He swore.

He was standing, just then, in one of those soggy spots of the lawn. He stepped, tripped, almost fell. A hole, damn it. How could there be such big holes and such big lumps in the ground, suddenly? Was this vandalism, damn it? Or some bastard sabotaging him? The newspapers were full of sick people sabotaging things.

Bob looked down and saw a piece of trash. Kids were always tossing trash on the lawn. He picked it up: a gray strip of something like fur. It *was* fur. And he recognized whose. This was—yes—Princess's tail.

With a gasp of understanding, he threw it from him. The mower tilted to the left, sinking, and Bob's left leg sank, too, all the way to the knee. He pulled his leg out—the skin was burning, as if from liniment or jellyfish—and then, as the lawn groped for him again, he ran, stumbled, staggered to the safety of the driveway. He looked back at his mower. It was on its side now and slowly disappearing into the green. The expensive five-horsepower Honda he had bought only last year. Jesus Christ.

Teeth clenched, hands trembling, Bob Petruzzo pulled open the garage door and got the ten-gallon can of gasoline and a box of wooden matches. This, damn it, was war.

15

A motel conference room. Gray walls; the conference table in the center also gray; all the chairs empty except one. A man reading a newspaper. Joe Smith enters stage left, ill at ease. Looks at his wrist, shakes his head as if he did something stupid again, looks around. A minute of silence. The man in the chair slowly wets his thumb and index finger with his tongue, and slowly turns a page.

JOE, *finally:* Uh, excuse me—is this—the support group?

MAN *looks up from newspaper, smiles:* Yes.

JOE: I guess it's eight-thirty. It's the damnedest thing, I keep looking at my watch, and there's no watch.

MAN *nods:* Right.

JOE: You're the only one here? It hasn't started yet? They told me it was Thursday at eight-thirty. Although how anyone can tell what time it is . . . I can't figure that one out. Or the day, for that matter. There are no calendars, either, are there?

MAN: Hardly.

JOE: It doesn't make sense.

MAN: I know.

Joe takes a seat at the table, at the far end from the man. Looks at the door, looks around the room, but there's nothing, really, to see. There's just one framed print on the wall, and it's so gray—an etching or a watercolor—that it's practically indistinguishable from the wall. Joe drums his fingers on the table, looks at his wrist again, and again shakes his head.

JOE: Wonder why they're late. Do you think maybe it was canceled?

MAN *shrugs:* Probably the traffic.

JOE: Yeah, the expressway's murder. I was lucky, I was able to take the service road, because I live right near here. *Laughs.* I said "live," didn't I, "I live right near here." *Pause.* This is weird.

A longer pause. Joe starts to look at his wrist again but stops himself.

JOE, *to make conversation:* The service road wasn't any bargain, either. Everybody was trying to use the shoulder. Even the grass. Lucky there weren't any cops around. By the way, do they have cops here?

MAN: Oh, sure. *Nods.* Why not?

JOE: And people still lose their temper, too. Blow their tops. Not what I expected.

MAN *smiles, nods.*

JOE: One guy, whew, I cut in front of him . . . But I guess guns is one thing people don't have down here. I mean, what would be the point? It's really strange. I don't know how you take it all in stride.

MAN: I don't take it all in stride. That's why I'm here.

JOE, *half to himself:* I suppose I could look up people, too, Mom, Dad, Billy. Old Mr. Giambucci. *Chuckles.* This is going to take some getting used to.

The man returns to his newspaper. Joe sighs, looks around the room, drums his fingers on the table.

* * *

JOE, *finally:* Uh, excuse me. *Pause.* Mind if I ask you a personal question?

MAN *looks up from newspaper.*

JOE: Just curious. I was wondering how you . . . I mean, were you hit by a truck, or had a heart attack, or was it some crackfiend in an alley? The crime has got so bad, even out where we are. My sister was attacked . . . I was just wondering how you went. We all go in different ways.

MAN: Cancer.

JOE *makes a face:* That's tough. I guess I was lucky, going quick. No pain. Didn't know what hit me. Cholesterol, a stroke. Like somebody turning out the lights. You suffered a long time, had tubes in you, and all that?

MAN: About three months.

JOE *tsk-tsks:* Awful. A lot of pain?

MAN: Oh, yes.

JOE: That's the worst thing. That's gotta be the worst thing.

MAN: I kept wishing it would be over. I prayed a lot.

A group of people enter. They all take seats. The number of people and the number of seats are exactly equal, and each person goes straight to his or her seat, as if they've done this many times before. William, the leader, sits in the middle, looks at everyone, smiles, and consults his clipboard.

WILLIAM: Sorry we're late. The traffic was murder. There was an accident between Exits 17 and 18A going south, and a lot of rubbernecking, as usual. Have all of you filled out the disclaimer forms now and the 740-H?

JOE *raises his hand:* I'm new.

* * *

William passes some papers to him down the table; they go from hand to hand, with an efficiency that shows that this has been done many times before. As William continues, Joe takes out a pen, reads the forms, frowns, fills them in.

WILLIAM: Now, a major problem, which we haven't discussed, but which Eugene brought up last week, is boredom. Eugene, you recall what you said?

EUGENE: Well, I said I was bored.

WILLIAM: Yes.

EUGENE: I miss my stamp collection. When I was bored . . . before, up there, you know . . . I'd get out my stamp collection. I specialize in American stamps, nineteenth century, most of it's after the Civil War. The 1870s. It's worth a fortune.

WILLIAM: And you don't have your stamp collection here.

EUGENE: The stamps here are all the same.

WILLIAM: Yes, that's my point.

EUGENE: Gray.

WILLIAM: Precisely.

EUGENE: You can hardly read them.

WILLIAM: Thank you, Eugene. As I was saying, boredom is a major problem here. That is why we encourage people to seek employment. A nine-to-five job is a great way to make time pass, though time, strictly speaking, doesn't pass here, as no doubt you've noticed. Nevertheless.

ETHEL *raises her hand:* William.

WILLIAM: Yes, Ethel?

ETHEL: I was a buyer for a department store. Thirty years. They gave me a silver serving tray, from Tiffany's.

WILLIAM: And?

ETHEL: There just aren't any openings for buyers at the mall. And to Rosewood, or to the city, it's too far.

PEGGY: Nothing in Maplehurst, Ethel?

ETHEL: Not a damn thing. So what am I supposed to do, sit in traffic three hours a day breathing exhaust fumes? It's not healthy for you.

JOE: You're worrying about your health?

WILLIAM: Retraining might be a good idea for someone like Ethel. The job market here is bound to be a little different. Supply and demand, after all, supply and demand. Now, our bureau offers postmortem career counseling . . .

The scene fades slowly as William drones on, until his voice is disembodied, and that, too, blurs and fades into the featureless gray, which is like a television screen after the station has signed off, except not as bright and with no jumping or flickering lines.

16

On his first outing, Power Man was flying over the notorious Kingston suburb of the city, that den of violence, drugs, AIDS, child abuse, and organized crime, when he saw, with his telescopic vision—and his infrared vision, too, since it was dusk and the pollution hung black and heavy in the air—a woman on an apartment building rooftop being attacked by several greasy, swarthy types in bandannas, leather jackets, and nose rings.

"Hot dog," said Bernie, and swooped down on the group with a triumphant whoosh.

The woman was naked and apparently had already been raped. She was babbling incoherently, holding her hands together as if in prayer, pleading with the despicable creeps not to throw her off the roof, which they were now trying to do, chasing her and laughing.

Power Man alighted on the roof with a satisfying crunch of gravel under his boots. He immediately dispatched two of the creeps with a particle beam from his right index finger. Two stabs of the finger, and two bodies were blown apart into floating ashes, just like that.

Another creep he blew off the roof with his superbreath.

Then he charged the remaining four creeps, who

only now—this had all happened so quickly—turned to face him. Power Man punched the closest creep in the head, which split apart like a pumpkin, spraying the others with blood and bits of brain.

"Oops, don't know my own strength," he said, quipping the way heroes did in the Marvel comics his son had recommended. Heroes and villains always exchanged wisecracks as well as blows in their rooftop duels. But these Latin American scum probably didn't even know English.

Power Man took one of the men by the scruff of the neck and hurled him in a high, wide arc into the street below. A creep, cursing, tried to stab him, but the knife blade snapped in two; Power Man gave him a brief laser stare and fried his face; the creep threw up his hands with a scream and fell to the gravel, lifeless.

The last creep fled, but Bernie caught him, said, "This'll teach you to rape innocent people," and impaled him on one of the poles on the roof used for clotheslines. The man gurgled, kicked and twitched a few times, and was dead.

Bernie flew back to the woman, but she shrieked in wide-eyed terror and jumped off the roof herself. This took Bernie so completely by surprise that by the time he thought of flying down and catching her in midair, it was too late, she was a limp, broken doll on the ground, barely visible in the dark alley that ran along the side of the building.

"Shit," said Bernie. "I haven't got the hang of this yet." And he took off, skyward, into the gathering night.

17

It wasn't until the severed human head was produced and placed on the lectern that Clifford realized—he hadn't really been paying attention—that this was not only not a Christian service, it was an anti-Christian service, of the Black Mass Satanic variety. He was sitting, in other words, in one of those witch-cult congregations he had read about not that long ago in the magazine section of the Sunday papers.

Mr. Nagel, noticing Clifford's uneasiness, leaned over and whispered, "This is only sympathetic symbolism. We don't go in for human sacrifice. We're fundamentalist, yes, but within reason."

Yet the head looked absolutely real. Had they got it from a medical school or what? It gave Clifford the shivers. The whites of the eyes showed between half-open lids. Dirty, dull, spoiled-milk whites, which somehow seemed, even without pupils, to have the power of sight. They seemed to turn and regard Clifford with irony, as if to say, "And what are *you* doing here, Koussevitzky?"

Brother Cain went on intoning his sermon, which had a great deal more to do with fund-raising and the congregation's parking problem than with the Prince of Darkness. Clifford didn't catch all the words anyway. The chugging of the AC unit overhead was very loud—an old BTU unit—and every so often a train whistle would blow, and the whole church would shake as the train passed, because the tracks were less than twenty feet away, in the back. Added to this ambient racket was the constant yelping from the dog pound next door. You could hear the dogs even over the AC.

The service concluded with an invocation and then a psalm sung backward and upside down. The upside-down part was done by everyone standing on his head. Clifford had a moment of acute embarrassment when he saw legs kicking in the air, skirts falling over heads, showing panties, pink, violet, apricot, so he hurriedly got down himself and did his best to stand on his head, too, which he hadn't done since high school, in gym. The floor in the pew was dirty, sticky. Like the floor in a movie theater, it had cigarette butts and black globs of old chewing gum. Clifford sighed with relief when the psalm was over.

Then everyone filed out, and proceeded to a rec room where coffee and coffee cake were being served. Brother Cain stood at the doorway, smiling, shaking each worshiper's hand, and saying, "Damn you."

To Clifford he said: "Haven't seen you before, I don't think."

"I came with the Nagels," Clifford replied, forcing himself not to grimace, because the man's hand was cold and clammy. The hand of a corpse. "I'm, er, visiting."

"Well, damn you to hell for coming." And, almost as an aside, "We can always use new blood."

Clifford laughed, nodded, and stepped into the rec room.

He wanted to talk to Mr. Nagel, but others came over—everyone knew everyone here, it was a close group—and there was a stream of gossip and chitchat that Clifford couldn't see how to interrupt, it was so friendly. Mrs. Nagel introduced him to the Sparks and the Mullers, who congratulated him on his upcoming marriage. "Isn't that lovely." "So few people get married these days." Mrs. Spark was fascinated with what he did for a living. "My goodness, is it hard to do? But of course it must be. Where do you get your ideas? How did you ever decide, of all things, to be a songwriter?"

It really wasn't all that glamorous, he explained. He worked in an office, with nine other songwriters.

"I just love your song about the dolphins," gushed Mrs. Spark. "It's so refreshing to hear something positive for a change. The songs these days on the radio, they're all about murder and mutilation, murder and mutilation. It's disgusting, don't you think?"

Clifford would have thought that a Satanist wouldn't object to a little murder and mutilation in a popular song, but he kept this remark to himself and said only that that was the whole idea of the Upbeat label: to look on the positive side of life.

The conversation turned to Brother Cain's sermon and the parking crisis. Mr. Muller's opinion was that the members ought to carpool more, or even look into buying a used bus, which had been done by a congregation up in Franklin.

"I didn't know they had witches in Franklin," said Mr. Spark.

"They don't," said Mr. Muller. "It's an Episcopalian congregation. My friend told me about it. He's Episcopalian."

"I guess that witches and Episcopalians," Mr. Spark said philosophically, "have some of the same problems."

"A used bus would cost us next to nothing. A few million dollars."

Clifford finally got Mr. Nagel off to a side, where they could talk. He told him, awkwardly, hurriedly, what he wanted: to explain things to Mrs. Feldman, to let her know what kind of person he was, and that he didn't mind converting, not even to the most orthodox form of Judaism. That he would devote himself to Marsha totally. If Marsha wanted to go on taking courses in anthropology instead of working, that was fine with him. His only desire was to make her happy. He was an old-fashioned man, believed in the old values, in the family gathered around the hearth on Christmas Day. Hanukkah, that is. He meant Hanukkah. Christmas or Hanukkah, it didn't matter, not as long as they all loved one another and kept together. His children, true, were not home at the moment. Josh rarely dropped in; he was, Clifford admitted, a space cadet. The boy was usually either in some seedy dive with undesirables or else on a planet in another galaxy, dueling with God knows what kind of sentient rollmops. Kids that age, it was hard to bring them down to earth. And Trish, his daughter, was even farther away, unfortunately. She had become one of those teenage Flying Dutchman shoppers. He had never thought that such a thing could happen in his family. It was Jeannette's fault, walking out on them like that; divorce was so damaging to children. But Clifford was confident that with a woman in the house again—a wife, a mother—his children would return. And if they didn't, he would go and find them, reclaim them, bring them back, and they would stay. He was determined to have a family again, his family again. Didn't Mrs. Feldman want the same for Marsha: a family, children? Surely she did, she was old-fashioned, too.

Mr. Nagel fidgeted. He wrinkled and twitched his nose like an uncomfortable, puzzled rat. It was an embarrassment for him, hearing all this personal stuff from a virtual stranger.

"You can't," he finally muttered. "You can't communicate with the dead, not to that extent. Unless of course you—" He was going to say something, but changed his mind.

"Unless what?"

Mr. Nagel shook his head. "It really is not possible, Mr. Koussevitzky—"

"Kay. I'm changing my name to Kay. Or maybe Kaplan."

"Mr. Kay, Mr. Kaplan. I'm very sorry. I do sympathize with your problem. But you saw the difficulty I had, today, with the mother. Even the mothballs didn't work. She's an extremely stubborn woman. Mothers can be stubborn enough, you know, impossible to get through to, even when they're alive."

Clifford sighed, nodded. It was true. He remembered his own mother, the way she had insisted he snort fairy dust because all the other kids were snorting fairy dust. She didn't want her son to be branded eternally a chicken wimp. How would he ever get a good job? "I'm sorry, Mr. Koussevitzky, but our files show that you didn't snort fairy dust in elementary school. It says here plainly on your transcript, CHICKEN WIMP." But all the drug did was give him a splitting headache and a trickling nosebleed that got all over his pillow. He had hated it.

"No fairy dust, no television," his mother would say, stabbing an implacable finger at him when there was only five minutes to go before one of those fabulous *Sesame Street* special rerun festivals starring Kermit.

"Mr. Nagel, you said 'unless.' Unless what?"

Mr. Nagel squinted in such a way that the long black hairs of his brows bristled like whiskers. He looked around furtively, obviously hoping that someone would come and interrupt this conversation. But everyone else was chatting and sipping coffee in different groups.

"Well, unless," he finally said, with great reluctance, "a person is really desperate."

"I am really desperate," Clifford assured him. "Marsha won't marry me as long as her mother objects, and I can't live without her. I mean, without her as a lawful wedded wife in a traditional ceremony, veil, bouquet, something borrowed, something blue, and rice thrown."

"You would do anything? Risk anything?"

"I would go to hell and back for Marsha."

Mr. Nagel gave him an odd look, then said, "Well, yes, in a manner of speaking, that's it."

"You mean—?"

"The only way you can say everything you want to say to Mrs. Feldman and be sure she's listening is to go in person. Pay her a visit."

"In the land of the dead? The hereafter? That's possible?"

"Oh, yes."

"To go, I mean, and return?"

"And return, provided you're careful about following the rules."

Clifford didn't hesitate. He smiled a broad smile, gripped Mr. Nagel's bony shoulder, and said, "And you can show me how? Tell me what to do? I'll be forever in your debt!"

Mr. Nagel rubbed his nose. "Well, all right, Mr. Koussevitzky, or Mr. . . ."

"Call me Cliff."

"Seeing as you're determined . . ."

The method was certainly peculiar, but not all that complicated. It didn't involve, thank goodness, hard-to-get materials or equipment, such as buzzard-beak powder or Chaldean alembics. While Mr. Nagel spoke,

Clifford had the nagging suspicion that the exorcist was pulling his leg. But the little man seemed completely in earnest. He didn't once crack a smile, and not a glint of humor, not once, showed in his beady eyes.

Then Mrs. Nagel came over, gave her husband and Clifford each a danish on a paper plate, and introduced Clifford to the Rassmussens, who had just got back from China. Mr. Rassmussen imported ties, and Mrs. Rassmussen collected delft shepherdesses.

18

Sing to me from your house of blue,
Brother Dolphin,
Brother Dolphin.
Sing to me from your house of blue,
And I'll sing you a song of me and you,
A song of survival.

Give me your flipper, I'll give you my hand,
Flipper and hand.
Let there be peace between water and land,
Water and land.
Let there be peace between me and you,
Brother Dolphin.

Kindness and laughter in your eye,
It says, Come play,
Come play in the waves.
It says, I'll carry you, little fry,
Little two-legged,
Slow-swimming,
Knob-headed guy,
Across the roof of my house of blue,
Where there are no nets
And no pollution.

Carry me, then, on your roof of blue,
Salty blue,
Over the treasure chests, over the waves,
As you carried my father,
And his father too.
And I promise,
Tomorrow if not today,
I'll carry you,
Yes, I'll carry you,
We'll all carry you,
Out of the doom of extinction.

Sing to me from your house of blue,
Brother Dolphin,
Brother Dolphin.
Sing to me from your house of blue,
And I'll sing you a song of me and you,
A song of no nets
And no pollution.

19

You got to the land of the dead, Mr. Nagel said, by taking the subway, the D train, D for Dis, which in Clifford's mind did not conjure up mythological images of Pluto and Proserpina sitting sternly on thrones of ebony with smoldering, sputtering torches to their left and right. Instead, Dis, like a broken record, echoed in his thoughts as a prefix. Denoting separation or parting from. A privative, negative, or reversing force. A loss, a lack, a deprivation, an undoing, the opposite or absence of. His cursed loneliness.

Of course, thousands if not millions of people every day took the D train, and they did not end up in the land of the dead. Unless occasionally someone suffered a heart attack, during the rush hour, while pushing desperately through sardine-packed fellow commuters to exit at the 89th Street stop—because if you didn't get off there, the next stop was 31st Street, where the crush was often so great, people couldn't get on or off, period, impassed. Even using your fists didn't help. And if you missed the 31st Street stop, God forbid, you had no choice but to get off at 4th Street, the end of the line, miles from your office and in absolutely the worst part of town.

Beggars, drunks, thieves, roaming packs of grinning teenagers on razor sprees, and gaunt Florida druggies on their last legs. The 4th Street station was so awful that even in the middle of the day, every second person was abnormal. On a platform or at a newsstand, you could easily look up and suddenly find yourself surrounded by stubbled chins and wolf eyes closing in. People were murdered there all the time, for no reason. Clifford had lost two friends that way—and an aunt, his father's sister. A Koussevitzky from the old country. Aunt Milena, may she rest in peace, had a mustache, her English wasn't too good, and she never married. She used to take him out for sundaes. She would order extra scoops, have them pile the ice cream on, higher and higher, and then she watched her little nephew closely while he ate, making him feel that by causing the giant sundae to disappear he was doing her such a favor, she would never be able to repay him.

He once wrote a song about Aunt Milena. "Love and Ice Cream." But it didn't rise in the charts, maybe because—as Mr. Drucker said—everyone these days was anticholesterol.

Clifford got off the bus and approached the steps leading down. He had butterflies in his stomach. "But maybe," he said to himself, "this whole thing is a joke." In his right hand was the black token.

Thousands if not millions of people every day took the D train, but they didn't put a jet-black token in the slot at the turnstile, hold their breath, and subvocally say, three times, *Omnia sunt perdita,* as they pushed aside the revolving arm with their hand or body.

"And where do I obtain one of these magic black tokens?" Clifford had asked Mr. Nagel.

"They're not magic," Mr. Nagel replied. "You take a regular token and paint it black."

"Paint it?"

"You can buy one of those little square bottles of

black enamel that people use for hobby kits. You know, to build model planes or cars. Or India ink, for that matter. Whatever holds on metal. I'm not sure about India ink. As long as the token is completely black when it goes in. You can't miss any spots. And you have to watch out for scratches—not in the token, in the paint. No metal must show."

If any metal showed, the symbolism wouldn't work, and therefore the token wouldn't work. One would get off at 217th and Fortune streets, or First Avenue near the planetarium, but not Dis, the land of the dead, the realm of the departed.

There was so much garbage on the steps, Clifford had difficulty finding places to put his feet. Because of the strike, people were dumping their garbage everywhere: in stairwells, in doorways, off bridges. Manna for the rats. The strike was in its seventh week now, and the stink was unbelievable, worse each day, the garbage ripening and cooking in these unprecedented hundred-degree-plus oven temperatures. Even the flies seemed a little dizzy.

Inside, Clifford saw a few down-and-outers sprawled in rags in the corners and along the walls. They had a stink all their own, an overpowering, sour, stale-cheesy stink, familiar to him, because his job took him into the city frequently. But two of them were lying in the middle of the walkway, right in his path. He looked more closely and saw that they were not down-and-outers at all but men in uniform. Soldiers. Dead soldiers.

Then he noticed the bullet holes in the walls. There were so many bullet holes in the brick and plaster, you couldn't even read the graffiti.

Of course: the war. He had forgotten all about it, with his personal trouble. Were these corpses American or Soviet? Or one each? As if two fallen soldiers could give him an idea who was winning. As if anyone could win, in the nuclear holocaust. Although apparently not everything was vaporized or radioactive yet. "Unless we're all afterimages," he thought.

In his mind's eye, Clifford saw Marsha's face. Behind a lacy white veil, she blushed happily as she said, "I do."

Just before he reached the turnstile, a man on the platform saw him and called out. This was a live soldier. The shout sounded like an order. Stop? Come here? Go back? Unfortunately, the echoes in the subway tunnel distorted the words into an unrecognizable bark. Either that or the order was in Russian.

The soldier shouted again, angrily, and lifted his rifle. There were other soldiers there, too.

Quickly, Clifford put the black token in the slot and, as he pushed through the turnstile, held his breath, closed his eyes, and said subvocally, three times, "*Omnia sunt perdita*," praying that a bullet wouldn't cut him down before he stepped into Dis. He would reach Dis in either case, true, but he didn't want the trip to be one-way.

20

Power Man pulverized a couple of crackfiends as they began to kick a little old lady who refused to let go of her pocketbook. But it turned out that they weren't crackfiends. They were neighborhood kids, high-school kids, on the basketball team, and one of them, named Frederick Michael, was an A student bound for college. Early acceptance, with a scholarship, too. His mother, a big black woman with a gold tooth, told reporters, tears coursing down her round cheeks, that Frederick Michael had been a good son, a good brother, always looked after his little sister, helped her with her homework, and he was active in church and the charity fund-raisers. Maybe, in his senior year, he had got in with the wrong crowd a little, feeling his oats like a lot of boys his age, but that was normal; he never would have done anything really wrong, not Frederick Michael. The whole community was so proud of him. She showed the reporters photographs of Frederick Michael, and these appeared in all the papers the next day. His picture in the school yearbook, smiling. His confirmation picture, serious and mature, with a tie. Frederick Michael on the basketball court, intent on a foul shot. Frederick Michael, age eleven, with a new bicycle on his birthday. Frederick Michael, seventeen, last year, with his girlfriend at a car wash for muscular dystrophy, both of them holding sponges and mugging, mouths wide and full of teeth, at the camera.

"They were stomping this little old lady!" Bernie Rifkin said to the cop, who was also black and writing grimly in a pad as the lights flashed and a voice crackled on the two-way radio at his hip.

"Just my luck," Bernie thought. "A black neighborhood."

The cop asked for identification, a driver's license.

"Look," said Bernie, trying to keep his temper. "Maybe you haven't noticed. I'm a superhero, I'm wearing a tight superhero outfit. I can't carry a wallet because I don't have any pockets. I don't even have a fucking credit card on me." Batman was the only one, as far as he knew, who had pockets. Bernie would have to ask his son about that when he got home.

"Couldn't you have stopped them, Mr. Rifkin, without doing this?" The cop, still writing, moved his head. What he moved his head at was all the blood in the street, and the ambulance people carefully putting pieces of body into plastic bags with carefully plastic-gloved hands because they were afraid of AIDS.

"Officer, I'd really prefer it if you called me Power Man. That's my official name."

And the press was even worse, with such sneering remarks as "What do you feel gives you the right, Power Man, to take the law into your own hands?" or "Do you advocate vigilante justice?"

"What is your opinion, we'd like to know, we're just curious, of white supremacy and the Ku Klux Klan?"

"Where did you get, sir, that funny costume?"

"No patience, it would appear, with our legal system and trial by jury."

"They were kicking this little old lady," Bernie said for the tenth time. "They were kicking her, because she didn't give them her pocketbook." He might as well have been talking to a wall. Goddam bleeding-heart liberals.

Goddam stupid superior one-track black militants. It got him so angry, his face went numb and he had trouble talking.

Which made him sound even more like the redneck retard they were trying to turn him into, shoving their microphones in his face.

The papers had a field day with him. On television, too. It was awful.

For two weeks after that, Bernie didn't touch his superhero suit. It hung in his closet, the big red P on royal blue surrounded by the ten white stars that stood for both America and the Ten Commandments. At one point, he seriously considered throwing it in the garbage.

"What's the matter with people?" he muttered beerily into his pillow at night. "I'm on the side of Good, Justice, Decency. Isn't that what we all want, for Chrissake?"

On Poker Night, no one spoke as the cards were dealt and played and reshuffled, or as the chips were stacked, then clicked down one by one, then tossed in the center of the table by twos and threes. You could almost see the cloud over Bernie's head. It was like being at a wake.

21

Lucy was pleasantly surprised at the number of people who showed up for Mark's funeral. As if he were some kind of important person. At least a dozen from Shaw were there, including Dave's vice-president brother, who was sporting a new pencil-line mustache. The Karpinskis were there, all seven of them. Dr. Wong was there. George Lyons the anchorman was there and had his makeup on. He looked unbelievably glamorous, as if there was a spotlight on him no matter which way he turned.

"Is that George Lyons?" Bertie whispered in her ear.

"Yes," Lucy said, pretending she had been expecting George Lyons and it was no big deal.

"Are we going to be on television?" Bertie wiggled with excitement. The stainless-steel balls of her earrings made little circles. She was young.

And the Davidsons were there, and the Randolphs with their new foreign-exchange student from Lisbon, and Barb Humphrey, in mourning herself and looking terrific.

"Barb, you've lost weight," said Lucy. "What a wonderful dress."

"I've been working out," Barb explained. "They have a new machine at the club. You wouldn't believe what I can lift."

And Father Jackson was there, and Mark's half brother from New Mexico, the car salesman, with his new Japanese wife. And Clifford, the only one present— bless his heart—in a jacket and tie. He had a haircut, too, that made his ears stick out.

Lucy, laughing, took his hand and gave him a kiss. "What brings *you* here, Clifford?"

"The loss," Clifford said, groping for a suitable reply and doing his best to look condolent, though he had never cared for Mark, nor had Mark cared for him. "The loss that you have suffered."

True, they had been married seven years, a pretty long time to be married, all things considered. Lucy's marriages before Mark had all run one or two years at most—one or two years was standard—and his marriages before her had been about the same. He and Edith, the bimbo with the balloon bazooms from Connecticut who preceded her, had tied the knot for only two months. Long enough for Edith to kill them, long distance. Mark now, Lucy in a year, maybe.

Unless it was Janice's boyfriend Bill who had given them the lethal retroviral oncogene. Janice right now was in a hospital in Compton, a chart at her feet and a hundred tubes, yuck, in her arms and up her nose. Well, she had asked for it.

But what difference did it make, really, whether it was Edith or Bill? It made no difference.

Lucy was glad she had taken a couple of Quiets that morning. This day was going to be on the annoying side, no question. And old sentimental Clifford Koussevitzky in jacket and tie was certainly one of the annoyances, with his basset-hound face and "loss that you have suffered" intoned an octave too low and gurgling, as if underwater.

Clifford and Jeannette had been together—how

long? Three years? Four? No, seven years, also seven years. Ah, so that was why. Mark's passing, because of the seven years, had touched a nerve in Clifford's old sorrow.

It was mercilessly hot as everyone trudged up the hill where the open grave was. Some of them, like Art, had on AC helmets, the new type, which wasn't so bulky and spaceman-looking. Still, it was not exactly the sort of thing you'd want to wear to the opera or the regatta. A blue-black plastic beetle-head. Sleek, but a beetle-head nevertheless. Of course, if the weather continued like this, and it was still only April, if you can believe that, everybody and his second cousin would be wearing one, and beetle-heads would become de rigueur.

Might not be a bad idea, either. You could go out without having to worry about your hair. Without having to spend half an hour getting your lashes straight. Just pop the helmet on, honey, and you're all set.

The cemetery was grungier than when Lucy had been here last, two weeks ago, for Jack and Saul's funeral. Jack and Saul had died in each other's arms, how romantic. Two skeletons hooked up to monitors, with charts at their feet, the graphs going down, down, down.

Litter between the tombstones—shameful—and the grass was pathetic. Clumps of ugly weeds, patches of dirt; you could hardly call it a lawn. You'd think, with all the business they were doing here these days (it's an ill wind, ain't it, that blows no good?), they could maintain the grounds.

The weeds were not only ugly, Lucy thought, they were weird. Like something out of one of those dubbed campy Philippine science-fiction flicks that were shown three in the morning on TV. *The Killer Kohlrabi from Planet Bingo*. The stalks and blades were greasy, more gray than green, and had a lumpy, pulpy shape, like fingers of much-chewed chewing gum clutching at you, ugh. But Mark would have just said, not even looking up from his book, in his calm, computer voice, that it wasn't the cemetery's fault. It was the greenhouse effect, those ultraviolet mutations, and no high-tech sprinkler system could do anything about that.

Know-it-all Mark was six feet under now, or would be in a few minutes. Maybe that would shut him up.

When they were assembled around the rectangular hole and the coffin was lowered slowly to the bottom with creaking ropes, Reverend Bennison handed Lucy a trowel.

"What, are we planting crocuses?" she asked.

"It is customary, Mrs. Hoff," said the reverend, talking as if his mouth were full of caramel, the way old Clifford did when he got solemn, "to cast a handful of earth upon the coffin."

She saw now that there was soil in the trowel she held. Shrugging, she took a handful of it and tossed it in the hole. Not taking off her white glove first. Damn it, how stupid, getting the glove dirty. And then it occurred to her that—of course—she was supposed to have just dropped the soil from the trowel, not using her hands, her white-gloved hands. That was what the trowel was for, stupid.

"They could have told me," she thought. They could have had a little rehearsal or something, instead of making her look like a jerk in public, and this was all probably being televised, since George Lyons was here in his makeup. Smiling for the camera, wherever it was, Lucy dropped the rest of the dirt from the trowel into the hole. It went plonk-plonk-plonk on the varnished blond wood that covered her dead husband. Pieces of earth bounced and scattered on the wood.

That was the signal for the grave diggers to start their shoveling to fill the hole.

"What do I do with the trowel now?" she thought. It was the Quiets that were making her such an airhead today. Hoping no one was looking, she dropped the trowel into the grave. Then noticed, too late, that Reverend Bennison was holding out his hand to retrieve it. "Oh, well," she thought, "they can add the trowel to the bill." Which would be huge. But she didn't have to worry about that, not with Mark's insurance. A damn good thing he had got the policy before he tested positive. And she, too. Screw the insurance company for a change.

Lucy turned, as if not seeing the reverend, and waved at a make-believe friend. A couple waved back. They were trudging up the hill, hurrying, late. The Baxters, of course. Mona and Dave would probably die only after everyone else in the group did. And miss the big sex party in hell.

22

The lawn screamed as it burned, a horrible high-pitched scream. He thought that that would be the end of it, but it turned out he was wrong, because evidently the roots hadn't been killed, at least not completely. By next morning, there was half a foot of grass everywhere, dark green, too, lush.

"Jesus Christ," he said, looking out his bedroom window, blinking. "What am I supposed to do, call the national guard?"

From the bed, his wife said: "Bob, what's the matter with you? Yesterday you torched our lawn, almost burned down the goddam house, set off all the smoke detectors, I couldn't hear myself think, and now you're standing at the window naked and talking to yourself. Are we going to have to have you committed, or what? Tell me, please, I'd like to know."

He was going to say something sour to her, but just then there was an awful racket downstairs—glass breaking, Jimmy howling bloody murder—so he pulled on his blue-striped boxer shorts and, muttering, went down to see what trouble the kids had got themselves into this time.

In the kitchen, glass all over. Jess was sitting on the floor, crying and hiccuping.

"What happened?" he yelled. There was a huge mess

for them to clean: cereal, milk, pieces of glass, which would take forever to pick up. And a whole window to repair, because he saw that the kitchen window had been completely smashed. The curtains fluttered. The jungle heat of the outside was billowing in like steam, filling the house.

Little Jess, hiccuping, pointed and said, "A big green Hulk arm got Jimmy."

"A big green Hulk arm? What the hell are you talking about?" Bob was pissed because of the mess and the trouble—the trouble of having to replace a window, buy the glass, apply the putty, when there was so much else to do this weekend. When all he wanted right now was to sit down and read the morning paper and have his coffee before he went to work. Except, if the newsboy tossed the paper on the lawn, say good-bye to the paper. Bob was so pissed, he bent over to swat the kid for talking comic-book nonsense on top of everything else. But a light went on in his head and stayed his hand.

It was the lawn. Of course. Taking revenge. Bob could picture his children having breakfast at the kitchen table. The lawn rearing up outside, breaking in with its arm or tentacle, or whatever it was that killer mutant lawns had. Then snatching up Jimmy, the last of the male line of Petruzzos in Woodhaven. (There were a few Petruzzos in nearby Terryville, but they were unrelated.)

Jimmy had gone the way of Fluffy and Princess.

Was, even as we speak, in the stomach—stomach?— of the Petruzzo lawn.

Bob shuddered.

"Damn," he said, a little stunned by this development. And how was he going to break it to his wife, who didn't even know about the greenhouse effect because she never watched those nature or science shows on television?

"Just what the hell is going on?" his wife said, coming down in her bathrobe.

"The lawn is alive," Bob told her. "It ate Jimmy."

She gave him a look, was probably going to say something sarcastic again, but a big green arm appeared in the window, so instead of saying something sarcastic she gasped, her eyes got wider and wider, and her mouth fell open in a large O.

Jess screamed. Bob pulled his daughter out of the way, in the nick of time. The big green arm reached in, amazingly swift for a vegetable organism, and snuffled, as if the tip of it were a sloppy snout or melted vacuum-cleaner head. Jimmy, apparently, had only whetted the lawn's appetite.

"What in God's name is that?" gasped Bob's wife, pointing a rigid finger.

Bob whacked the green arm a couple of times with a shovel he got from the garage. This only seemed to make the thing angry. It flailed, reaching for him. It growled.

"Everybody out of the kitchen!" Bob yelled.

What now? Block off the kitchen with a barricade of tables stood on end, plus other furniture? No point; the lawn could break in through any of the windows on the first floor, the living room, the dining room, the utility room. The goddam thing surrounded their house, with the exception of the driveway.

"Out the front door!" he yelled.

But when they went out the front door, his wife and daughter screamed. There was a wall of green on the driveway, a wall of malevolent green between them and the street.

"Into the car, quick!" Bob yelled.

In bathrobe, pajamas, and boxer shorts, they piled in, rolled up the windows, and locked the doors as the green came at the car, hit it, rocked it. Bob's idea was to back out, flooring the gas pedal. The lawn—he was sure—he crossed his fingers—couldn't be that strong, not strong enough to stop the car. How strong, after all, could grass be, even with complicated chemicals in it?

"Oh no, oh shit," he said, punching the dashboard, "I don't have the keys." The car keys were in his pants, in the house. "Shut up, will you?" he said to his wife, who was screaming at the top of her lungs. "I can't hear myself think."

The front door would be locked, if they had closed it after them, and they probably had. Shit, shit. The keys, goddammit, were in his pants, upstairs, in the bedroom. Meanwhile the lawn was clawing at the car, covering half the windows now, making his wife hysterical, and all stupid Jess could do was bawl.

"Would you please shut up, both of you, for just a minute?" he pleaded, but they didn't hear him.

"Okay, here goes nothing," he said to himself. "You two stay here," he told them, and took a deep breath. As quickly as he could, he opened his door, pushed his way out, closed the door, fought through clutching green to the house, and tried the front door. It was locked, all right, so he punched the glass out of the closest window as the lawn chewed at his legs and burned them with its nasty vegetable acid. He climbed in, cutting his knees and shins on broken glass, limped upstairs cursing, stepped into his pants, took the goddam keys, ran out again to the car, tore the green off the driver's side as another bunch of it tried to tackle him from behind. In a fury, he kicked and spit at it, but the lawn spit right back, a rain of teeth in his face, little teeth, Jimmy's.

Finally in the car, Bob started it up, put it in reverse, and floored the gas while he ripped away the green that was trying to wrap itself around his throat.

The car shuddered—there must have been grass in the tailpipe—but then the engine roared, and they were thrown backward into the street, crashing into a car.

The other driver—no surprise—started shooting. Then began a chase in which they drove half on the sidewalk, or sometimes completely, he and the car he had rammed, because the street was filled with traffic, almost bumper to bumper, even though it wasn't rush hour yet. Bob kept hitting garbage cans overflowing with garbage, and the garbage flew—beer bottles, banana peels, coffee grounds, magazines, chicken scraps—and got on the windshield and obstructed the view. But he couldn't stop, not with the bullets—they seemed high caliber, too—zinging off the roof or making holes thwock-thwock in the upholstery, because the rear window had been blown out first thing, little bits of glass everywhere. "Another broken window," he said to no one in particular as he swerved to avoid a mailbox.

"Keep your heads down!" he yelled, remembering his family, what was left of his family. It occurred to him then that they hadn't been screaming and bawling for some time. Not a peep. Fainted, maybe? Speechless with terror?

He took a quick look to the side, a quick look over his shoulder: nobody was there. On the seats, only a few blades of wriggling grass.

When in hell, had his wife and daughter jumped out, after the crash, maybe, because of the shooting? No. They hadn't been in the car at the time of the crash. They hadn't even been in the car when he came back with the keys. He had been too busy to notice. Or maybe he had tried not to notice.

The lawn got them.

Bob Petruzzo, though bereaved, chuckled at the

sudden thought that now he wouldn't have to feed his lawn this spring.

Another thought, a worry: he ought to warn Maury Bergholz. Maury had a monster and a half next door and didn't know it. It would be only neighborly to tell him. He would phone him.

The cars were all honking in anger, and other drivers were starting to shoot, too. One of them must have got the guy chasing Bob, because that car abruptly turned and went into a chain-link fence. A bullet caught Bob in the shoulder, but he stayed at the wheel and by a great stroke of luck was able to take a small, unexpected side street away from the traffic and the gunfire.

His seat was covered with blood. He hurt in a hundred places. He was dizzy. All he could think of was to go south, to Elton Beach, to the boardwalk and the ocean, where there was lots of sand, sand everywhere, long sweeping rows of white or gray or brown or yellow dunes, and the hard tan sand at the water's edge. The main thing was that sand, no matter what its color, was never green, and that at the shore, in sight of the ocean, there would be nothing remotely like a lawn.

He didn't want to see a lawn for the rest of his life.

Was it his imagination, or did he really see, in the rearview mirror, far back, behind the intervening houses and fences and cars, an enraged emerald carpet coming after him?

"Jesus H. Christ," Bob Petruzzo whimpered.

23

Joe got a job selling shoes at the Maplehurst mall. It wasn't that unpleasant. Dead people, though their feet smelled just as bad as the feet of the living, turned out to be a lot less picky. If a shoe wasn't perfect, wasn't exactly what they had in mind, they didn't make a face and ask to see something else. They didn't walk out muttering and without a word of thanks after you had fetched and laced and unlaced for more than half an hour. That is, for what seemed more than half an hour, because time was virtual here, only virtual, not real, as had been explained at the support group, though it still didn't make sense to Joe. But, then, he wasn't exactly a genius in physics. The dead customers sighed wearily and bought the damn shoes, as if they didn't want to go to any more trouble.

"Those don't fit either," one lady said, "but screw it, I'll take them."

"Don't you have anything more colorful?" said another lady. "Oh, never mind."

Toward the end of the day, his lower back would ache from all the bending over. How was that possible? The ache must have been out of habit or expectation, a kind of ghost-ache, the way people sometimes felt their toes burn and tingle years after their legs had been amputated.

A few mall zombies drifted by, now and then. You

could tell them from the other shoppers not only because they were transparent but also because there was nothing in their faces, not even boredom. But this was no different from the way it had been before, up there. The zombies never bought anything, of course. The Catholic Church, Joe remembered, ruled that they had no souls. He remembered reading about it in the papers last month. A month, that it, before the Mexican pizza faded out on him forever.

But if the mall zombies didn't have souls, what were they doing here, in this place of souls? Joe shrugged. He was no better at religion than he was at physics.

At least he could go to the Taco Bell as much as he liked now and not have to worry about cholesterol. There was a Taco Bell right in the mall. It was just like the Taco Bells back home, except that the red on the sign and menus and in the decor was more brown than red. A kind of dull maroon. Even the tomato sauce and the hot peppers were maroonish. But the food was fine, the same as it always was. On his lunch break, after selling shoes for what seemed a week, he went there and had a superburrito. And followed that up with a Mexican pizza, not because he was hungry but for old times' sake. And perhaps, too, to thumb his nose a little at the cholesterol: Nyah, nyah, you can't get me now.

Imagine his surprise when suddenly he felt a sharp pain in his chest, to the left, a pain so severe that he had difficulty breathing. The next thing he knew, he was on the floor, his face in the half-eaten pizza. "How in the hell," he thought, "can I be having a heart attack?" The next thing he knew after that, someone was looking down at him and he was lying on his back on one of those padded tables doctors used for examinations. "What is this?" he thought. "Back to square one?"

The unisex nurse helped him up. The doctor came in with a clipboard, said, "Joseph David Smith," and made a couple of breezy remarks that the nurse didn't approve of. Then Joe was given a Coke to drink. Then he went to a desk to get a packet of papers, which included a form that looked a lot like an application for a Social Security number. But he discovered that this was not back-to-square-one, after all. He saw, outside, the diner on the corner of Broadway and Teller Avenue, and the sign said not NICK's or RICK's but J-CKS, the A missing and no apostrophe. The grass of the lawns, also, was a much darker gray, almost charcoal, though the sprinklers were going as usual, as if nothing were wrong. As if the summer sun were beating down, which of course it wasn't.

At the Holiday Inn—it seemed to be the same one, off the expressway—he was asked to fill out a 7040-HH and advised to take postpostmortem counseling and get a job, because the boredom here was even worse. He got the same job selling shoes at the mall. The only difference was—aside from the fact that the customers were a little more apathetic—but that was to be expected—the only difference was the money he was paid with. The bills were so washed out now, you could hardly see George Washington's face. Or Lincoln's, or Hamilton's, or Jackson's. But everything was hard to see. It was like being in a brownout. He squinted so much throughout the day that even though he was twice dead now, or doubly dead, if that made any sense, and it didn't, he got a throbbing headache and had to take a couple of aspirin and lie down in a cool, dark place.

24

A vortex of magenta dragon bears—there must have been several thousand of them in the sky—swooped down, baring fangs, belching fire. They were armed, too, with what appeared to be high-power submachine guns, as if the fangs and claws and fire weren't enough.

"Duck," said Josh as a hail of bullets came rattling and pinging across the strange ceramic roof on which the two young space cadets found themselves.

They ducked.

The bullet holes in the roof all smoked, and the air turned acrid.

"Poison bullets, too," observed Josh, drawing his blaster.

"Holy shit," said Bobby Bergholz. His eyes glittered with excitement. This was great. He couldn't remember when he had had so much fun. Maybe bobsledding once, at Uncle Max's up in Vermont.

The roof was white and very rough, like stucco, and in addition it had lots of odd humps and slopes here and there, with mushroom protuberances of unknown purpose and function. Josh saw nothing that looked like a doorway down, or a hatch or ladder to safety. He grabbed Bobby and pulled him and dived. Fire roared where they had stood a moment before. The roof hissed and crackled, a black circle of flames.

To the right, a head appeared. Someone gestured to them: Here, this way. They ran toward whoever it was, as fast as they could.

It was a close thing. A dragon bear, wings beating, tore at Bobby's back with its claws, ripped off his jacket and half his shirt. An expensive shirt, too, the kind that had one of those fancy Dublin labels and cost a couple thousand dollars. Bobby went in for clothes like that, on the money he stole from his dad.

Josh zapped the attacking creature, and another two that were right over his head, and made more than a dozen of the nearest dragon bears hesitate with the bloodcurdling war cry that was his specialty. He had perfected it at the age of ten, in the mandatory drug fights on the school playground at lunchtime. This gave him the second or two he needed to scramble down the steps after Bobby and shut the armored trapdoor against another hail of bullets and fire.

"Whew," he said.

"This is already a lot of action," said Bobby, breathless, "and we only just got here."

"You're bleeding," Josh told him.

There were three ugly welts across Bobby's back, and one of them oozed blood.

The native who had given them refuge introduced himself—his name was Phex Plowg—and said the wound should be attended to immediately, because the dragon bears from Moon Two were filthy beasts and known carriers of a host of fatal diseases. One could not tell, of course, what degree of immunity—or lack of immunity— an Earthling might have, but better safe than sorry, *n'est-ce pas?*

"You speak perfect English," Josh remarked.

Phex waved his hand impatiently, meaning: Yes, but the explanation, my dear boy, is too involved to go into now. He led them to a room where there were towels, a sink, a television set, and a medicine chest filled with tubes of ointment. While he cleaned and dressed Bobby's welts, which made Bobby wince once or twice—the ointment evidently stung—the native filled the space cadets in on the situation.

This planet had three moons, Phex Plowg told them, all quite large. Large enough to support atmospheres, seas, and—in the case of moons One and Two—life. The creatures of Moon One, the closest satellite, were no more highly evolved than a chicken or a cow and never gave anyone any trouble. But those of Moon Two, unfortunately, had evolved more, and into several species, each intelligent enough to develop a technology and wage war, and this they had done, hammer and tongs, for several centuries, until only the dragon bears were left, curse them.

"For centuries," Phex mused, "we watched the fireworks on Moon Two, which sometimes were quite beautiful, quite colorful, on balmy summer nights. We did not prepare ourselves for the eventuality—it never crossed our minds—that the victor on that distant bellicose body would run out of opponents someday, and seek them elsewhere."

"Why are your roofs in funny shapes?" Josh asked.

"Tidal forces," Phex replied. "Besides three moons, we also have two suns, a binary made up of a red giant and a yellow Sol-type star. We have, in addition, an erratic green gas-giant planet with an orthogonal double ring—orthogonal means that the rings are at right angles to each other—most unusual—and occasionally it passes between us and the suns. Not a very stable system, but it makes for some interesting eclipses."

"How much will you give us to wipe out these dragon bears for you?" Bobby Bergholz asked. A natural question, especially considering his indebtedness to Captain Jack Zodiac.

"Ten quid," said Phex Plowg.

Bobby frowned. Ten quid didn't seem like a hell of a lot. "How does that convert into dollars? I mean, American dollars. Also, our expenses—"

Phex waved his hand impatiently. "It's all in the contract. Boilerplate stuff."

"You have many space cadets coming here, then, to take care of your dragon-bear problem?" Josh asked, feeling a sinking in his stomach.

"About two a week. Not many Earthlings. All kinds of races, from different planets, different galaxies. Kids, like you."

"And they don't . . . survive?"

"Most of them don't even make it to Moon Two. As I was telling you—the tidal forces. When all these heavenly bodies line up, and the configuration is such, you know, with the houses and the cusps, the tidal forces can get pretty nasty. For certain hours every day, our women don't put their laundry out to dry. All the flowerpots are taken off the sills. The airports are closed, the planes bolted down, the flags lowered."

"Every day?"

"It's inconvenient, but we're used to it."

Josh now noticed that the native wore a hat, a kind of derby, blue-black felt. It had a reinforced, no-nonsense chin strap. The strap was a chain.

25

The danger was that on your way to Moon Two you'd be pulled off course by an unexpected gravitational current, and that that current would in turn be unexpectedly preempted by a current even more powerful and swifter, if gravitational currents can be thought of as swift, and you'd find yourself pulled inexorably in an even less desirable direction, perhaps toward one of the suns, or perhaps, instead, you'd be hurled out into deep space beyond this solar system, ending up millions of parsecs from the nearest call box.

Or another possibility. Two or three different currents in different directions might intersect at your position and literally pull you limb from limb. Such intersections were not common, but they did occur.

"I'm surprised," Josh said, "that with all this, your moons and planets are still in one piece."

Phex Plowg smiled wryly. "Our system used to have twenty-three planets. There are only four left, and one is more a comet than a planet. The instability increases exponentially. When I was a child, in school, and that wasn't so terribly long ago, there were fifteen planets. I had to memorize their names, circumferences, and rest masses, in order, for tests."

He began to recite the names, circumferences, and rest masses, but Bobby interrupted him and asked if they could please sign the contract now. "We don't have all day," Bobby said, fidgeting with his blaster. There was no telling how long the lemon and vermillion pill would last, and they had paid so fucking much for it.

Phex shrugged, led them to an office, where another native had them fill out a form, some kind of disclaimer. Then he led them to a third native, who fingerprinted them and took their pictures. "Routine," said Phex. "You'll be done in a minute." From there they were ushered into a big room with a big desk, and a native with a potbelly, pudgy hands, and deep voice introduced himself—Seph Glowp—and gave them the contract to sign, several pages, in triplicate.

The contract was not in English, so there was no point worrying about the small print.

"Jesus, how many places do we have to sign?" said Bobby, because there were X's followed by dotted lines, dozens of X's and dotted lines, it seemed, on each page, front and back.

"It's just a formality," said Seph Glowp with a big, hearty, confidence-inspiring, lawyerlike laugh. "This, and the waiver, and the loyalty oath, and you're on your way, gentlemen."

"What are we waiving?" asked Josh, suddenly smelling a rat.

26

Even when she was two years old, she had a washed-out look, perhaps because her skin was so pale, her eyes such a light blue, and her hair so wispy. A normal-enough child, but with never a whole lot to say. If she cried, she cried very quietly. When the other kids teased or tormented her, she didn't run and tattle; she just took it, took whatever happened—the usual sticks and stones of childhood—without a murmur. And you couldn't tell, watching her face, if she was feeling any kind of anguish afterward, in that private, locked place inside her head. She was always glued to the TV. Clifford would walk into the den and see that pale little face, as fixed and bloodless as a moonlit statue, bathed in the flickering light. Trish sat, unmoving, throughout the commercials and the sitcoms, throughout the news and the prime-time off-color talk shows.

"Maybe we should get her on a soccer team or something," Clifford suggested to his wife. "And feed her more red meat. She looks anemic."

There was nothing Trish was really interested in at school. She had no favorite color, no favorite food, and no special friend—just the usual whispering, giggling girls and the occasional wan boy bringing a box of chocolates to her birthday party.

It was in the tenth grade that Trish began to go to

101

the mall every day. Sometimes missing dinner to go to the mall. Clifford tried to explain to her that it was dangerous. Malls these days were filled with homeless people, muggers, gangs of teenage rapists and slashers, not to mention old spacesalts who sold those polka-dot pills from the Philippines to young children, ruining their lives forever. He tried threats and he tried sarcasm, but it was as if she didn't hear him. She needed a blouse, she said. She needed socks that matched. A new pocketbook. A scarf.

One Wednesday evening—it was eleven o'clock—they had brushed their teeth, got into their pajamas, and were ready to go to bed, and still no Trish. Jeannette said the kid would come home when she came home, but Clifford, growing more and more uneasy, finally decided to get dressed again and go to the mall. The image of his daughter lying spread-eagled, shit-smeared, and with her throat slit behind a decorative hedge in a dim corner of some loading area became more vivid with each passing minute. Sleep was out of the question, even though he had to be up at five next morning, like every morning, to avoid the worst of the rush hour. So he drove to the mall.

He cruised around it a couple of times, went through the maze of loading areas behind the stores. A carful of Hispanic crackfiends leered at him once. A police car with a spotlight stopped him. "I'm looking for my daughter," Clifford said into the glare, showing his license and registration.

Then he walked up and down the promenades inside. Only a few stores were still open, but there were shoppers wandering from display window to display window like ghosts, like tormented souls unable to rest. Some of them, he saw, were transparent.

He didn't know how it happened, but he found himself running and calling, "Trish! Trish!" at the top of his voice, and hearing eerie echoes of her name down the dimly lit promenades. It was like a scene out of a horror movie, one of those nightmare sequences where everything gets blurry and distorted as the character runs and screams on the brink of his sanity.

By a pattern shop, someone turned to look at him. After a halting second, he recognized his daughter. He almost sobbed with relief. He ran to her, took her by the arm, said, "It's almost twelve. Why didn't you come home? Are you all right?" Her arm was cold and oddly inert. Her face was as expressionless as a fish. "You're not on drugs, are you?" he asked.

She shook her head. "I was just looking," she said.

"But, dear," he argued with the aggrieved love of all the fathers in the world, "if you don't eat, you'll get like one of those suicide anorexia types."

Was it his imagination, was it a trick of the eyes caused by fatigue, or did he really see the tile-reflected neon sign blinking purple Coke, Coke, Coke—through her shoulder?

That weekend, he made an appointment for Trish to see a doctor. And he put his foot down: No shopping for a month. Or at least not until she was checked out and maybe a psychologist had a look at her, too. She didn't protest. After school, for a few days, she lay in bed listening to the radio. Then she seemed to get a little color back in her cheeks—not that there had been much color to begin with—and to take an interest in a trip her class was going on, to an amusement park in Delaware. The doctor didn't find anything wrong. "She should straighten up more," he said, "and stop slouching. Good posture gives the internal organs more room."

The psychologist, after some tests, talked to Clifford for an hour without saying anything: it was a stream of unfamiliar words, whose only purpose, it seemed, was to make Clifford painfully aware of how little he knew about psychology. Not a word from the man about mall zombiism.

But, then, mall zombiism was more a spiritual affliction, a metaphysical affliction, than one that had to do with the psyche or mind. Clifford probably should have gone to a priest. But he didn't know this at the time. Besides, he was a nonbeliever. When he went to church, it was for tradition and ceremony, not to ask a white-bearded Deity to drop everything, all His cosmic business, please, and pay a little more attention to the Koussevitzkys.

Trish went to the amusement park in Delaware. Went to the mall again. Missed a few dinners again. And vanished without a trace. The police told him, when he finally called them, what the story was. "You see, sir," explained some lieutenant with an impersonal-sympathetic manner, which suggested that he had said the same thing to hundreds if not thousands of parents, "she could be almost anywhere. There are malls all over the world. Ankara, Timbuktu, Seattle, Bucharest. These people—people like your daughter, sir—they go from mall to mall instantaneously. It's sort of a genius loci thing, all the malls being essentially the same, if you know what I mean. So these people are, in a way, in the same place, whether it's Ankara, Timbuktu, Seattle, or Bucharest. And even if you found her, sir, she wouldn't know you. Your hand would go right through her, too, since she isn't really there, or she is, but she's also in all those other places at the same time, if you follow me, sir. I'm awfully sorry."

Clifford looked up the phenomenon in the local

library and read that it was similar to electron smearing. Not that he knew what electron smearing was. His hands trembled for weeks. He saw Trish at night, her two-year-old face unsmiling and completely without color. Staring at him, staring through him.

27

My life is a bowl
Of cherry ice cream.
Oh give me a spoon.
It's a sundae dream
Of a lovely moon
High on a wonderful Sunday night
With you,
With you.

My life is a free ride,
A ring-toss throw
In an organ-grinder, hurdy-gurdy
Carnival show.
A pink cotton-candy
Spinning Sunday, a wonderful sundae
With you,
Oh you.

My life is a boardwalk
Of flashing lights
And arcade
Space-invader fights
And roller coasters that scream
Through the wonderful starry night
With you,
Yes you.

And my love is a cherry
Ice-cream hill,
A tumbling Jack
And laughing Jill,
A child's rhyme,
A Sunday wedding chime,
A wonderful fairy tale come true
With you,
Ah you.

My love is a bowl
Of cherry ice cream,
A sundae dream,
A wedding ring,
So high and white
In the Sunday night
So grand with the wonderful moon
And you,
And you.

28

Jiménez Quindío Vichada "Dusty" Colón, the Colombian cocaine kingpin and one of the world's most feared tsars of violence, stepped from his limousine and took out a cigar. His four pantherlike bodyguards assembled around him as the cigar was lit by Percy Barnes-Smythe, Colón's right-hand man and one of the world's most highly paid assassins. (Barnes-Smythe, using only hair dye, a fake mustache, and a plastic stiletto, had killed the president of Chad under the noses of both the CIA and the KGB and made his escape in downtown Fort Archambault on, incredibly, a motorized skateboard.)

"The Third Street exit covered?" asked Dusty Colón, puffing.

"Sí, boss," said one of the bodyguards with a nod that was a bow. "Is covered."

"And Carlos and Miguel are on the seventh floor, corner window, Dusty," said Barnes-Smythe. "With their scopes." Even Barnes-Smythe bowed when he spoke to Dusty Colón.

The Colombian kingpin was short, a little under five feet in his socks, but unusually broad and squat. His hair was black and straight as crow feathers, and his high-cheekboned face was flatter than a pan and almost orange. The face of an Aztec god that has looked unblinking upon innumerable human sacrifices—palpitating hearts torn from chests. He blew out fragrant blue smoke and turned slowly, surveying the alley.

"So where," he said, "are the Wops and the Japs?"

As if on cue, two other limousines appeared, their powerful engines hardly making a sound. Out of one stepped Emilio Ventimiglia "Padre" Pisticciani, the Corsican don of dons, whom the government could not lay a finger on though it had tried for twenty years, employing snoops even more microwave high tech than those in the Soviet embassy and offering the sun and the moon to one sleazeball informer after another. The Padre, too, was accompanied by four pantherlike bodyguards, and a right-hand man who glittered eerily about the face, more bionic, probably, than human.

From the last limousine emerged, decorously and with tremendous dignity, Masanari Kagoshima-Yakamatsu, addressed even by his closest associates, even by his wife, as "Mr. Yakamatsu, sir." He was over eighty years old, incredibly rich, and said to have half the world's dictators in his pocket. His henchmen were no less pantherlike than those of the Colombian kingpin or the Corsican don of dons, but far better groomed and dressed, in impeccably tailored suits and Irish pinstripe silk lamé shirts. They were better educated, too. One could tell from their otherwise studiedly inscrutable faces that they had been to Oxford or Cambridge or Harvard or perhaps even the Charles University in Prague.

Such was the air of authority given off by Mr. Yakamatsu, sir, that both Dusty Colón and the Padre, in spite of themselves, nodded deferentially.

"This is a historic meeting," Mr. Yakamatsu intoned in a gravelly voice, leaning on an ebony cane. But before the three underground warlords could exchange a few gangster civilities and get down to business, an oddly dressed figure with a potbelly dropped from the sky and landed between them with a thud.

"Looks like I lucked out," said the man, laughing. "A lot of big fish here."

In less time than it takes to blink—because their reflexes were so extremely well honed—the bodyguards all had their Holcombs out. Armor-penetrating, cadmium-cased, high-humming needle bullets converged on the intruder from every direction. Had he been a tank, he would have been riddled beyond recognition, a Swiss cheese of hardly any cheese to speak of. Yet (amazingly) the unstoppable needle bullets were all stopped, they vaporized around the man in fleeps of light, from the heat of impact, and he was unscathed. Not a mark on him, though his peculiar uniform had been reduced to a crumbling web of charred threads.

Power Man—it was none other—looked down at himself, grimaced, and said, "Aw." A lot of hours had gone into that suit. Thank God, at least, there weren't women present. Bernie was not painfully modest; he had no problem in communal gym showers; but that didn't make him the type to go parading around on nude beaches, letting everything hang out in mixed company.

Momentarily distracted by the loss of his costume, Power Man was unprepared for the attack of the bionic bodyguard, who came at him with a small laser cannon blasting from his/its open mouth. The yellow beam bounced off Power Man's hairy chest, and the ricochet brought down a rain of bricks as one of the alley walls began to crumble.

Meanwhile, several bodyguards sprang, launching themselves at Power Man with professional karate shrieks.

And overhead, there was the crack of sniper fire.

Dusty Colón and Mr. Yakamatsu both shot poison

darts—the Colombian kingpin from his trick cigar, the Japanese baron of evil from his trick cane—but they didn't shoot at Power Man: each, suspecting a double cross, shot at the other. Emilio Ventimiglia "Padre" Pisticciani, however, a veteran of a hundred such encounters, ducked and, with a curse of many guttural syllables that only his ancestors in the maquis could have appreciated, dove back into his limousine, which took off, jets and afterburners roaring, like the proverbial bat out of hell, except faster . . .

That evening, Bernie Rifkin sat in his armchair reading the papers and drinking one St. Pauli Girl after another. The headline banner said GANGLAND MASSACRE.

"What's wrong?" his wife asked, because he was silent, his forehead all knotted up, and because, although it was almost eleven, he still hadn't had his shower and got into his favorite bathrobe. "Where'd you find those clothes? What happened to your superhero clothes?" She knew he'd been out flying, yet here he was in a fancy businessman's suit, which was dirty, crumpled, and had a couple of very noticeable bloodstains. The shirt was one of those Irish pinstripe silk lamé things that were so expensive, the ads in the magazines didn't give their price. "You ought to take a bath, Bernie. Soak a little. You'll feel better," she said.

"Fucking papers," he said. "They don't get anything right."

Not a word about the druglords, the international traffickers who were destroying America's youth despite the best efforts of the men in blue in every state, despite the valiant undercover narcs, despite the guardsmen patrolling by sea and air at great taxpayer expense. All the reporters could talk about, damn them, was this self-appointed executioner who went into action without trial, jury, due process, right of appeal, or stopping to ask himself if maybe there was a shadow of a doubt.

"What shadow of a doubt are they talking about?" Bernie asked the air. "People meet in a dark alley, in limousines, filthy rich, armed to the teeth, and not one American among them. What are they supposed to be, a PTA group selling cookies? Give me a break."

Outside, a squealing of tires. It was the Popovic kids again, in their Jeep, drunk and tearing up lawns. Bernie jumped from his chair and made for the window.

"Now, don't do anything you'll regret," said his wife. "You're in a bad mood."

But he had already thrown open the window—with such force, it shattered into a hundred pieces—and the next instant Power Man was swooping down through the air, after the Jeep, an unholy light in his eyes.

29

A living room. A gray-haired lady, in her fifties or perhaps sixties, sitting in an armchair by a lamp and reading a magazine. A knock at the door.

LADY, *not looking up:* I don't want any.

After a moment, another knock, polite but determined.

LADY, *louder:* I don't want any! *To herself*: It's probably one of those Jehovah's Witnesses. *Tries to read again.*

A third knock, a fourth.

LADY *sighs:* All right, damn it, I'm coming. Can't leave a person in peace. *Gets up and goes to the door.* Trying to convert me. Fat chance. I know the Bible better than any of them. Chapter and verse. In the original. *Opens the door.* What do you want?

CLIFFORD: Mrs. Feldman?

MRS. FELDMAN: So?

CLIFFORD: I'm Clifford Koussevitzky.

MRS. FELDMAN: You don't say.

CLIFFORD: Although, with the war, I was thinking of

changing it. But changing it also because . . . Actually, that's the reason I'm here. Your daughter Marsha and I . . .

MRS. FELDMAN: Oh. *You're* the one.

CLIFFORD: Could I come in? I thought we might talk. If you have a moment.

MRS. FELDMAN *shrugs:* A moment? I have more than a moment, young man. Much more than a moment. I was reading the *National Geographic*.

CLIFFORD: They have the *National Geographic* here?

MRS. FELDMAN: Only back issues. It's like a doctor's waiting room. You've read all the magazines before, ten times. Thank God they don't pipe in music. I'd really go out of my mind, if they piped in music.

CLIFFORD: Could I come in, Mrs. Feldman?

MRS. FELDMAN: All right, then. Come in.

Clifford enters. Mrs. Feldman resumes her seat in the armchair. He looks around but sees no other place to sit. He looks around again, thinking he must have been mistaken. But there really are no other chairs. A couple of end tables, a magazine holder, and, against the back wall, a dresser. That's all. He tries to adopt an unselfconscious pose, as if it were perfectly natural for him to be standing in the middle of a living room while talking to someone seated in an armchair.

CLIFFORD: Well, Marsha and I want to get married.

MRS. FELDMAN *looks at him:* You mean, "wanted" to get married.

CLIFFORD, *after a puzzled pause:* No, want. Still want. I gave her a ring, went down on bended knee, the whole thing. She's a wonderful woman.

MRS. FELDMAN: Of course she's a wonderful woman. You don't have to tell me that.

CLIFFORD: She's so intelligent, so sensitive. Artistic.

MRS. FELDMAN: We gave her a good education.

CLIFFORD: Mr. Feldman has no objections. He's given us his blessing.

MRS. FELDMAN *snorts*.

CLIFFORD: And I'll convert. I was thinking of changing my name to Kaplan. Clifford Kaplan. I could change the first name, too, if you like. Something like Seymour. Seymour Kaplan?

MRS. FELDMAN: You poor thing. You haven't got used to it yet. I understand. It takes getting used to. Like jet lag. It took me a week before my head cleared.

CLIFFORD: Excuse me?

MRS. FELDMAN: Being here. You know.

CLIFFORD: You mean—? Oh, I see. You think I'm dead.

MRS. FELDMAN: Of course you're dead. If you weren't dead, you wouldn't be here.

CLIFFORD: It's a misunderstanding. No, really, Mrs. Feldman, I'm not dead. I'm only visiting.

MRS. FELDMAN: Visiting.

CLIFFORD: Yes. Mr. Nagel showed me how.

MRS. FELDMAN: Mr. Nagel. Ah, Ben Nagel, the Nazi exorcist.

CLIFFORD: Nazi? Oh, he's not a Nazi, he's a very nice person. I met his wife. They're churchgoers . . . witches. Churchgoing witches. There was an article about it recently in the Sunday papers. Everyone's entitled to his own religion.

MRS. FELDMAN *snorts*.

CLIFFORD: You mean, because he's German. But that doesn't make him a Nazi, you know.

MRS. FELDMAN: All Germans are Nazis.

CLIFFORD: Now, Mrs. Feldman, don't you think that's kind of a prejudiced thing to say?

MRS. FELDMAN: It's not prejudice, it's a fact. Scratch a German and you have a Nazi. Witch or no witch.

CLIFFORD: Anyway, Mr. Nagel told me about the black token and the D train, so I decided to come here and talk to you.

MRS. FELDMAN: Then you're not dead?

CLIFFORD: No, I'm a songwriter. I have two children by a previous marriage. I'm not rich, but I make enough to get by, though the inflation these days is murder. I own my own house, in Woodhaven. It's not a bad neighborhood. I'm Slovak, Catholic. Was a Catholic. I mean, I'd be glad to convert. I've always respected Judaism. I was brought up to be tolerant.

MRS. FELDMAN: Any relation to the conductor?

CLIFFORD: Sergey Koussevitzky? Actually, yes. I'm a second cousin of his grandson, Harry, who's in Seattle now. Harry works as an accountant for a clothing company. Men's suits. I haven't seen him in twenty years.

MRS. FELDMAN: I have a nephew in Seattle. Had. Meyer Halperin.

CLIFFORD: He died?

MRS. FELDMAN: No, I did.

CLIFFORD: Seattle's a nice city. More relaxed. The people are friendly.

MRS. FELDMAN: What bothers me the most about this place is that you never know when *Shabbos* is.

CLIFFORD: *Shabbos?*

MRS. FELDMAN: That's Jewish for the Sabbath. I always lit the candles, went to *shul*. Religiously.

CLIFFORD: *Shul?*

MRS. FELDMAN: The synagogue. But here—no calendar, no clock. It could be *Shabbos* right now, and I wouldn't know it.

CLIFFORD *sighs, nods:* It's hard to keep up traditions nowadays.

MRS. FELDMAN: I'd offer you something to eat, but this apartment has no kitchen.

CLIFFORD: No kitchen? How is that possible?

MRS. FELDMAN: I don't know. Space is at a premium. Too many people. Too many bodies. They pack us in.

CLIFFORD: I've seen. The traffic is terrible.

MRS. FELDMAN: And getting worse.

CLIFFORD: Well, I guess so. More people dying every day, after all. It must build up. But why don't I take you out—what time of day is it?—for lunch? Is there a restaurant or diner nearby? A place we can sit and talk? Oh, I suppose it has to be kosher. Is that a problem?

MRS. FELDMAN: Young man—

CLIFFORD: Please, call me Clifford.

MRS. FELDMAN: Clifford, you don't know what I have to put up with here. There's no kosher. None. Well, I complained, of course. "I'm Jewish," I said. "I've been keeping kosher all my life. Thou shalt not boil a calf in its mother's milk." I went to the county offices.

CLIFFORD: They have county offices?

MRS. FELDMAN: Yes. And they looked at me like I was crazy. A young clerk there said, "Ma'am, we don't have any religion here. There are no Jews, no Catholics, no Moslems, no Presbyterians. Everybody's the same." Can you imagine that?

CLIFFORD: That's terrible.

MRS. FELDMAN: Everybody's the same. Well, that's nonsense. I know what *I* am.

CLIFFORD: I assure you, when Marsha and I are married, I'll see to it that we're very observant. We'll go to—what was it?—a kind of school?

MRS. FELDMAN: *Shul*.

CLIFFORD: We'll go to *shul*, on . . . *Shabbos* every Sunday, I mean Saturday, of course, and keep kosher . . . *Nosh* kosher?

MRS. FELDMAN: Close. *Glatt* kosher. But kosher-shmosher, you can forget about marrying my daughter, young man. That's quite out of the question. I'm sorry, but there's no point beating around the bush.

CLIFFORD: We love each other. I'll convert. I'll be Orthodox.

MRS. FELDMAN: You can be Orthodox until you're blue in the face. My daughter's already married. Didn't you know that? Didn't she tell you? You must have seen his photograph on our hutch. Philip.

CLIFFORD: Hirsch, yes. The anthropologist.

MRS. FELDMAN: The Pygmy expert. I never liked him.

CLIFFORD: His plane went down, ten years ago.

MRS. FELDMAN: According to Jewish law, she's still married.

CLIFFORD: Surely he's dead.

MRS. FELDMAN: Disappeared, missing. No body. That makes Marsha an *agunah*.

CLIFFORD: A what?

MRS. FELDMAN: If she marries and has children, and Philip returns—maybe he was held captive by the Pygmies, who knows?—then her children are *mamzerim*, and that's my grandchildren we're talking about. Even though, may I rest in peace, I'm no longer among the living. Living or not living, I don't want *mamzerim* for grandchildren. Thank you but no thank you.

CLIFFORD: Then . . . suppose we don't have children. I mean, I already have a family, two teenagers. Marsha and I don't need any of our own. So you wouldn't have . . . *mamziree*, whatever it is, for grandchildren.

MRS. FELDMAN: Birth control, too, is against Jewish law. "Be fruitful and multiply." The first commandment. But Philip—*shakes her head*—the man was one of those yuppie types, nose in the air. Didn't want to be too Jewish. Embarrassed by his roots. Didn't eat gefilte fish.

Didn't say *oy* when he stubbed his toe. Didn't use his hands when he talked.

CLIFFORD: I know. The kind of people who don't like messes and smells. And children are messy and smelly.

MRS. FELDMAN: You're right. That's it. Hit the nail on the head. *Looks at him with interest*.

CLIFFORD: My children. *Shakes his head*. It's hard bringing up children without a mother. She left us, also ten years ago, to save the whales. Not as much as a postcard or a phone call on the holidays. Nothing. Just turned away and never looked back.

MRS. FELDMAN: Shameful.

CLIFFORD: It's hard bringing up children anyway. Pornography on television. All the drugs. All the violence. Our world is so polluted. And now war with the Russians.

MRS. FELDMAN: We're at war with the Russians?

CLIFFORD: You didn't know?

MRS. FELDMAN: How am I supposed to know? There are no papers here. I really miss the Sunday papers, the funnies. The news I can do without.

CLIFFORD: And the way the papers pile up. You wouldn't believe it. I must have two hundred pounds of newspaper at least on my back porch, tied up in bundles. There's no point putting it out, because of the garbage strike.

MRS. FELDMAN: What is it with those people?

CLIFFORD: They want more money.

MRS. FELDMAN: A garbage collector nowadays makes more than a neurosurgeon. And he has better hours. You ride a truck in the morning, take the rest of the day off, go to the beach, get a tan.

CLIFFORD: Josh and Trish, they're like lost souls. They're so far from me now. What they need, what we need, is a mother. A mother in the house. What's a home without a mother?

MRS. FELDMAN: Absolutely.

CLIFFORD: When Marsha and I marry, and I bring her home, my children will have a mother.

MRS. FELDMAN: Too bad it's out of the question. But tell me, Mr. Koussevitzky—

CLIFFORD: Please, call me Clifford. I'm changing the name anyway, because of the war. And the converting. Kaplan.

MRS. FELDMAN: You can't be a Kaplan. A Kaplan is a *cohen*, a priest. A convert can't be a *cohen*.

CLIFFORD: That's a Jewish law, too, I guess.

MRS. FELDMAN: We have a lot of laws. Hundreds. A whole book of laws.

CLIFFORD: It makes living difficult, sometimes.

MRS. FELDMAN: You wouldn't believe how difficult. What I used to have to go through on Passover.

CLIFFORD: So there are Jewish priests? I thought you had only rabbis.

MRS. FELDMAN: Only rabbis since the fall of the Temple. If the Temple ever gets rebuilt, they'll need priests again, to do the burnt offerings.

CLIFFORD: I guess I have a lot to learn about Judaism.

MRS. FELDMAN: Being Jewish isn't a picnic.

CLIFFORD: I'll work at it, I promise.

MRS. FELDMAN: You said you're a songwriter, Clifford?

CLIFFORD: Yes, ma'am.

MRS. FELDMAN: What kind of songs do you write? You know, a lot of songwriters are Jewish. Irving Berlin. Maybe you have some Jewish blood in you and don't know it.

CLIFFORD: It's possible. I'm mostly Slovak, but a little Russian, on my father's side. My father's father was from Russia.

MRS. FELDMAN: Where in Russia?

CLIFFORD: Riga.

MRS. FELDMAN: Lots of Jews in Riga. A lot of inter-marriage. Unfortunately, that doesn't help. If it was your mother, it would be a different story. Maybe you should have another look at your family tree, Clifford.

CLIFFORD: Well, maybe, except I don't think my parents wrote any of that down.

MRS. FELDMAN: An aunt, an uncle?

CLIFFORD: I don't think so. I'm sorry. *Pause*. But to answer your question, I try to write positive songs. Songs of hope. So much of what's going on in society today is so negative. The negative things seem to feed on themselves. I try to look on the bright side. My friends say I'm an anachronism.

MRS. FELDMAN: And these songs, they're on records?

CLIFFORD: Tapes. They don't make records anymore, Mrs. Feldman. It's all tapes and discs. And now there are those new things, from Angola, rolls.

MRS. FELDMAN: This I haven't kept up with. But you must be uncomfortable, standing there.

CLIFFORD: Well. It's all right.

MRS. FELDMAN: There just aren't any chairs. Not that I need any, usually, except this one. I don't entertain. No one comes, except Jehovah's Witnesses, and them I tell to go to hell.

CLIFFORD: Your ancestors don't drop by? Old friends who passed away?

MRS. FELDMAN: I guess they have other fish to fry. Or haven't got around to it yet. There's plenty of time down here, you know, all the time in the world. Although, strictly speaking, there's no time at all, because time has ended. At least that's the line they gave us at orientation. It doesn't make a lot of sense.

CLIFFORD: Marsha and I will come see you every day—I'll make a point of it—when our turn comes.

MRS. FELDMAN: Well, that's very nice of you, Clifford. But you really can't marry her, as I explained. Too bad, too. You would have made a first-rate son-in-law.

CLIFFORD: I'm sure Philip's dead. Nowadays, communication systems are good, even in Borneo. You can call anywhere by satellite. If a man doesn't show up ten years after a plane crash in a jungle . . .

MRS. FELDMAN *takes his hand, gives it a squeeze:* I'm sorry. But you can find someone else, Clifford. You shouldn't have any trouble. You're young.

CLIFFORD: I'm in my forties.

MRS. FELDMAN: That's young yet. You have a lot of years left.

CLIFFORD: Marsha and I want to get married.

MRS. FELDMAN: Maybe we should change the subject.

CLIFFORD: Look, if Philip's dead, then he must be here. Right? I'll look him up in the phone book.

MRS. FELDMAN: Not everyone here has a phone. And a lot of deceased people—you'd be surprised—have unlisted numbers. I guess they want to be left alone. Rest in peace, as it says in the cemetery. *Looks at her phone.* Mine hasn't rung once. Well, once it did, the first day I got here. A wrong number. A man spoke in a foreign language. With funny clicks. Or maybe he was some kind of pervert.

CLIFFORD: I can still look. It's worth a try, isn't it?

MRS. FELDMAN: You're not a giver-upper. That's good.

CLIFFORD: I just want a normal life, a family.

MRS. FELDMAN: Clifford, I'll tell you what. I'll take you up on that invitation to lunch. There's a reasonable diner around the corner. A Greek place.

CLIFFORD: But it's not kosher, is it?

MRS. FELDMAN: I stick to the falafel or the hummus. I close one eye. Don't tell on me.

CLIFFORD: Humus?

MRS. FELDMAN: Not humus, hummus, with two *m*'s. The Middle East chick-pea stuff. Not soil. We may be six feet under here, but we're still people, thank God, not worms. *Gets up, puts a shawl around her shoulders.*

CLIFFORD: I'd be delighted. *Gives her his arm.*

MRS. FELDMAN: That way, we can both sit and talk. Your feet must be killing you.

CLIFFORD: It's all right.

MRS. FELDMAN: And maybe you could sing one of your songs for me.

CLIFFORD: I didn't bring a guitar or keyboard.

MRS. FELDMAN: So sing without it. What's to be embarrassed? I'm just an old woman.

CLIFFORD: You're not that old, Mrs. Feldman.

MRS. FELDMAN: Please, call me Emma.

CLIFFORD: I'd like most of all to call you Mother.

MRS. FELDMAN *laughs lightheartedly as she lets him lead her out:* Over my dead body, Clifford dear, over my dead body.

Not sure, under the circumstances, whether this is a yes or a no, a categorial refusal or a jest that offers grounds for hope, Clifford laughs nervously, watching her carefully, and they both exit.

30

The wedding took place at Temple Beth Shalom in Rosewood, Rabbi Kipple or Kippel officiating, who, although he was not super-ultra-Orthodox, was the grandson or the great-grandson or possibly the great-great-grandson of some extremely famous and revered Jew in Lithuania, and that satisfied Mrs. Feldman when they told her this, using Marsha's old Ouija board.

It was in the middle of July. Clifford was on his feet again, though still a little shaky after his combination circumcision and vasectomy. The vasectomy, to allay Mrs. Feldman's fear about having *mamziree* for grandchildren and because of her strong religious scruples, as well, about contraception, although Rabbi Kipple or Kippel pooh-poohed that.

"Jews don't have a problem with birth control," he had said at the prenuptial interview.

"The Hassids do," Mr. Feldman, at Clifford's shoulder, put in.

"The Hassids," said the rabbi with distaste, raising one eyebrow at Mr. Feldman.

"The point is, gentlemen," Clifford said quickly, to forestall religious contention (of which there seemed to be a lot, in Judaism), "that Mrs. Feldman must be satisfied. We can't have Marsha living in a house where the sugar bowl is constantly exploding and the faucets drip blood."

And they couldn't very well argue with that.

The ceremony went off all right, though Clifford needed considerable prompting with the Hebrew, and his Aunt Bea from the Cherokee reservation in Oklahoma kept glaring at him. When he took her aside later and asked her what was wrong, she said that he should be ashamed of himself for renouncing Jesus.

"But, Aunt Bea," he said, "we all worship one God."

"They're Christ-killers," said Aunt Bea. "But don't worry, I won't make a scene." And she gave him a dry peck on his cheek. "I hope you'll be very happy, Clifford."

Mr. and Mrs. Nagel were there, and the Rifkins, and Mrs. Popovic, still in mourning. There was a bad moment at the reception, everyone standing around awkwardly with their canapés, because Mrs. Popovic had dropped her anchovy-and-cream-cheese on the rug and turned away very conspicuously after Bernie, in response to a question, made some statement about the necessity for discipline in dealing with today's youth. Mrs. Packard, another neighbor who had been invited, caused everyone to squirm even more when she gasped and said, "Oh, my! Of course! Poor woman!" In the silence that followed, the guests could see the large headline in the local newspaper six months ago: POWER MAN DISMEMBERS TWO TERRYVILLE HIGH-SCHOOL STUDENTS.

Lucy Hoff was there, introduced all around by Clifford as "my former sister-in-law." She was so thin now, it was a wonder she could stand up. A mummy, all stooped and desiccated, but with gleaming, feverish eyes. She laughed constantly, an unnatural, mirthless laugh, and made one joke after another about AIDS. People smiled politely and excused themselves. Lucy didn't seem to notice or care.

It was inhumanly hot, even with the AC grinding away. The temperature outside was in excess of a hundred and twenty degrees. Clifford kept wishing he could take off his clothes and get into the shower. And he worried about his guests. Were their helmets all working? Did everyone have a helmet? In this heat, and with the three-day pollution alert, the air was impossible to breathe. Just looking out the window made you feel stifled. And there were two months of summer to go. No relief in sight.

"Your honeymoon," asked an old gentleman, some relative of Marsha's on her father's side, "will it be in Niagara Falls?"

"Yes," said Clifford, thinking of the famous Falls and longing for a shower. "We hope so. There was fighting there, you know. But the last we heard, the Soviets were driven out of the area. We'll keep the radio on the news as we drive up."

"Sounds a bit risky," observed the gentleman.

"Well, I suppose it is," said Clifford. "But what isn't risky nowadays? Why, you take your life in your hands just going to the mall."

"True, true." The old man shook his head and sighed.

"A person," Clifford went on, "has to try to live a normal life. Otherwise, what's the point?"

What was a wedding, after all, without a honeymoon in Niagara Falls? No, Clifford wanted to do the thing right. Correctly, completely, from A to Z. There had to be rice thrown as the couple left the building—it didn't matter if the grains rattled against their helmets instead of getting in their hair. There had to be tin cans tied to the back of his Audi—it didn't matter if the cans were dragged silently in the inch-by-inch traffic on the expressway north. A wedding wasn't a wedding without rice and tin cans. It was as simple as that. At his urging, Marsha had worn something old, something new, something borrowed, something blue. And, of course, a demure veil, though she wasn't a virgin. But all brides were virgins, in a way. It was traditional.

"Where are your children, Mr. Koussevitzky?" asked another relative, a fat woman in a flower-print dress, holding a drink.

Clifford said they weren't able to make it.

"Couldn't come to their father's own wedding?" asked the fat woman, tactless. There was a tactless questioner in every family.

He hadn't seen Trish now for—what was it?— twelve years. And Josh hadn't been home since March, no, January. Only for one evening, and a few mumbled words. His son stopped coming home regularly three years ago.

"First thing after Niagara Falls," Clifford said, "I'm going to round them up, introduce them to their new mother." He set his jaw, and his eyes glinted with the hard light of resolve. A man who braved the hereafter to win his wife's hand in marriage could surely track down and reclaim one mall zombie and one space cadet. The trick was to think positively. Not to be, as Mrs. Feldman put it, a giver-upper. Faith can move mountains.

"God, it's hot in here," said someone.

The AC had stopped chugging. It happened a lot these days: units couldn't take the strain; they blew. Or there were outages. It happened in movie theaters, supermarkets, homes—and often meant fatalities, particularly among the aged and those with respiratory problems.

Everyone scrambled for his helmet, and Rabbi Kipple or Kippel distributed a few synagogue helmets to the few who couldn't get theirs working. Mr. Feldman suffered a heart attack, turned blue, and was declared dead by a take-charge relative who was a certified nurse.

Two other people passed out, but they were quickly revived with water from a garden hose and spray nozzle, which the rabbi kept on hand in his office. A simple funeral service was held. The eulogy was kept short, since most AC helmets had to be recharged frequently, like flashlights. Only the latest models were solar-powered, and they were beyond the pocketbook of all but trillionaires. There were no trillionaires present.

"Not an auspicious beginning for a marriage," Clifford thought as the bride at his side wept and blew her nose inside her helmet.

When Osborn Feldman was lowered into the ground, the heat at the cemetery was so fierce and the humidity so oppressive, everyone longed to be lowered with the dead man. That deep rectangular hole, how invitingly dark and shaded it was, how wonderfully cool it seemed, like a cave where a man could have a quiet moment to himself after all the fever of the day.

31

Bob Petruzzo kept seeing green out of the corner of his eye. He was convinced the lawn was after him. Like Frankenstein, the Mummy, or Moby Dick. The psychologist told him he needed a change of scenery after the shock of losing his family, so Bob moved to California, where he stuck to the beach and the pavement and carefully avoided parks. After a couple of weeks, he met a woman, a little retarded, perhaps, but sweet as could be, and he began going with her. The psychologist he saw there said that was a good sign. He said Bob should work on not being so paranoid. But Bob remained vigilant, which turned out to be a good thing. On his wedding night, when he entered the bedroom and saw, on the bed, no wife but only a green blanket, he put two and two together immediately and dived backward into the motel corridor. And not a moment too soon. The lawn had indeed crossed the continent in pursuit of him, but thank God its intelligence was not equal to its hatred. Disguising itself as a blanket when the mercury yesterday had reached a hundred and thirty, a new record, was not particularly bright. The lawn, snarling, leaped for Bob, but Bob was running full tilt to his car—and this time, even though he was only in pajamas, he had his car keys. He kept them now on his person at all times, even when he showered. Some lessons we don't have to learn twice. He drove off, tires squealing, toward the harbor, toward the sea. He would be safer on water; he would spend the rest of his goddam life on a ship, if he had to. Lawns couldn't swim, and even if they could, they couldn't swim fast, having no flippers or fins. But on his cruise to Alaska, and then on his cruise to Panama, Bob couldn't relax. He would stand on the deck day and night watching the ocean through expensive infrared binoculars, looking for suspicious patches of seaweed. The ship psychologist gave him Quiets, but Bob didn't take them, which was a good thing. The next evening, when the moon was hidden by dark clouds and most of the vacationers were either drunk, stoned, or glued to their television screens, there was a muffled knock on the door of Bob's cabin and a sound like rustling. "Who's there?" Bob asked, but the only answer was another muffled knock. Had his mind not been clear, he would have unlocked and opened the door, assuming it was a repairman or else some recreation assistant inviting him to join the captain's all-night poker game. Instead, Bob held his breath and crawled out the porthole. He snuck around to the personnel area, where in a closet he found, sure enough, one of the repairmen bound and gagged, in nothing but his skivvies. The gag, moreover, had grass stains on it. Bob realized, with an awful chill, that the greenhouse effect, which was growing worse with each passing day, causing the earth to be bombarded by all kinds of harmful radiation on account of the ozone layer's being depleted by chlorofluorocarbons, was causing his former lawn to mutate at an alarming rate toward greater intelligence. The goddam thing might even have an opposable thumb now. Losing no time, Bob dove off the ship and swam like one possessed to the coast of a Central American country, which luckily was not far from the ship. He changed his name, acquired a phony passport, and with the last of his money took a plane to the Philippines, to Davao. Not to be in Davao, but simply to leave the ground, to get into the air and stay in the air as long as possible, because lawns couldn't fly, no matter how much they evolved. You couldn't develop wings until you had arms, and you couldn't think about arms until you had bones and a whole skeletal structure, for Chrissake. True, a boneless creature might get itself airborne, after a fashion, by flapping hard, but it wouldn't have a prayer, no matter how hard it flapped, keeping up with a supersonic jumbo jet at forty thousand feet above sea level. Bob looked out the window and smiled. Miles and miles of uninterrupted sky. Absolutely nothing for a monster to hide behind. The clouds were all far, far below. He sighed with relief, for the first time in months, and let his head fall back against the cushioned headrest. The only fly in the ointment was that he wouldn't be able to take another plane after this flight; he had used his last traveler's check, and there was nothing left in the bank account from his first wife's insurance. Not a cent. "What the hell," he thought dreamily. "I'll become a hijacker. Everybody does it these days. I'll say I have one of those plastic bombs in my pocket and want to go to Murmansk or Ankara, and then I'll keep changing my mind." He would go from airport to airport, stopping only to refuel, and while refueling make damn sure there wasn't any green on the runway. He'd have them spray the place first with Agent Orange. Twice, three times with Agent Orange. Bob chuckled. A shapely flight attendant pushed a cart down the aisle, offering the passengers drinks. Bob got a Coke. The man next to him, sipping a martini, struck up a conversation. He was a psychologist, originally from India, on vacation to recover from a personal tragedy. It seems his wife had been eaten by a man-eating plant while they were visiting her sister in Jakarta. "It's the greenhouse effect," said the psychologist, "that has made our flora and fauna so dangerous and unpredictable." Bob thought, "What a coincidence," and was about to tell the man his own story, but was distracted by the fact that the Coke had a funny taste. Then, suddenly, his nose and cheeks turned numb. The psychologist from India, as if by accident, spilled—tossed, actually—his martini into Bob's face. The liquid in Bob's eyes was not only blinding but paralyzingly painful. There must have been more than just alcohol in it. The psychologist, apologizing profusely, waved his napkin and called the flight attendant, who came quickly, removed the top of the cart, and together they picked Bob up, the two of them, and stuffed him in the cart: all so deftly—they must have rehearsed it—that none of the other passengers noticed, with the exception of a nine-year-old boy in the seat directly across the aisle, but he decided, wisely, to keep his mouth shut. The flight attendant put the top on again and wheeled the cart to the back, to a small storage area behind a curtain, and the psychologist from India followed her. A man in a low-brimmed hat, dark glasses, gloves, and trench coat paid them both off, putting a great deal of folding green—bill by bill, all brand-new and in impressively large denominations—into their held-out hands. In a hoarse, deep, blurry voice the man said, "Thank you. I'll take care of him now," and the flight attendant and psychologist from India both nodded, pocketed the bright-green money, and left, closing the curtain carefully behind them.

32

The dungeon was deep, dank, and foul. And the fact that hours passed and nothing happened strongly suggested that it was not for show but the real thing. A real dungeon. That more hours would pass, even days, months, years, and nothing would happen except sitting in the dark on uncomfortable stone and listening to the drip, drip, drip of water somewhere.

Bobby Bergholz was fit to be tied. "What the fuck is going on?" he said. "I mean, what the fuck is going on? Is this the action we get for seven hundred thousand dollars? I can't believe it."

It wasn't seven hundred thousand dollars, it was twice that, one million four hundred thousand dollars, almost one and a half million, for the two pills, a pill for each of them, and Bobby hadn't even paid for his. And—let's face it—he probably wouldn't, no matter how much action he got. Josh would have to come up with the whole amount, the million and a half, for the privilege of sitting in a cold, wet, stinking dungeon until the pills wore off. Was this the captain's idea of a joke?

"Why did they throw us in here?" Bobby Bergholz whined, shifting on the clammy stone because his behind hurt. "Just because you wouldn't sign a couple of papers. I don't get it."

Josh didn't say anything, but his suspicion was that

the lawyers, and perhaps all the natives of this planet, were in cahoots with the dragon bears. That they worked together, luring space cadets from different galaxies, innocent kids in search of a little adventure. Kids who wanted the fun of saving a world from the vile clutches of a race of monsters. So the dragon bears played the monsters, and the lawyers made sure that the planet couldn't be sued. And maybe the dragon bears took the space cadets prisoner, hostage, demanding an arm and a leg in ransom from the parents or the legal guardians, and the lawyers were the go-betweens, forwarding the money from parents to dragon bears—but in reality splitting it with them fifty-fifty, or sixty-forty . . . "Why am I so cynical?" Josh thought. He could even see Captain Jack Zodiac in on this operation, getting a percentage, a cut.

The captain says to little Johnny, "Now here's a pisser. This pine-green pill with the pastel gold dots— lovely, ain't it?—will whisk you parsecs farther than you've ever been whisked. Maybe even beyond the Crab Nebula. It's amazing what those people in Manila can cook up in their chemical laboratories."

(Travel to the stars, we probably should explain here, was made possible through the discovery, by an anonymous Scottish graduate student at Ohio State back in 1983, that certain aromatic peptides in the presence of chromium ions caused the thalamus and pineal gland in adolescent males to set up gamma-wave rhythms that in turn triggered the dramatic but still poorly understood hyperspace displacement known as the Davis Effect. The graduate student received no credit for his pioneering work, because he disappeared mysteriously, shortly after he accused his professor, at a Christmas party, of unprofessional conduct in the publication of a research paper on cortisone and sheep. The student's academic records also disappeared, both at Ohio and in Edinburgh. The professor has since retired and lives in Manila.)

Captain Jack goes on, scratching his gray head under his faded blue cap. "But this baby is expensive. It'll cost you . . ."

Little Johnny pays, of course, swallows the pill, finds himself in the system with the weird tidal forces on account of the binary star and the erratic green gas-giant planet with the orthogonal double rings, and as soon as he signs the contract and waivers that Phex Plowg and Seph Glowp give him, and takes off for Moon Two, the dragon bears, laughing, pounce. They pluck him out of space, tie him up, and say so help them and no kidding they'll stick hot pins in his young testicles until he's dead unless Mom and Dad cough up twelve billion dollars in a brown paper bag by tomorrow noon. The lawyers, pretending to wring their hands in distress, call or telex the parents: It's not our fault, we warned him, he signed on the dotted line in front of witnesses, and send the twelve billion in stacks of hundreds, please, and unmarked, or those awful dragon bears will do what they say, they have absolutely no conscience, having evolved without it. The parents, cursing, send the cash, which is divided three ways: four billion for the dragon bears, four billion for the lawyers, and four billion for Captain Jack Zodiac, who already took a half million or so from the kid to begin with.

It was because of the inflation, Josh thought. When people felt fear, they grew desperate, they showed their teeth. Get the money, as much as possible, get it while it's still worth something, which won't be long, and buy that house in Costa Rica or that ranch in Danang or that yacht or that Sharper Image two-seater spaceship. This is your last chance, before the bottom falls out of everything and we all have to stand in line to get even the dark smelly tuna fish that used to be only for cats.

It wasn't the captain's fault; it was the world, the stock market, the evils of capitalism, as the captain often said. The captain had to be a capitalist in self-defense, had to outcon the cons, outshark the sharks, not only for the money but because of his personal honor and revenge. The oath he had sworn when the bank repossessed his house in Compton, having no respect for the old spacesalt's war medals.

Josh sighed, and wished—what? That he was back at Farmer Carver's pumpkin stand? No, anything was preferable to that, even sitting in this fetid black tomb of a dungeon with nothing happening.

33

This time, at the Taco Bell, the red on the signs and menus and in the decor was dark brown, not even remotely red, and the counter where you got the food was very crooked, more than five degrees off, though no one seemed to mind. Joe figured a Mexican pizza would be safe now. What else could happen to him? Stroke, heart attack—that was it, wasn't it, in the way of health hazards, from cholesterol? As far as he knew, there wasn't anything that linked Mexican pizza to cancer. So he bought one. But he was nervous as he ate it, perhaps because in the back of his mind there was that saying that bad things always happen in threes. He was still all right after he finished half, then three quarters of the pizza, which was farther than he had got in a long time. "This is ridiculous," he thought. "I'm all in a sweat." Perhaps he felt that if he made it through this pizza without dying again, it would break a jinx. Perhaps that was the reason he hurried, and ate without chewing properly, and breathed too much while he ate, and inhaled a piece and choked. He knocked over a couple of chairs and a table, and, eyes bulging, looked around in panic. But even though there was a poster clearly displayed that demonstrated all the steps, one, two, three, of the Heimlich maneuver, the diners in the Taco Bell all looked at him with disgust and turned away, as if hoping the son of a bitch would unchoke himself, sit back down quietly, and not cause any more trouble.

So Joe went through the routine again of the unisex nurse, the doctor with the clipboard, and the Coke. Dis 3 was a lot shabbier and dimmer, but his eyes eventually adjusted to the lack of light. The main difference was that the place was noticeably less crowded. Which made sense, after all. If most of the world's population in history was contained in the present generation, because of the exponential curve in the birthrate—he had read something to that effect, in a dentist's office once—then it followed that most of the deceased hadn't got to the end yet of their second existence, so to speak. The farther down in afterlifes you went—afterlifes or afterlives?—the more Ancient Greeks and cavemen you would bump into. Occasionally there would be someone, like himself, who had had a lot of accidents, a run of bad luck, or someone, maybe, who kept committing suicide because he wasn't normal in the head. Sinking from Dis to Dis, like taking an elevator down. Was there a bottom Dis? Or did they go on infinitely?

Joe liked the idea of less people. He liked it so much that eventually, with a bemused smile on his face, he went to the nearest Taco Bell—barely visible lettering on old boards, gray-black on gray-black—and ordered, yes, his nemesis: a Mexican pizza.

34

Fortunately, the nuclear winter—because of all the bombs—provided an effective counterbalance to the greenhouse effect, which lately had seemed out of all control, sending the temperature to incredible new heights with each passing day. A hundred and thirty-five degrees, a hundred and thirty-six degrees; a hundred and thirty-seven degrees . . . Now the weather was more moderate. Though, of course, the radioactivity presented a problem. All these inconvenient siren alerts. People had to run inside before it rained, and wait the rain out, even if they had an important appointment on the other side of town. And if it rained all day, too bad, you had to stay put. Because if you got wet, you got cancer; it was that simple.

Clifford Koussevitzky—who, now that he was married and converted, was thinking of changing his name to Kahn, Clifford Kahn, although Kahn, too, was a priest's name in Judaism—but perhaps Mrs. Feldman didn't mind now, or perhaps her attention was being taken up these days by her husband, who had just joined her, presumably, in the hereafter—because when Clifford and Marsha asked her about Kahn on the Ouija board, she didn't reply—

Clifford, anyway, kissed his new wife on the nose and took off for Reykjavík, full of optimism. At the mall in downtown Reykjavík, he showed shoppers a photograph of his daughter. They looked at the photograph politely, smiled, and shook their heads. No, they had not seen, doubted that they had seen, could not recall ever having seen, sorry, a mall zombie that bore any particular resemblance to the picture of the pretty young girl. Mall zombies, anyway, all looked alike; they all had the same expression, which was a lack of expression. The blankness in the eyes, the puffiness about the eyes and lips, the loose jaw, the thick tongue, the way the head and arms moved as through soup or a dream.

A few people approached him. They, too, were looking for their daughters; they, too, had photographs. Clifford clucked with commiseration. Seeing his photograph, they clucked with equal commiseration. A short, careworn lady from Bavaria had been everywhere, from Grand Rapids to Marrakesh, in search of her Hannah, so far in vain. But she would not, could not, refused to give up. "This is worse," she said, "than a funeral. It is a funeral that never ends. With the dagger of hope always in the heart, twisting." Clifford agreed. They all agreed. If you did not have a mall zombie for a child, you could not understand, not really, this pain of always mourning and always hoping.

Coincidentally, the next day, he was musing about daggers in hearts when a gang of razor boys came running through the mall slashing people's throats and cutting off their ears. "Even in Iceland," he thought with surprise, because Iceland had one of the lowest incidences of juvenile violence in the world. A couple of the boys made for him. He could not outrun them, they were too fast, so he dodged into a women's clothing store and tried to hide in an aisle of long dresses. But the boys were too close and saw where he went, and followed him, were right behind him, at his heels. One of the boys struck at him with a razor. Clifford threw up an arm to protect his throat and felt a pain in his hand. Suddenly he was very tired, and it seemed to him then that it was all over. He would be killed, butchered, in the next second or two, and have to spend his evenings, forever after, reading back issues of the *National Geographic* and listening to Emma Feldman complain about the absence of things Jewish in Dis. Not that he had anything against the woman. A lot of what she said made sense. She had her heart in the right place. There were certainly worse people to spend one's eternity with.

But apparently Clifford, fallen and tangled in the dresses, sprawling under the dresses between the narrow aisles, was hard to get at, because the razor boys lost interest in him. They had easier prey at hand, namely, the screaming women in the store. He was tremendously relieved when they stepped away, and couldn't help feeling a rush of satisfaction when he heard the gurgle of one of the women as she was having her throat cut. It's horrible, yes, unspeakably horrible, but better your throat, dear, than mine. Clifford went on all fours, quietly, like a mouse, to an exit in the back, tiptoed down a corridor, and opened a door that led back into the concourse of the mall. No razor boys in sight. The police had finally arrived, with their clubs and dart guns, and everything was under control. Clifford noticed that the doorknob in his hand was red, and that his clothes were all red. The red was in fact blood, his own, and he was missing a couple of fingers. He must have fainted then, because he woke up in a hospital, comfortably bandaged, sun streaming through the window.

The doctor, a cheerful, overweight man with a goatee, came in and told Clifford that he was minus the fifth finger of his right hand. Both the fourth and the fifth had been severed. The rescue medics had been able to locate only the fourth, which was sewn back on and should be good as new in a month or two, with therapy. "There were parts of folks all over the place," said the doctor, chuckling. "Not easy to match them up. Just thank your stars," he added, "that you have both your ears. Those bad boys collect ears the way the American Indians used to collect scalps. The leaders have whole chains of ears. I saw an ear chain once. It looks like a string of dried mushrooms. I hope you're not put off by my sense of humor. We might as well laugh, don't you think? Otherwise, we are going boo-hoo all the time."

Looking in the mirror, Clifford saw that he had received a cut on the forehead, too. The zipper stitches went from one side of his forehead to the other. "This," the doctor told him, "is no problem. A little plastic surgery, and no one will ever know."

A telegram for Clifford Koussevitzky. It was Mr. Drucker, his boss. They needed a song, quick, on world peace. Clifford composed, humming to himself, in his hospital bed. It was a little difficult holding the pencil, with the bandages, but not that difficult. After a while, absorbed in the song, he forgot about the missing finger and the slash on his forehead and the despair he had felt, earlier, listening to the other parents of mall zombies, whose tales of woe were all the same and whose photographs all, every one, resembled Trish.

35

She saw a new doctor standing over her bed, with a clipboard. "Lucy Hoff," he said, more a statement than a question. "Maiden name Tyler."

"What is it this time?" she asked. "Another kind of experimental drug?"

"Had nine husbands, I see," said the doctor with a grin, almost a smirk. "Well, things should be a bit quieter for you here."

"I'm tired of the IV and all the goddam needles," Lucy said, surprised that her voice was so strong. Lately, it was a feeble croak, hardly a voice at all, and the nurses had to 'ean over to hear her. Though most had stopped bothering. She couldn't blame them, being nine-tenths out the door, so to speak, of life. What did it matter if the patient was a little uncomfortable, if she wanted a swallow of water or wanted the television channel to be changed because the superhero cartoons were getting on her nerves? Her discomfort would last only another day or two at most, and she probably couldn't feel much of anything anyway, with all that medication percolating drip, drip, drip through her bloodstream . . . "What business is it of his," Lucy thought, "how many husbands I've had?" She didn't like doctors. They were so goddam smug and superior all the time. Had the advantage of you while they shoved things up your orifices and asked for your Social Security number.

The doctor helped her sit up, and she found that she could sit up without having the room spin. Was she actually getting better? Impossible.

"You've passed away, Mrs. Hoff," he said. He took her left hand and had her press two fingers to the side of her neck, where the carotid artery was. No pulse. "My name is George," he said, and a flat-chested nurse held a pocket mirror to Lucy's mouth. There was no clouding. "You won't be needing any more needles," he said, showing her the thermometer that had been in her mouth, under her tongue, for five minutes. The reading was far, far below ninety-eight point six.

When she saw there was no clock on the wall, she realized she was not in a regular hospital. "What, is this some kind of special guinea-pig institute?" she asked. "I didn't sign my name on anything." At least, she didn't remember signing. Maybe she should call her lawyer. Maybe, Christ, they were planing to cut her up and use her liver for science.

"You've passed away, dear," said George, giving the nurse a side wink, as if to say: This one's not too swift. The nurse frowned disapprovingly.

"What are you trying to tell me?" said Lucy. "Is it bad news? I can take it. I'm used to bad news."

They gave her a cold, fizzy Coke, which had—as it always did, God bless Coke—a bracing effect.

"It's been nothing but bad news," she said, sipping the Coke, "ever since that party, when Janice brought Bill and went upstairs with him. I think only the Baxters are left. A damned stupid thing for her to do."

George patiently told her that she had kicked the bucket. Was six feet under. Pushing up daisies. Gone west. Deceased, departed, defunct. And for proof, he produced the death certificate, put it practically in her face, as if she were nearsighted.

"I'm not blind," she said.

The document looked official, was on parchment, had an embossed seal and signatures. Her name was spelled correctly, and they even had her birthday right.

"You mean . . ." she began, and looked at them, and George nodded, and the flat-chested nurse nodded.

"It's a joke, isn't it?" Lucy said. "You're playing a joke on me. You had this printed up the way they make fake newspapers." The headline saying something like LUCY HOFF WINS SIX QUADRILLION IN LOTTERY.

But George shook his head, and the nurse, too, with a sad, sympathetic smile, shook her head.

"When you check out, at the desk," George said, "they'll sign you up for postmortem counseling. A lot of people—you'd be surprised—have trouble coming to grips with it. Nothing to be ashamed of."

Lucy went for counseling and to her support group, but she didn't really believe that she was where everyone was telling her she was. She said to herself: "Maybe I've gone bananas, maybe the retrovirus has now got into my brain." She didn't believe, refused to believe, until she threw her first party and suggested, when the party warmed up, that everyone take off their clothes. Bill and Barb Humphrey were there, and Art and Janice Peppo, and Jack and Saul, and Mark (her former husband or still her husband? it was confusing), and Edith, too, whose enormous breasts were gone. Poor bimbo, she looked lost without them, like a cat in the rain. Lucy, on the phone, had told everyone it would be a reunion, and they came, looking as good as ever and in some cases better. Mark was the same old calm, collected Mark, though Lucy didn't understand why he brought his former wife. Anyway, they could all have a little orgy for old times' sake. Why not? And if they were all supposed to be dead, then they didn't have to worry about AIDS anymore, did they, and sex could be free again, the way it was supposed to have been in the first place.

But the people were strangely reluctant to drop their pants. You would have thought they were virgins. Lucy insisted, taunted, so down went the pants finally, and when she saw what she saw, she realized that this had to be the afterlife, because that was the only possible explanation. No penises. No vaginas. Not even, God help us, pubic hair. Smooth skin. Like dolls before the days of anatomical correctness.

"What are we supposed to do for all eternity," she said, aghast, practically in tears, "sit around and talk dirty?"

She went to the city hall in Maplehurst—though it wasn't Maplehurst, exactly—at the intersection of Broadway and Teller Avenue, across from the Greek diner, and asked to talk to somebody in charge. After the usual bureaucratic go-here and go-there, she was shown into the office of a woman who wore granny glasses and had her hair in a bun. And not a thing in the chest area.

"I don't think it's fair," Lucy said.

The woman explained, in a dry, hard, mechanical voice, as if she had given the same explanation countless times before. There couldn't be gender here, she said. Or sex, because there couldn't be babies—new babies, that is. It wouldn't make sense for people to be born to people who were dead, now would it?

Lucy didn't see what babies had to do with it. Making babies was an awfully old-fashioned, and boring, way to look at screwing.

The woman said, a little huffily, that Dis was an old-fashioned place, having been around since the Dawn of Man, since the Quaternary, which was a long time, relatively speaking. They didn't go in much for fashions here, or perversions, or swingers.

Lucy, her chin trembling, said there was no reason to call her names. She was an honest person, and in her opinion life—or death—had played one hell of a rotten trick on her. "What the fuck else, I mean, do we have going for us? Garbage strikes? War? Those little nasty biting flies that make it impossible for you to sit out on the patio?"

The woman supervisor took off her glasses, put her dry hand on Lucy's, and suggested, in a voice that was a little less hard and mechanical, that Lucy consider therapy.

36

You couldn't establish eye contact, Clifford found, let alone enter into a conversation, with a mall zombie. It was like trying to get the attention of a goldfish in a goldfish bowl, through the thick curved glass. Tapping with your fingernail didn't work. Making faces didn't work. Jumping up and down and shouting didn't work. Clifford must have cleared his throat, held out the photograph of Trish, and said, "Excuse me but—" a hundred times. It was as if he weren't there. As if he, too, were a child of limbo. But of a different, separate limbo, not this public one of concourses and store windows and the endless segueing of semitransparent figures back and forth between Oslo, Detroit, Belize, and Liège like puffs of subetheric mist.

Even real people looked through him: not wanting to have anything to do with sorrow. Or maybe they thought he was selling something, or begging. Panhandlers in three-piece suits and polished shoes were not that rare these days, what with all the unemployment, on top of the recent insane deregulation of the dollar.

He tried making friends, in the malls, with teenage girls who were plainly on the verge of zombiism. He reasoned that through them he might have a link, when they became zombies in a month or two, with other zombies and ultimately with his daughter. Assuming that mall zombies communicated with one another. Though it didn't look that way. It didn't look like they had anything to communicate. He tried such gambits as "There's a great sale at Macy's, I hear," or "Where did you get that neat panda?" But the mall girls hardly seemed to see or hear him. Sometimes, indeed, he mistook a flesh-and-blood girl for a zombie, and vice versa; the response—the lack of response—was so very similar, a slow-motion cottony vacuousness, which he remembered well from Trish when she was fifteen, fourteen. How time flew.

One girl, Bettylou Annamarie, let Clifford buy her a soda and talk to her for half an hour about Trish. But as he talked, he realized that she wasn't listening; she just sat there with a peculiar, unpleasant half smile. The next day, she pointed him out to a teenage boy, probably her boyfriend, and half laughed in an insinuating way, and the boyfriend leered. "They think I'm a pervert," Clifford thought, and suddenly he was painfully aware of his bald spot on the top, his paunch, and his skinny middle-aged legs with varicose veins.

After trying a couple of malls in Pakistan and then sitting for six days straight in a sour-smelling, cheap hotel in Damascus, unable to leave because of the radioactive rain that refused to let up, filling the rooftops and streets at night with an ominous ochre phosphorescence, he took a plane home. To consult with Mr. Nagel. Maybe the kindly German exorcist-warlock knew of a charm or potion that might help in this case.

Mr. Nagel shook his head, winced apologetically. "Mall zombies," he said, "are neutral, nonvalent, nonaffiliated beings. They have no focus. None." He shrugged. What could one do with a thing that had no focus? A thing that was less even than a shadow or a reflection; because shadows and reflections, at least, were connected to places, to solid objects. Also, what leverage, magically speaking, could one possibly have against a phenomenon that belonged to no mythological or ideological system? "With television zombies, for example," Mr. Nagel went on, "you can use advertisement. Television is basically capitalistic."

"And malls aren't capitalistic?" said Clifford.

"They are, of course," said Mr. Nagel. "But, you see, mall zombies don't buy anything. That is the whole point. They shop without buying." They were tangential, in other words, to consumer goods. Whereas television viewers, in the very act of switching on the set, became consumers and thus willy-nilly joined the ideological system of consumerism.

"Then there's no magic that will work?" asked Clifford in a stricken voice.

Mr. Nagel looked at him and sighed. "There is one thing you could do," he said at last, "but I don't recommend it." He looked at Clifford again, at the desperate pleading in Clifford's eyes, the awful scar across Clifford's face, and the missing finger on Clifford's right hand. He sighed again. "It could be throwing away your life," he said. "It means using drugs." Then, after another long pause and very, very reluctantly, the little ratlike man wrote a name and a number on a piece of paper. He folded the paper and handed it to Clifford while looking the other way, as if he were doing something highly immoral and there were vice-squad cops nearby.

Clifford unfolded the paper and read the name. Captain Jack Zodiac. It rang a bell.

37

For their twentieth anniversary, the Rifkins went to a fancy French restaurant, La Moufette. It was one of those places where you had to make a reservation two weeks in advance, and where a single glass of wine, the house wine, was memorable but cost a thousand dollars. It was one of those places where you waited an hour for a course so small, you could hardly find it on your plate. Where the waiters kept coming around and making you feel like an asshole who didn't know how to hold his melon fork or what to do with his napkin after it got vichyssoise on it in four or five places. Still, the Rifkins were celebrating twenty years of marriage, no small achievement in this day and age, and so they wanted to do something special and not worry about the expense or the awkwardness that went with class.

Halfway through the appetizer, which was toast strips and an assortment of minuscule pâtés, they heard screaming outside, in the parking lot. From the sound of it, someone being murdered, mutilated, or raped. Possibly all three. Mrs. Rifkin raised an eyebrow at her husband. He pretended not to notice. After a particularly awful scream, she cleared her throat and said, "Dear, perhaps you could do something about that."

"I'm all dressed up," said Bernie. "I'll get blood on my shirt. Blood doesn't come out."

Another scream, even more awful.

"But someone's being hurt," said his wife. Probably the understatement of the year.

"People are being hurt all the time," said Bernie, concentrating on a toast strip. "Don't you read the papers?"

A scream, now, so high on the scale of agony that even the sickest mind would have been hard put to imagine what form of torture had caused it.

Mrs. Rifkin set her napkin on the table. "I can't eat with that going on."

No one else in the restaurant seemed to be having a problem with it. The diners didn't miss a beat as they chewed their escargots à la bourguignonne, sipped their châteaux Latour-Neuilly, and discussed in muted tones the recent use of carbon dating in the renovation of the opera house in Turin.

Bernie sighed, got up, and went outside. It was over a hundred again, like an oven, and the air was gaggingly sour with pollution. The greenhouse effect was gaining, again, on the globe's nuclear winter. God knows what that meant. Whatever it meant, it was probably bad news. The sprinklers were going like mad. There was a mountain of garbage behind the restaurant, poorly concealed by a faded plastic-slat fence. Above the garbage hung a cloud of unusually large flies, hairy and iridescent.

At the far corner of the parking lot, Bernie saw one of those psychedelic vans and a couple of bearded longhair freaks with cowboy boots, Jesus beads, and spiked bracelets. He went over and saw that they had pulled apart what must have been one of the patrons. The gentleman or lady—it was hard to tell now—had either stepped out for a smoke, since the restaurant didn't allow smoking, or perhaps went to get something in his or her car.

"What can we do for you?" asked one of the freaks,

grinning like a drunk baboon. His mouth and beard were covered with spittle and blood.

"Just keep it down, all right?" said Bernie. "My wife is trying to eat."

Back at the table, he told her that it should be quieter now.

"Did you save that woman's life?" she asked.

He grunted noncommittally, and thought to himself that, really, after all the abuse he had taken from the press, he no longer gave a shit, when it came down to it, about crime. Sad but true.

On the way home, Bernie zapped a persistent tailgater. Turning around with a curse and a particle beam from a jabbed finger, he took out his own rear window but also put a satisfying six-inch-diameter hole in the head of the driver. The man's wife and children were sprayed with bits of his hat, cerebrum, and cerebellum.

"Can't stand those impatient sons of bitches," Bernie muttered.

Mrs. Rifkin grimaced. They had already had to replace the rear window twice this month, and car windows weren't cheap.

"Sorry," he said after a while. It would be a shame to spoil their anniversary, spoil the evening.

But then, as he pulled into the driveway, a few kids ran from the house. He thought that they were some of those pill-popping punks who were plaguing the neighborhood lately, breaking into homes and taking jewelry, antique lamps, and VCRs. So before they could get away, he rolled down his window and fried them with a glare. They made little piping noises and sizzled like steaks as they fell, dropping their bags.

"What did you do that for?" said his wife. She had

that chill in her voice, which meant she was really disgusted now.

"Space cadets," he said. "Making off with Billy's Nintendo, I bet." And they had probably broken a window, too, the brats, to get in.

"Trick-or-treaters," she said. "It's Halloween."

"Oh," he said. "I forgot."

Halloween. Now there was a pain-in-the-ass holiday: eggs on houses, lipstick on cars, shaving cream all over the place. And the knocking at the door until twelve or one.

These three kids, worst luck, were all still-innocent elementary-schoolers. The only things in their bags were candy bars, ampules, and a couple of coins.

"Our neighbors," said his wife, "will not want to have anything to do with us."

"We never see them anyway," Bernie retorted. People in Woodhaven kept to themselves, damned unsociable. If you said hi to them on the street, how's it going, they gave you the fisheye.

"You didn't have to kill those children," she said.

"Aw, come on. It was a mistake. It was dark. Look, I'm sorry. I'll have the window fixed first thing in the morning. Come on, Momma, lighten up. It's our anniversary. Hey, twenty years." He put his arm around her, but she was stiff.

"You've changed," she said, with that hardness he hated. "You've changed, Bernie. You're not the man I married."

He had, so help him, half a mind to wring her neck then and there, because she made it sound like it was his fault, and it wasn't his fault at all. He was a decent guy. He didn't like people trying to make some kind of monster out of him, just because he had a short temper and a few powers.

But of course he didn't wring his wife's neck. He clenched his fists instead and apologized, calling her in his heart a stupid bitch as he held open the door for her meekly. Because the truth was that Power Man, even when he was brimful with St. Pauli Girl, didn't wear, as they say, the pants in the family.

38

One of the welts on Bobby's back got inflamed, and the next thing you know, he was running a fever and talking funny. Then he was on the wet stone dungeon floor grring like a dog through clenched teeth. Probably foaming at the mouth, too, but Josh couldn't see that in the dark. An infection, as Phex Plowg had warned, from the filthy, disease-carrying claw of the dragon bear that had scratched Bobby in the attack the moment they arrived here. An infection, in spite of Phex Plowg's ointment. Or maybe because of Phex Plowg's ointment. Maybe Phex Plowg had really rubbed not an antibiotic into Bobby's scratch but some slow-acting poison. People were capable of any treachery. "This way," Josh imagined Phex Plowg thinking, "in case the kid does manage to get rid of the dragon bears for us, we don't have to pay him the ten quid." Josh they would dispose of in some equally underhanded way.

But no, the disposing had already taken place. The two space cadets had been thrown in here to rot, or to pop back to their planet of origin when the pills wore off. Josh would have to get Bobby to a doctor first thing when they popped back, because Mr. and Mrs. Bergholz, he now recalled, were on vacation, visiting her sister up in Vermont, where Mr. Bergholz liked to fish. The Bergholzes did that every August, for a week and a half. Over the mantelpiece in their living room was an enormous rainbow-colored fish with fins like wings, large-eyed, arched, and all shiny with shellac. Josh had been impressed by that fish when he was younger, but then decided that Mr. Bergholz couldn't have caught it himself. Mr. Bergholz was not well coordinated. There didn't seem to be anything, really, that he was good at. Maybe he paid a professional fisherman to catch it for him, or maybe he bought the fish, already shellacked and mounted, at a garage sale for eighty dollars.

A bad smell came from Bobby: he had crapped in his pants. Had some kind of awful diarrhea. Then he started jerking and kicking. "Maybe," Josh thought, "he isn't going to make it." This looked—sounded, that is—more and more like final throes, and the fancy lemon-and-vermillion pill they had paid a bundle for might not wear off yet for another week or two. Space pills were unpredictable. Poor quality control, because the government wouldn't legalize them. Sometimes you flicked in and out, and got nothing for your money but a splitting headache. Or you saw plaid for days afterward. Once, a pill gave Josh breasts for a month, and hair on the end of his nose. Captain Jack Zodiac would shrug and say, "What do you expect? It's a crooked world. Some lab technician kept the good stuff for himself. And why not? It's dog eat dog out there."

Josh felt a little sad at the thought that he might never see Captain Jack again. There was something comfortingly solid and reliable about the crease-faced old spacesalt. He was always there when you came back, shaky in the knees, from the asteroid belt or Alpha Centauri or the Coalsack, and though he never said he was glad to see you, or asked how you were doing, you knew, in a quiet way that didn't need words, that you belonged to him and he belonged to you.

Bobby Bergholz was definitely not going to make it. Yes, there was the death rattle. Josh had heard it many times before. The perils of space travel. Not everyone came back. A last kick or two, a squirting noise, an even fouler smell, then silence. Then a sudden foop and a breeze from the implosion as the body, finding itself free of the Davis Effect and obeying the laws of conservation of energy, momentum, and location, returned like a slingshot to the planet from which it came.

Leaving behind, in the cold, dank dungeon, Josh Koussevitzky, all by himself, alone with his thoughts and a smell of shit that persisted for hours.

39

Clifford didn't like the look of the man, but shook the horny hand that was extended when Clifford introduced himself. Introduced himself, using the name Katz. Clifford planned to make Katz official as soon as he got his family together again. A new family, a new name. Clifford Katz. Marsha Katz. Trish Katz. Josh Katz. A nice sound to it: perky and kind of neighborly.

Clifford and the dealer sat together on a bench in the mall, among potted tropical trees that were too green and dust-free to be real. The man said nothing, and his face showed nothing—not surprise, not sympathy, nothing—while Clifford explained what it was he needed.

Finally Captain Zack Zodiac pursed his lips, nodded, and said, "That's not easy."

"But you do have such a pill, don't you?" Clifford asked, his heart in his mouth. If this didn't work, what else could he do? Where else could he go? So much depended, now, on this sleazy, seedy character, who for all the cracks in his weather-beaten face probably had not been on a ship, space or otherwise, a day in his life.

"Such a pill," said the captain. "Not really."

"But . . . I thought you had pills to go anywhere."

"It's supply and demand," said the captain, scratching his head underneath his faded blue captain's cap and wincing as if from an old wound. "The law of supply and demand. One of the pillars of our cursed capitalistic system." He put his teeth into *cursed*, said it with two syllables. Cursèd.

Space cadets, the captain elaborated, were all teen-age boys (females having the wrong kind of pineal gland), and naturally, being teenage boys, they all wanted to go to Titan or Ganymede or Betelgeuse or the Andromeda galaxy. That was where the action was. They didn't want to go shopping in a mall, nossir.

And since the money came from them, since that was where the market was, that was where the research was done, in those state-of-the-art sweatshop labs in Manila. "If a chemist wants to try something different," said Captain Jack Zodiac, "he's not going to be funded. The company won't want to hear about it. Companies like their profits quick, and as sure as possible." He spat.

But once in a while, a chemist did a little something on his own time. On the side, for fun. Experimental was putting it mildly. So there were prototype pills now and then, though not often. Very hard to come by. Collector's items. With them, you could go to places not on any map. If you were lucky. If they didn't kill you instead, or burn out your brain, or turn you into something horribly alien.

"I'm prepared to take risks," said Clifford, and that was the truth.

The captain nodded, seemed to think awhile, and finally dug into his jacket pocket and took out a small dirty envelope with some words and numbers scribbled on it. Inside the envelope were a few pills. The captain looked at the pills, squinted, pursed his lips. "Well," he said, "this one might do the job." And he picked out a pill and let it fall into his leathery palm. It was pale brown, a coffee-with-lots-of-cream brown; the brown, almost, of a chicken's brown egg.

"That'll do the job?" Clifford asked, nervous, because he had never liked taking drugs, not even as a kid, and this pill, somehow, looked potent.

"Might. I'm not promising anything," said Captain Jack Zodiac. "Even with the regular pills, I don't give guarantees, and this . . ." He shook his head and, as he shook his head, closed one eye, the right eye, which spoke volumes about the pill's unreliability.

"All right, I'll take it," said Clifford. If the brown pill was the only pill that could help him reach his daughter, what choice did he have? No choice. He would do it for Trish. Grasping at straws. So be it.

Clifford would need hormones first, the captain told him. Because he was no teenage kid. The pineal gland needed juicing up for the kind of traveling he had in mind. If Clifford liked, the captain could sell him some hormones, too. Generic, but good quality, from Singapore. No nasty side effects, or at least not very many.

"I'd rather not," said Clifford. He didn't like the thought of having his penis shrink, or growing breasts the way Josh did once for a month. Particularly not now, just married. Marsha wouldn't understand; she would take it personally. In some ways—many ways—Marsha was a traditional woman, despite her courses in anthropology. As traditional as her departed mother. She would not be philosophical about her new husband's penis shrinking or his growing breasts.

The captain raised a gray eyebrow. "I think you'd better take them."

"I'll do without them."

"It's your funeral, Mortimer," said the captain sotto voce, with a shrug.

Then there was a long silence.

"What are we waiting for?" thought Clifford—and realized what they were waiting for. Of course. So he asked: "How much?"

The answer was in English, and each word, taken separately, was perfectly distinct and intelligible; yet, when put together, their combined meaning eluded Clifford completely. Perhaps he hadn't been paying attention.

"Come again?" he asked, leaning forward a little.

"Seven hundred and fifty million," said Captain Jack Zodiac.

"I'm sorry, seven hundred and fifty million what?"

"Dollars."

"Seven hundred and fifty million dollars."

"That's right."

"For a pill."

The captain smiled. He was no doubt accustomed to sticker shock from his clientele in such transactions, but this Clifford Katz seemed to amuse him. A middle-aged, middle-class parent turning pale and slack-jawed. Eyes going wide and out of focus.

"Are you really asking," asked Clifford, "seven hundred and fifty million dollars for *that*?" Pointing to the brown pill, which looked very small now in the captain's hand.

"As I told you," said the captain, "it's one of a kind. Or maybe one of two. On the cutting edge of the technology."

"Three quarters of a billion bucks for a pill. You must be joking."

Slowly, the captain put the pill back in the envelope, put the envelope back in his jacket pocket, and zipped the pocket shut. He sat, impassive, staring at nothing in particular as people in the mall walked by with their packages.

"I don't have that kind of money," Clifford said. His tongue was thick in his mouth.

The captain shrugged. He didn't really care, said the shrug. Clifford could buy the pill or not buy the pill. Clifford could get a second mortgage, or rob a bank, or sell his soul to the devil, or all three, or none of the above—it didn't matter to the captain.

"I'll have to talk to my wife," Clifford said.

The captain shrugged.

40

It'll all work out in the end, my friend,
It'll all work out in the end.
Yeah, it'll all work out, it'll all work out,
It'll all work out in the end.

We'll put down our guns in the end, my friend,
We'll put down our guns in the end.
We'll put down our guns, and all shake hands,
We'll all shake hands in the end, oh yeah,
We'll all shake hands in the end.

And we'll all have food in the end, my friend,
We'll all have food in the end.
And no one will starve, and no one will grieve,
No, no one will grieve in the end.
Or shiver with cold or fear or disease,
No one will shiver again.

It'll all work out in the end, my friend,
It'll all work out in the end, oh yeah,
It'll all work out in the end.

And our children will love us, and we'll love them,
And our children won't die,
And our babies won't cry,

And we'll all have food in the end, my friend,
Plenty of food in the end.

And our neighbors will love us, and we'll love them,
We'll love them all in the end, my friend,
We'll love them all, like the Bible says,
Love them all like ourselves in the end,
And never make war again.

It'll all work out in the end, my friend,
It'll all work out in the end, oh yeah,
It'll all work out, it'll all work out,
It'll all work out in the end.

41

Marsha thought he was crazy. "You're not being rational," she said. She could understand his attachment to his daughter, of course. "But what you're talking about sounds like suicide," she said. And the money. They would have to go into hock up to their eyeballs and over. Seven hundred and fifty million dollars, for one pill, from a disreputable character, with no guarantees. And Clifford wasn't a young man anymore, to go popping in and out of strange, dangerous places. "You have responsibilities," she said. "To me, at least, your new wife." And she pulled his head down and gave him a kiss on his bald spot.

"There's no other way to get to Trish," Clifford said.

"You're a noble man," said Marsha, looking at him with fond surprise, with pride, as one might look at one's dog that has just received a blue ribbon, on the bandstand in front of everyone, even though the dog isn't pedigreed. See what my darling little pooch has done. She told him to have a long soak in the tub and take a couple of Quiets with bourbon. He had had a hard day, had had to fight all that traffic, coming home, because of a detour after Soviet paratroopers used an incendiary device at a shopping center off Newcomb Highway.

Next day, at work, Clifford asked his boss if he could talk to him in private. Mr. Drucker raised an eyebrow, twisted his mouth, but finally nodded and ushered Clifford into the office that held all the archive file cabinets, the extra fans, and the water cooler that broke last year, was replaced, but still hadn't been removed from the premises. This office, more a storeroom than an office, was used for serious gossip, for saying things off the record, and occasionally for quick sexual acts.

"I need a lot of money," Clifford began, feeling how stupid it sounded.

Mr. Drucker raised an eyebrow again, as if to say, darkly, "Don't we all, my boy, don't we all. Have you seen what they're charging now for a head of lettuce?"

"About five hundred million dollars," Clifford said.

To this there was no reaction, not even a blink.

"More, if possible," Clifford added.

Mr. Drucker cleared his throat and said: "You know, Koussevitzky, that last song you wrote—I've been meaning to tell you—wasn't up to the high standard we try to maintain around here. Too repetitious. And kind of, well, simpleminded. It almost looks—I hate to say it—like you're running out of ideas. Like the old creative well is drying up."

"I'll work extra hard to pay it back," said Clifford. "I'll work overtime and weekends." He saw himself writing five, six, seven songs a day. The strain would be tremendous. All those rhymes and similes seething in his brain as minute after minute ticked by. Normally, a couple of songs a week was pretty good. Even one a week was fine, if it made the charts.

"And I have to tell you, too," said Mr. Drucker in a lower voice, "though, you understand, I don't want this getting around just yet, it's strictly *entre nous* . . ." And the dusty, dented file cabinets seemed to hunch over to hear the secret . . .

With a schedule like that, seven songs a day, seven

days a week, Clifford thought, he wouldn't have much time with his family. Not for many years, until he paid off the debt. They would all want to go to the beach, and he wouldn't be able to join them. But it would be worth it, it would be worth it twice over, to get Trish back.

"Our sales are down," his boss was saying. "Way down. Frankly—I hate to say this—but it looks like people out there are losing interest in the whole upbeat idea. Maybe it's the war. Who knows? We get letters telling us our songs are corny."

Clifford began to realize, with a slow sinking in his stomach, that Mr. Drucker wasn't going to come up with the five hundred million dollars Clifford needed to buy the seven-hundred-and-fifty-million-dollar experimental pill that was the color, almost, of a chicken's brown egg.

"Mr. Hillsworth-Fenwick," his boss went on, lowering his voice even more, "wants to close down the whole department. It's not fair, after all the years we earned our keep, but you know how the company is, with its damned bottom line."

"Then . . . I'm fired?" Clifford asked.

Mr. Drucker put an arm around him—but didn't hold him too close, as though Clifford had bad breath or body odor. "It hasn't come to that," he said, "at least not yet. We have a month or two, maybe three, to try to improve the figures. To rethink our strategy, to switch gears. The label's changing its name. Starting next week— this is confidential, now, not a word to anyone—we'll be The Downbeat. Not a bad sound to it, really. Kind of contemporary, don't you think?"

"The Downbeat."

"Yes. And in order to keep our staff intact, you understand, in this emergency situation, and keep Mr. Hillsworth-Fenwick off our back—Christ, I hope the man gets transferred to California or kicked upstairs—

we have to do some really unpleasant belt-tightening, I'm talking a twenty-percent cut in pay. Sorry, Koussevitzky." And Mr. Drucker shook his head, nodded, shook his head again, twisted his mouth, and sighed. But the sigh didn't quite come off.

Clifford also shook his head and nodded, as if he understood perfectly and appreciated his boss's efforts to save his job, although in fact his head was in a muddle as he tried to figure out what impact exactly, in dollars and cents, a twenty-percent cut in salary would have on his biweekly paycheck. It was confusing, too, this mention of Mr. Hillsworth-Fenwick, whose name Clifford had never heard before, and Clifford had been with the company more than twenty years and thought he knew all the executives.

He shook Mr. Drucker's hand, thanked him, and on his lunch break went to his bank, which was just across the street. He asked to speak to one of the assistant managers, and was directed to a desk where a young woman sat. She had purple punky hair, a cheek flower tattoo, and looked all business and very upwardly mobile. When Clifford told her that he needed five hundred million dollars at least—but, what the hell, he might as well ask for the full seven hundred and fifty million—she made a tart moue and said: "Do you want that in hundreds, in a brown paper bag?"

"No," he said, "a bank check will be fine."

"And I suppose you have a gun?"

He looked at her questioningly. He had missed something—which was not surprising, given all that was on his mind lately. "Excuse me?"

"I suppose you have a gun?"

"A gun?"

"I mean," she said, "this is a stickup, isn't it? I mean, no one in his right mind, with the balance you have in your account, Clifford"—and she pointed a long purple fingernail at the sleek monitor beside her desk—"would ask for a loan of that size. You're not exactly in the corporate raider category, if you know what I mean."

"I see," said Clifford, regretting that he didn't have a gun on him.

42

An old-fashioned radio console. The mahogany cabinet full of scrollwork at the top and corners, and with a carved Corinthian column on either side. Across the large speaker, a wood grille and a fabric containing a scene in petit point: the Ponte Vecchio, in tans and greens, faded oranges and rusty grays. Boats on the river below; a young curly-headed boy and girl sitting together on a wall overlooking them. Clouds in the sky, above the battlements, all very picturesque. Behind the radio is drab dark-green wallpaper, probably a floral print, but it's so old, it's hard to tell. Centered above the radio is a framed sepia etching, a woodland scene as nondescript and dreary as the wallpaper. Nothing else on stage, or at least not visible. The radio is on, and in the dim light its dial glows cheerily.

ANNOUNCER: And now the news. *He speaks, but on and off is drowned out by static, due to some atmospheric disturbance:* . . . up to three-hour delays on Interstate 28, north of Exit 43. Carter union spokesman Bruce Riley today accused Essex County officials of failure to . . . and three divisions are reported retreating to their stronghold north of Morristown after heavy . . . down a full eight points against the yen in heavy trading, despite the intervention of several . . .

no end in sight . . . Partly cloudy, a high of a hundred and twenty-six, which should provide us with some relief—right, Dan?—after yesterday's blistering . . . a possible breakthrough in the war against AIDS, researchers say, with the discovery of a new autoimmune suppressant drug developed at Drake Damon University in Botswana, but Dr. James Oliver . . .

SECOND VOICE: The most frequent question is, "Is the water safe to drink?" . . .

THIRD VOICE, *louder, static subsiding:* Our next guest is Senior Detective David Ferrucci of the Los Angeles Police Department, the author of the recent bestselling book *What Is Eating Our Children?* Welcome, Dave, to Speak Your Mind.

DETECTIVE FERRUCCI: It's nice to be here, Jane.

JANE: Well, I'm sure it must be, Dave, after that awful smog you people had this week. That was incredible. Nitric acid and cyanide.

DETECTIVE FERRUCCI: Yes.

JANE: I don't know how you people in L.A. put up with it.

DETECTIVE FERRUCCI: Well, it's tough sometimes, Jane, but you get used to it. Wherever I go, even if it's just to the convenience store around the corner, I take my gas mask with me.

JANE: Wow, incredible.

DETECTIVE FERRUCCI: Detroit has the same problem now, you know.

JANE: Detroit.

DETECTIVE FERRUCCI: The humidity's not as bad, but with all that industrial stuff being pumped into the air by the power plants, and now with the greenhouse—

JANE: Well, I don't know. What did you have, ten thousand dead? I think the press said ten thousand in L.A.

DETECTIVE FERRUCCI: Closer to nine thousand, actually. Nine thousand four hundred and something. But those were mostly senior citizens with respiratory problems and—

JANE: Dave, our listeners would like to know about the mystery of the disappearing children. You wrote this book, *What Is Eating Our Children?* Well, it's really fascinating. Creepy. I'll never be able to look at a playground again without freaking out.

DETECTIVE FERRUCCI: The publisher is Putnam. And it's coming out in paperback soon.

JANE: This month alone, more than a million children were reported missing in the United States. Between the ages of two and twelve, I believe.

DETECTIVE FERRUCCI: Well, yes, as a rule. They can be younger or older, but the idea is, playground age.

JANE: Something's eating them on the playgrounds. Eating our children. But I don't want to give it away. Dave, tell us your crazy theory.

DETECTIVE FERRUCCI: It's not crazy at all.

JANE: I didn't mean that. It's just . . . mindblowing.

DETECTIVE FERRUCCI: There's a lot of good hard evidence. Labwork. Data. The Los Angeles Police Department has some of the finest pathologists and forensic chemists in the country.

JANE: Oh, I'm sure.

DETECTIVE FERRUCCI: The first real clue we had that something unusual was happening was those strange blades of grass we found that moved—

JANE: Grass that moved, folks.

DETECTIVE FERRUCCI: Wriggled. Like little worms, almost. A few pieces of this grass were noticed in a sandbox shortly after the disappearance of Jimmy Pliscou and his sister Suzy, ages ten and seven, in Boston.

JANE: Boston.

DETECTIVE FERRUCCI: Right, uh, Brookline.

JANE: Arthur's from Brookline. Aren't you, Arthur?

ARTHUR: Yep.

DETECTIVE FERRUCCI: Anyway—

JANE: But, I mean, Dave, how did you get interested, involved, in these disappearances? I mean, Boston isn't L.A. Why L.A.?

DETECTIVE FERRUCCI: The Los Angeles Police Department, Jane, has one of the finest criminal laboratories in the country.

JANE: Yes.

DETECTIVE FERRUCCI: We did a bunch of NMRs on the grass.

JANE: Pardon my French.

DETECTIVE FERRUCCI: Oh, sorry, NMR, that's nuclear magnetic resonance. It's—

JANE: Dave, you must be great at parties.

DETECTIVE FERRUCCI: —uh, it gives us information on the, uh, molecular structure. Each atom, you see, has its own—

JANE: Most of our listeners, Dave, are mindless couch potatoes and housewife dweebs. Plus a few retard psychos, God bless them, who keep calling in about Bigfoot, fish oil, the Irish, and capital punishment. If we could keep our explanation down to words of one syllable . . .

ARTHUR: How can the man explain, dear, if you keep interrupting him? Why, he's getting positively purple around the edges.

DETECTIVE FERRUCCI: No, not at all, I'm fine.

JANE: You're a darling. He's really quite handsome, folks. Broad shoulders, wavy hair—

DETECTIVE FERRUCCI: An analysis of the DNA showed us that we were dealing with a totally new organism, which, however, is clearly related to the kind of grass you can find in any—

JANE: In other words, folks, it's somebody's lawn that's eating our children.

DETECTIVE FERRUCCI: Well, yes. We think that the current high levels of ultraviolet radiation, in combination with the new chemicals used in—

JANE: Can you picture it? The lawn that ate the Bronx. The killer lawn. The lawn from outer space. Just when you thought it was safe to go on a picnic. I mean, can you picture it? Mr. and Mrs. Jones and the kids find a nice shaded spot in the park, spread out the tablecloth, sit down with their basket, and before they can open the potato salad, whammo, *they're* the potato salad!

ARTHUR: Ants are bad enough. And Lyme disease, those little ticks you can't see.

DETECTIVE FERRUCCI: In all seriousness—

JANE: I think you have movie potential here, Dave.

ARTHUR: Absolutely. With commercial tie-ins. Ortho. Snapper. Weed-n-Feed.

DETECTIVE FERRUCCI: As a matter of fact—

JANE: Well, our time's about up, gang. Tomorrow we'll be talking with Jeannette Kay, the convicted assassin of Oregon Governor Daniel Hawks. Remember that? Jeannette's on a tour to raise money to save the orcas in the northern Pacific, an endangered species.

ARTHUR: Sounds like Oregon governors are an endangered species.

Laughter, music, static.

JANE, *over the music:* Thanks, Dave, for joining us. Senior Detective David Ferrucci of the Los Angeles Police Department, author of *What Is Eating Our Children?*

DETECTIVE FERRUCCI: Published by Putnam.

JANE: Published by Putnam.

DETECTIVE FERRUCCI: It was a pleasure to be here, Jane.

JANE: So to all our listeners out there with young kids, if the little bastards don't behave, pack them off to the playground.

ARTHUR: And say "Excuse me" before you mow, next time. Better make that "Excuse me, sir."

JANE: This is Jane Olsen of Speak Your Mind on WTAQ, twelve hundred twenty on your dial, wishing you a pleasant day and a pleasanter you. Stay tuned for Sex Problems Hotline next, with Dr. Peter Hackett.

Music, static. A sudden burst of louder static, then a long rumble in the distance, stage left. The etching above the radio shakes a little on the wall. The console itself, a solid piece of furniture, doesn't shake.

43

The next several days he spent in confusion. His head hurt. Pounding headaches. At one point, he went back to the mall, found Captain Jack Zodiac, and asked him if he couldn't come down a little in the price of the brown pill. Down a little—actually, to tell the truth, down a lot. The captain shook his head, but so slightly, the gesture was almost unnoticeable. Then he looked away, as Clifford weren't there anymore.

About a week after that, Clifford went to talk to the captain again, but the captain wasn't in the mall. Clifford asked some kids. Finally, one little boy with a tattooed forehead, eight or nine, directed him to an old supermarket in Terryville. Off the beaten path. The place was so run-down—high weeds in front, flaking paint—that at first it looked abandoned, but Clifford saw a few people inside moving their carts around. Outside, the usual assortment of derelicts. One of the derelicts, on a half-broken bench, was Captain Jack Zodiac. Clifford approached him and asked, in a hoarse voice, if it would be possible to buy the pill on credit, on time. "I can give you a hundred million next Saturday," he said, because he had made up his mind to sell his Audi, his sound equipment, and his coin collection, which he had inherited from his father and never touched. The coin collection was supposed to help pay for the children's college, but at the moment college didn't seem to be a pressing need. For either Josh or Trish. First things first: get the children home in one piece, and get them human again. Then worry about their education.

The captain didn't blink. Didn't even hear the hundred million. Was deaf—would always be deaf—to such offers. The business he transacted was strictly for cash up front. And how could you blame the man, with today's inflation? Seven hundred and fifty million this week, the way things were going, could be a billion next week, if not more.

Clifford drove home and took some extra-strength aspirin for his headache. He looked in the yellow pages under "Guns," got back in the car, and drove to Mom-n-Pop's Gun Shop, which was on Valley Road, actually not far from Elton Beach, where Marsha and her father used to live. A young Portuguese couple with a baby now lived at the Feldman place. Clifford had met them when he helped Marsha move. Simple, down-to-earth people, their faces full of hope in the future. For them, America was still the land of opportunity. Clifford could write a good song on that. But the label, he remembered, was The Downbeat now. It would take some getting used to, writing songs about cancer, crackfiends, and incest. Would he still use rhymes? But perhaps the lyrics wouldn't matter that much, after all the synth effects and with the volume turned up to the pain threshold.

At Mom-n-Pop's, which resembled a corner delicatessen except that on the shelves behind the slanted glass there were firearms instead of chopped herring, roast beef, and noodle pudding, the selection was so large, Clifford didn't know what to ask for. It would be imbecilic to say, "I want a gun." That would have been like walking into a clothing store and saying, "I'm looking for something to wear." Yes, sir, you came to the right place.

"Can I help you?" asked a no-nonsense lady with a monocle on a ribbon (held in her squinted left eye). A tight, lipless mouth. This had to be Mom herself. In the monocle, cross hairs. After Clifford hemmed and hawed a little, she said, "You want something to rob a bank with, dear?"

"Not exactly," answered Clifford faintly.

"For robbing banks," she went on, " a person needs a gun with a lot of bang. High caliber, semiautomatic or automatic. A military piece. Impress the hell out of people, which is what you have to do, you know, in that kind of situation. Otherwise they won't open the safe for you and lie down on the floor in a row. The psychological effect of a weapon, its appearance, is so important."

"I'm sure," Clifford said, "but I really wasn't thinking of, uh, knocking off a bank."

Mom looked him over. "The overwhelming majority of people who come here, lately," she said, "have banks in mind. It's the inflation, of course."

"I'm afraid that's not for me." Particularly since the banks were beefing up their security systems. Just the other day—it was on the evening news—a man had been mowed down by a computer guard even though all he had done was ask for an extra lollipop for his daughter. His son was with him, but his daughter was at home with the measles. She had run a very high fever that morning. This was probably why the man's voice had had the pitch and intonation it did; he was upset about his daughter. The bank manager explained to the reporters that the security computer was programmed to respond to certain voice patterns. A lot of research had gone into it. "You can't go by facial configurations," the manager said, smiling at the camera, "because so many criminals, as you know, wear masks. And it is relatively easy to disguise one's face. A thick beard, a little putty or silicone. But one can't disguise one's voice. No, a voice is like a fingerprint." A reporter suggested that the program needed a little refining. The bank manager didn't agree. "Our system is, believe me, state-of-the-art. If one customer out of ten thousand is mistakenly stopped by the computer guard, that's an acceptable trade-off, I think, for the increased peace of mind we give to the other nine thousand nine hundred and ninety-nine regarding their savings. I need hardly remind you that in these uncertain times, liquid-asset repositories have become frequent targets of unlawful and armed acquisition." Clifford, when he watched this on television, thought about the little girl whose daddy wouldn't be coming home that day, or ever again, and it brought tears to his eyes.

"You're not interested in banks," said Mom, giving him the once-over, her left pupil dead center in the cross hairs of the monocle. A gray and penetrating pupil. A bird's pupil.

"No," said Clifford. "As a matter of fact, I . . ."

"It's an individual you have in mind, then."

Clifford shrugged, uncomfortable, not wanting to say "Yes." But he didn't have to, because Mom, nodding, took him by the arm and led him to a shelf filled with Saturday-night specials, all snub-nosed and silver-plated.

"You want to go cheap," she said. "Cheap and discreet. Do the deed in a dark alley. I understand."

"I'm not actually planning . . ."

"Relax, dear, I'm not the police," said Mom.

"Are these, er . . . how much are they?"

"Your intended victim isn't a drug dealer, I hope?"

"Well . . ."

"I only ask, because that's second to banks."

"Uh, second to banks?"

"Dealers walk around with so much cash. Millions, billions, typically. Not to mention their drugs."

"Yes, of course, but I . . ."

"The problem is, they're usually wearing special vests, so you'll need something a little more heavy-duty than these, if it's a dealer you're after, dear." She led him to another shelf, where the guns were larger.

"And for these," he said, dabbing the sweat off his forehead with a handkerchief, "what . . . is the price range?"

Mom put a pistol in his hand. The pistol, strangely, felt good in his hand. It made him feel that perhaps things weren't quite as black as he had thought. Where there was a will, there was a way. He would save Trish after all. And find Josh, too. Why not? He hefted the pistol.

"Now, that's a good one," said Mom. "Finnish. Notice its sleek design. You'll be able to hide it easily under your jacket. No telltale bulge."

"How much?" Clifford asked.

Mom took off his jacket, put a shoulder holster on him, tightened it, put the Finnish gun in the holster, put his jacket back on, buttoned it, and then brought him over to a full-length mirror. Indeed, no telltale bulge.

She stepped back proudly, removing her monocle and holding it up, as if she were holding a cup of tea at a cotillion.

Clifford heaved a sigh, thought, and said, "All right, I'll take it."

"Five and a half million," she said.

"Five and a half million."

"We'll throw in the holster, and a box of cartridges."

At the cash register, a tall billiard-bald gentleman

with a bushy gray mustache and a wrinkled scar on his neck rang up the sale. He handed Clifford the box of bullets in a shopping bag, and clapped him jovially on the arm. "Good luck, fella!"

That was probably Pop.

44

At dusk, Clifford found Captain Jack Zodiac relatively alone on the half-broken bench outside the seedy supermarket in Terryville. He sat down beside the dealer, pressed the muzzle of his new Finnish pistol into the man's ribs, and whispered between clenched teeth: "The brown pill, or I kill you, so help me God."

The captain turned slowly and smiled, crinkly-eyed, as if mildly amused. "Mr. Katz," he said. And that was all he said.

Clifford went home. He was so distraught, he nearly ran over a jogger, a young woman with narrow shoulders and a bobbing ponytail. She wore one of those jogger helmets, but even with it she was having difficulty because of the heat and the pollution. Half running, half staggering. To avoid a large pile of garbage on the side of the street—people were dumping everywhere now—she stepped out suddenly in front of him, tripping at the same time on a can of shaving cream. Not paying attention, he came within an inch of hitting her. He may have even brushed her.

She was furious. He couldn't see her face, with the helmet, or hear her curse, but she shook her fist, and as he pulled away, he looked in his rearview mirror and saw her drawing a gun from her belt. She fired at him, stiff-armed and with both hands, once, twice, three times. He counted the flashes. But the car, fortunately, wasn't hit. In his driveway, when he got out, he checked all around, to make sure. No holes, no creases.

Hands shaking, he took a couple of Quiets, then poured himself a bourbon. At the dinner table, as Marsha chattered away—something to do with Mrs. Helquist a few houses down—he was inattentive. In bed, later, he was impotent.

"What's eating you?" Marsha asked. "Is it that cut in pay?"

"I'm all right."

"It's your daughter. You're brooding about your daughter."

He thought: People shoot other people all the time. It isn't that hard to do.

At his trial, it would be pointed out that he had been under tremendous stress. That there had been great provocation. Seven hundred and fifty million dollars? To place a barrier like that between a parent and a child was unnatural. It was wrong. Your Honor, my client, Mr. Koussevitzky, had every right to act as he did. Ladies and gentlemen of the jury, he even underwent a vasectomy, a vasectomy and a circumcision, which for a man of his age, I can tell you, is not fun. He submitted to both procedures, submitted unflinchingly, to provide his children with a mother and a proper home. Regard this face. Is this the face of a hardened criminal? The face of an ordinary dust-sniffing druggie?

In the middle of the night, Clifford had the following thought. If he didn't act soon, the pale-brown pill might no longer be there, in the small, dirty envelope in Captain Jack Zodiac's pocket. Someone else might buy it. Or bump the captain off to get it. And the pill was one-of-a-kind, being so extremely experimental. That, at least, was what the captain said. But the captain may have been lying. All those pills, who knows, could be nothing but sugar. Sugar and sawdust inside colorful coatings. A complete fraud.

He got out of bed carefully, in order not to wake Marsha, and dressed. In the bathroom, he looked through the medicine cabinet. Perhaps, among Marsha's many bottles of pills, there were hormones he could use to juice up his pineal gland. Though if the hormones were for Marsha, they were probably the wrong kind. Estrogens, not androgens. Or was it the other way around? He looked for old birth-control pills. She didn't need birth-control pills anymore, of course, but perhaps she hadn't thrown them out. People often hung on to old medicine. He found two bottles. Pink pills. He filled a glass with water and took them. All of them, down the hatch. Too many to count. "I've finally gone mad," he thought. But mad was good. Madmen could do things others couldn't. Slashing their mad way, stepping over bodies, to get to zombieland and beyond.

He loaded the pistol in the kitchen. It took a while, because he knew next to nothing about guns, and the pistol hadn't come with an owner's manual. But it wasn't too hard to figure out. A simple mechanism, really. He put ten bullets in the magazine, snapped the magazine back into the pistol, and located the safety, which kept the trigger from moving. All systems go.

What to do with the other bullets? He filled his pockets with them. And what about a farewell note? Something like: "Gone to get Trish. If not back in a week, forgive me and forget me." He decided against a farewell note. Marsha would understand—or wouldn't understand. There was no time for letters and sentimentality. He was a man of action now. A quick salute in the direction of the bedroom, and out the door and into the night.

This time, if Captain Jack Zodiac smiled . . . This time, the gun was loaded, and Mr. Katz, no longer harmless, had a diabolical gleam in his eye. And determination and destiny in his desperate heart.

45

After a few more Dises, there were no hospitals. No George with the clipboard, no orientation packet at the main desk. No more Taco Bells, either. Which meant that to continue on, Joseph David Smith—who once upon a time had been married to Leslie Karen Giambucci from Apalachicola, Florida, and served as a purchasing agent at Burk Brothers fourteen years and six months before he was dismissed for embezzlement, though the company didn't press charges because the sum was so small—would have to do his suiciding now without the benefit of Mexican pizzas or steak fajitas.

He couldn't walk in front of a car or truck: there were no cars or trucks.

And he couldn't go to the next Dis by holding his breath; there was no breath to hold.

Hanging himself, therefore, was out, too. As was drowning.

There was no color now. Everything was in black and white. More precisely, in black and black—or black on black—because there was no light, either. Absolutely none. Nary a photon. But that didn't seem to matter. He managed fine without light, and without breath, and everyone else did, too.

This was, as he thought it would be, like traveling back in time. The people all had old-fashioned accents, and their dress was funny. Breastplates and halberds and farthingales. Unless it was Halloween and everyone was on their way to a ball. An odd thought: Halloween in Hell. The dead going as skeletons.

Joe met a couple of men—from his generation, more or less—who were having a duel. One duel, that is, after the other. Or, you might say, a duel that went on and on. These two were leapfrogging from Dis to Dis in their hunger to kill each other. The reason was that in life one of the men had cost the other his job, backstabbing, and the other, to get revenge on the first, had gone after his enemy's wife and bedded her. Whereupon the first, for this dishonor suffered, had murdered the second. When the first man finally died—of a bone disease at the age of eighty, surrounded by weeping grandchildren and great-grandchildren at a posh nursing home—the second man was waiting for him with a grin. Dead people, as a rule, can be very patient, as patient as boulders or doors. Joe heard this whole story from one of the men, at a bar, but could never quite get straight which of the men was the backstabber and which the wife seducer.

He dove off buildings a lot. Dove headfirst and with his arms at his sides, to get the full benefit of the impact. Not wanting to be merely injured and then have to walk around with a bandage and smile and say something polite when people asked questions and clucked their tongues in sympathy. It was unnerving at first, the diving off of buildings; it took getting used to. The old instincts of self-preservation still clutched you by the throat when you approached the parapet and looked down at the pavement several stories below. This method worked well, however, and sometimes he got through seven or eight Dises in a single day.

How many so far? He had lost count. Over a hundred.

But then the buildings grew closer to the ground, and then the highest roof was only two stories, no more than twenty feet up. Also, all the roofs were peaked now, and thatched, so they weren't easy to climb onto.

No cliffs in the neighborhood. No chasms worth the name.

He struck up a friendship—sort of—with a group of rough-and-tough Assyrian sailors. Nice people, but they lost their temper easily and would run you through with a sword without thinking twice. Joe found that by making remarks about their mothers he could be dispatched quite frequently. So for a while he went from one group of Assyrian sailors to another, continuing his descent in this fashion. Mother remarks took less effort than climbing stairs or ladders to roofs had—all you did was say a few words and maybe leer—but it was considerably more painful. The swords hurt going in, and unless you were lucky and got it in the neck or heart (the heart was relatively rare), it took several minutes to die, sometimes as much as an hour. And often, in the time it took, there were awful chills and awful nausea in addition to the agony of the wound itself.

Joe switched to a group of cavemen with clubs, thinking that a club over the head might be a much less stressful way of going. He was right. The cavemen, however, were disappointingly peaceful, infuriatingly hard to insult, and there was a language problem now besides.

"Your mother is a female dog," Joe might say.

"Thank you," the caveman would reply, as if this were a routine compliment.

"You are a coward," Joe would try again. "Your father is a coward."

"Good," the caveman would say solemnly, after thinking this one over.

"You have perverted sex with your father and with your mother. Your sisters are ugly, and your brothers are all women."

To this the caveman would shake his head, smile, as if there had been an understandable misunderstanding, and say, "No, no, we have plenty of berries to eat here."

"*You* are a berry!" Joe would yell, red in the face—and that might do it. That might bring the heavy gnarled club down on his head. But you could never be sure. Instead, you might be embraced and given a big wet kiss.

And a big wet kiss from a caveman made your gorge rise, made you shudder with disgust, sometimes for days afterward. A caveman's smell was ranker than anything anyone could imagine, and his saliva was sticky, too, even lumpy, like mucilage. (Apparently, the human race had evolved in the direction not only of less body hair but also of thinner spittle.)

Joe was on the lookout, as he descended the ladder of the afterlife, for famous men in history. Jesus, Socrates, George Washington, Napoleon. With less population, he figured, the odds of meeting someone important would be greater. But he didn't recognize anyone. The bushy beards made it difficult. One bushy beard looked like another. And people didn't appreciate being approached with the question "Should I know you?" Joe did meet Confucius. But the man, it turned out, wasn't very interesting. The conversation died quickly. They went their separate ways.

Past the Iron Age, suicide became a real problem. It wasn't easy opening your veins in a bathtub with a dull-edged bronze dagger or unwieldy piece of flint. It wasn't fun.

Then there were no bathtubs. Then there was no hot water.

He was walking alone on a dark road, enjoying the solitude and idly wondering what would happen when he ran out of ways, finally, to do away with himself. To get to the next Dis, would he simply have to wait for old age to finish him off? Though that didn't make a hell of a lot of sense, not if you thought about it: growing older when you were already cold and six feet under and watches and calendars no longer meant anything. He was walking and thinking about this—but not thinking too hard, because even in life you could never have called him the thinking type—when he came upon a new and totally unexpected object. The object was rectangular and made of metal, even though rectangles and metal presumably hadn't been invented yet, in this Dis. There were letters on it, and the letters made words. It was, in fact, a sign. The sign said: SIMULATION 97 TRIPLE PRIME, FRAME J.

Joe entered the building that appeared after the sign. An office building. Inside, hundreds of computers, monitors, and cables. A man turned around and gave him an odd look. "And who are you?" he asked.

Joe wasn't sure. Which wasn't that surprising, since he had died so many times, and death, after all, has an unidentifying effect. "Is this the bottom Dis?" he asked.

"Ah," the man said, "you're from the triple or quadruple prime." And nodded and smiled, as if that explained everything. "You're an explorer."

The man, Joe noticed, was not flesh and blood but, instead, all metal and plastic. A robot.

"You're a robot," Joe said. "I didn't know they could talk so well. And you move, too, just like a person."

The man smiled sadly. "A person. As it happens, my friend, my qualifications for personhood are far, far superior to your own. You have no idea how far. Though it's all relative, isn't it? Yes, it's all relative. We should keep that in mind. I apologize. A moment of arrogance. No call for it. And it's unbecoming. I should know better. Shame on me. Yes, my friend, you, too, are a person, shadow though you are. It took something to come all this way. Curiosity. Persistence. The two legs upon which the scientific spirit stands. Admirable, and touching."

The robot led Joe to a monitor, the largest monitor, and pushed a key here and a key there to show him something. What appeared on the screen had such a strong effect on Joe, despite the fact that he was deceased and not terribly intelligent, that he asked to be put out of existence permanently, without any more Dises, please, and the sooner the better.

Truth is generally a good thing, but some truths, like some pills, are hard to swallow. And a few truths, which get at the very heart of things, can be well-nigh unendurable.

With a faint smile, the man of metal and plastic obliged. It took only eight keystrokes, the click of one switch, and a wait that was so short, it was hardly a wait at all, for Joseph David Smith to cease. Had he had the time, which he didn't, he would have sighed with relief. The robot's right hand, two fingers together and curved slightly, made the sign of the cross in the empty air.

46

Captain Jack Zodiac wasn't on the half-broken bench in front of the seedy supermarket in Terryville. Clifford rode around for a while, on the chance that he might find him walking along a street nearby, but he didn't, so he tried the mall. Although it was two in the morning, the little boy with the tattooed forehead was still there, in the arcade. The air was so thick with cigarette smoke—marijuana, mainly—that it was difficult to see anything beyond a couple of feet. "You shouldn't be in here," Clifford said to the kid, who couldn't have been more than ten, eleven. "It's not good for your health."

The kid looked up at him. He was so short that to play the video games he had to crane his neck and stand on tiptoe. He reminded Clifford of Josh when Josh had been in the third or fourth grade and couldn't get enough of Nintendo, day or night. How time flew. Clifford could write, maybe, a nice nostalgic Downbeat song about time flying.

With luck, the song would do well—everyone related to nostalgia—and his boss might give him a raise after all, with apologies and a clap on the back, and Mr. Hillsworth-Fenwick might relent and not close down the whole department. Assuming there was such a person as Mr. Hillsworth-Fenwick.

"The captain," said the kid, squinting, "is faster than he looks, if you're thinking of gunning him down."

"I'll keep that in mind," said Clifford. And he gave the kid a few hundred dollars' worth of video tokens in exchange for the information that the old dealer was now somewhere in the vicinity of the Franklin train station. One of the places, no doubt, in which he carried out his capitalistic or anticapitalistic transactions.

Clifford parked on a side street. He walked slowly toward the commuter parking lot. The lighting was poor here, and there was garbage everywhere. A sour reek. The scurrying of invisible, nimble rodents. When would the garbage strike be over? This was getting ridiculous. A health hazard.

He walked in a smooth half crouch, like an Indian stalking a deer in a forest, a forest that hadn't existed now in the land of the free and the home of the brave for a thousand years, for two thousand years. The bullets made a muffled rattle in his bulging pockets, as if he had been at the beach collecting seashells. It would have been much more graceful, as he approached the lot, to have a quiver of arrows on his back.

Seeing a couple of people in the distance, shadowy figures conversing, their heads together, Clifford took out his gun and undid the safety with a click. If only his hands weren't so sweaty. He wiped his hands on his jacket. He took a couple of deep breaths to steady himself.

The lot was more than half full. These must be nightshifters. More and more people were nightshifting, to avoid the awful crowds. Or moonlighting, because of the inflation. No rest in the city, no rest in the suburbs. When was the last time he had taken a vacation?

A train—a row of dirty, tired lights—pulled into the station. One of the two people conversing, yes, was Captain Jack Zodiac. An unmistakable silhouette, with his stoop and his captain's cap. Clifford had to wait for him to be alone. Sneak up as close as possible behind him, shoot him in the back, take the pill envelope, and run.

After a while, the train blew its horn and began to pull out, chugging and whining, since it was one of those old diesels, not electric. The line out here couldn't go electric because that was too expensive. The taxpayers were already up in arms, and government funding was always being cut. A Downbeat song about government funding always being cut. The trains in Essex County were older than Clifford, twice as old. Meanwhile the other person, the one talking to Captain Jack Zodiac, was still talking. Showing no sign of leaving. Probably a teenage kid. Taller than Josh, though.

Clifford moved closer, from car to car. He wiped his hands again on his jacket. There was a flash and a rumble in the sky. Not lightning and thunder, but the war. That, too, was still dragging on. Odd, for a nuclear war to drag on. Then another train pulled in, its cyclopean headlight reflected in the glasses of some of the commuters waiting on the platform. Clifford tried to be patient. Count to ten. Count to twenty. The train finally blew its horn and pulled out, chugging and whining, and the teenager finally reached in his pocket and handed the captain a wad of bills.

It made Clifford angry: Why couldn't the kid have paid in the first place, dammit, and got it over with? Instead of talking and talking. Didn't he know you couldn't bargain with the likes of Captain Jack Zodiac, who always held all the cards? Except that Clifford now had, on his person, a trump. A trump of trumps. Loaded, this time. He gritted his teeth and moved closer as the youth walked away with whatever space pill he had purchased.

A sudden stab of ice in the gut: Could the space pill

have been the pale-brown pill, the one that was the brown, almost, of a chicken's brown egg? Of which there might be only one in existence. In that case, Clifford would have to shoot the kid, too, and quickly, before he swallowed it, which could happen any second now. If the kid swallowed it, farewell forever to any chance of bringing back poor Trish. Forever.

It was this possibility that made Clifford run out from behind the gray Toyota where he had been concealed, and point the gun at Captain Jack Zodiac, and pull the trigger.

The first thought that came to him, when nothing happened, was that Mom-n-Pop had sold him a defective weapon, a piece of junk, for five and a half million dollars. They were laughing at him right now. What a sucker, what a sucker. And how could he complain to the Chamber of Commerce? "I wanted to murder someone, you see, and they sold me this gun that doesn't work."

The second thought that came to him, quietly, like a modest footnote at the bottom of a page, was that the reason nothing had happened was that there was no bullet in the firing chamber. To move the first bullet into the firing chamber, he had to slide something on the top of the gun, forward and back. Where he had picked up this bit of information, he had no idea. Television? Where else?

He did the sliding business, and the gun made a satisfying shuttling click, as if to say, "That's it."

The captain turned around and saw Clifford, and sized up the situation immediately. The kid with the tattoo had told the truth: the old man was quick. In less time than it takes to blink he had his blaster out, and a purple beam made the Toyota beside Clifford come apart quite suddenly in flame and sizzling fragments.

Clifford was thrown by the blast into the grille of

another car, possibly a Chrysler, but didn't lose hold of his gun.

The captain, down on one knee, followed Clifford with the blaster, so that Clifford was just barely able to dive under a nearby Porsche before the Chrysler followed the Toyota's fate with a deafening roar.

"A good thing," Clifford thought, thinking of his Audi, "that I didn't park here."

It was clear that the captain, spacesalt that he was, had seen plenty of action in his day and knew how to take care of himself. It was clear, too, that Clifford didn't have a prayer against such a professional.

He looked up. The captain was fleeing, running along a row of hedges at the far end of the parking lot, toward the train station. Another train, the third, was now pulling in.

Clifford had to stop him. He ran after him, and the bullets in his pockets swished furiously as he ran. Swish, swish, swish. He hoped he wasn't losing any; he might need them later. He gained on the captain, who was heavier then he, out of breath, and seemed to have a limp. The captain turned and zapped at him with another purple beam, which singed Clifford's hair as he ducked, and put a respectable hole in a building more than a hundred feet behind him. The air crackled.

Clifford, filled with anger—because he was such a poor excuse for a man of action and couldn't even protect and save his own children, bone of his bone and flesh of his flesh, by killing a scuzzy old hypocritical drug dealer—fired at Captain Jack Zodiac blau-blau-blau, and his anger increased as he fired, and it made him aim better. The anger also helped him dodge the purple beam when it went for him again, dodge it fast enough and completely enough to live, because damn if he was going to let this old bastard kill him and keep him from getting that brown pill.

He shot again, ran up to the captain, kicked the steaming blaster out of his hand, and put a few more bullets in the body to make sure. The train blew its horn and began to pull out, chugging and whining, but there was another sound over the horn, a siren, and Clifford saw the flashing lights of a police car, two police cars, no, three. Entering the lot from different directions, doors already opening, police jumping out.

He also noticed that the sky was growing light in the east. Dawn.

In a black puddle of oil lay a faded blue captain's cap.

"I'm a murderer now," Clifford thought with regret, because he had been a fairly moral person all his life, up to this moment.

In a frenzy of haste, because the police had seen him now, and seen the body, and were converging and shouting, he bent over Captain Jack Zodiac—may you rest in peace—and unzipped the bloodied jacket, and reached in for the envelope. A dirty, creased envelope, with some words and numbers scribbled on it. It was there, thank God. And inside it, the pills, yes, all there, including the brown pill. Did the brown pill have a spot of blood on it? Clifford probably imagined that. Must have imagined that. Too outré, such a detail. His nerves, taut to the snapping point. You can see things, close enough to the snapping point.

As the policemen told him to throw down his gun and the train pulled out, he poured all five pills from the envelope into the palm of his left hand, clapped the hand to his mouth, and swallowed. Convulsively, as hard as he could. All five together. Not one at a time, which is the way people are supposed to take pills. You could almost hear a mother saying to her son, "Take one at a time, dear."

But when a man goes off the deep end, beyond the snapping point, and is actually gunning down people in parking lots, he doesn't listen to his mother or to anyone else.

The first thin rays of the rising sun, a lovely yellow-gold, reached across the sky; the train chugged off, taking bored commuters to the city; the policemen dropped to one knee and raised their shotguns, ready to shoot; and Clifford Koussevitzky vanished with a pop, taking with him the Finnish gun, the blaster (it also might come in handy), a stomachful of old birth-control pills to juice up his pineal gland, and a wild surge of hope.

47

His first thought was that the train was filled with crazies, that the crazies were from Franklin State (the asylum was only a few blocks from the station), and that they were going on some field trip to the city. The circus, maybe, or a dog show. Except that the passengers really didn't have the glassy look of people permanently veggied with a shot of frog-green L-50, or only temporarily veggied with limeade-green L-45. The crazy look, Clifford now realized, was because they were aliens, most of them, with an eye in the middle of the forehead, or lips that went vertically instead of horizontally, or else they had hair that wiggled slowly and fitfully, like worms that had fallen into a puddle of cleaning fluid.

Out the window, deep space and stars. More stars than he had ever seen in his life. This was a space train, then. The pills had put him on a space train, maybe by association to the train pulling out of the station at Franklin when the police surrounded him with their shotguns leveled as he stood over the body of Captain Jack Zodiac freshly murdered.

Clifford stuck the captain's blaster under his belt, pirate-style (uncomfortable, but the weapon was too large for any of his pockets). He leaned forward and asked the person in the seat in front of him, "Excuse me, but where are we going?"

The alien half turned and said, "Ursa Minor," then went back to reading his paper, a tabloid full of scandal.

"Excuse me," said Clifford, "but what's the next stop?" Because he had to get off as soon as possible. It could take days, weeks, to reach Ursa Minor, and who knows how long the pills would last? He didn't want the Davis Effect giving out on him before he found his daughter.

"No stops," said the alien, not turning around. "This is an express."

Interesting a place as Ursa Minor might be, and Clifford had certainly not been there before, he just couldn't sit back with a sigh and let this detour in his plans run its course. Not that he had specific plans, but it was clear that there would be no mall zombies—at least not human mall zombies—in the vicinity of the Little Dipper and the North Star.

He would have to talk to the conductor, or to the engineer. He got up and walked forward down the aisle, and was not a little disconcerted by the passengers he passed. They were either outlandish rollmops that didn't even have heads, or people uncannily familiar to him. Uncannily, because if they were who they seemed to be, they shouldn't have been there, among the living. His Uncle Ralph, for instance. The man on the right was the spitting image of his Uncle Ralph: baggy pants, suspenders, thick glasses, the eyes behind the glasses like the eyes of an enormous staring fish in an aquarium. If Uncle Ralph were still alive—though why in the world would he be on his way to Ursa Minor? He who had never even gone to Atlantic City with the rest of the family because it was "too far." If Uncle Ralph were still alive, he would be in his nineties now, covered with wrinkles and shrunken and pale and palsied. He would not be the spitting image of Uncle Ralph as Clifford remembered him, no matter how much allowance you made for the relativistic effects of time dilation during cosmic flight.

Clifford wondered if he was dreaming all this. Maybe he was actually still back at the commuter parking lot and being hauled, at this very moment, twitching and drooling, into an ambulance or paddy wagon. Not a pleasant thought. He squared his shoulders. Think positively.

"You look just like my Uncle Ralph," he cleared his throat and said to the man casually as he went by.

"I *am* your Uncle Ralph," said the man, in Uncle Ralph's exact voice.

"No you're not," snapped Clifford.

The man, seeing the steely look in Clifford's eyes and the blaster stuck under his belt, decided not to argue.

In the next car, a seven-foot-tall amoeba thing with black tusklike follicles blocked the way: a cross between a football player and one of those television personifications of tooth decay. Clifford said, "Excuse me." But the thing, apparently engaged in conversation with another thing, a seated, wholly different species of thing but no more prepossessing, ignored him. Clifford raised his voice for the second "Excuse me," and tapped— carefully but firmly—on one of the formidable follicles. The hairy—spiked—amoeba turned around; the other side of it was all mouth. A cavernous mouth.

"Can I get by, please?" said Clifford.

"Sure," lisped the monster. "Sorry."

The conductor, a few cars farther up, was a headless rollmop that had to talk through a speaker clipped to the lapel, or whatever it was, of his uniform. He listened patiently, nodded sympathetically, as Clifford explained his problem (the nodding was done with the upper torso). But then the conductor shook his upper torso negatively and said, through the lapel, that not only were no stops scheduled on this train to Ursa Minor but no stops *could* be scheduled, for the simple reason that there were no stations between here and their destination. The reason there were no stations, he continued after a moment of static, was that there was no celestial body for a station to be placed on, absolutely none, inasmuch as this region of space, like most regions of space, was hard vacuum as far as the eye could see. "Your usual wash of photons, radio waves, and neutrinos," said the conductor, "and that's about it. Why, we could go for miles, and I'm not exaggerating, sir, without even hitting a hydrogen atom."

"Let me talk to the engineer," said Clifford. "It's a matter of life or death that I get back to Earth."

The conductor stiffened and said that that was out of the question: passengers were not permitted to talk to the engineer, not ever, not even when it was a matter of life or death.

"I know," said Clifford, "the engineer can't be distracted because he's responsible for hundreds of lives. But I won't take much of his time, I promise."

"Distracted has nothing to do with it," replied the conductor. There was static on his speaker again. He adjusted it and went on: "Didn't I just tell you that we could go for miles without hitting even a hydrogen atom? Why, the engineer could be asleep the whole trip, and no harm would be done. More than ninety-nine percent of the pulling into the station at Ursa Minor is done by computer, anyway. I'll tell you something, sir. A couple of years ago, an engineer who had been working for the line all his life passed away. A charming person. Everyone, even the signalmen, who are not a sentimental bunch, believe me, thought the world of him. Such was the esteem for him that he was not replaced. His body was carefully, lovingly embalmed and arranged in a seated position, most lifelike, in the locomotive cabin whenever he was scheduled to operate a train. It is a moving sight to behold him at the engineer's window, as vigilant as ever at his post, even more so, since now he doesn't blink."

The rollmop conductor dabbed at his upper torso with a red-and-blue plaid handkerchief, because a few tears of emotion were being exuded from that area.

"The engineer here," said Clifford, "the one on our train, you don't mean to say that's the same one . . . who was embalmed?"

"Oh, no," said the conductor, "a different one."

"Then I see no reason why I can't—"

"Etiquette," said the conductor, putting away his handkerchief and becoming once again all business and officialdom.

"Etiquette?"

"We're out in space, light-years out, smack in the middle of the interstellar medium, which is mostly nothingness. The void inchoate. And in these cars are hundreds of life-forms from all sorts of solar systems. How you hold your grapefruit spoon in the morning, sir, is not how the passenger across the aisle, from Deneb Seven, is going to hold his grapefruit spoon in the morning."

"I don't see—"

"We fail to preserve etiquette on the train, and the thin veneer of civilization cracks and the goblins of chaos and cannibalism break loose and run amuck."

"That's ridiculous."

"Let me remind you that we're tens of thousands of astronomical units from the nearest police station. From the nearest call box."

"Surely the people here—"

"Etiquette," said the conductor, pointing a rollmop finger and shaking it, "keeps a tight lid on the goblins of internal night and madness. It is the safety railing at the brink of the psychic abyss. Why, just last week, on the Sirius–Algol train, a conductor omitted to punch a passenger's ticket, and when the omission was pointed out to him, he reportedly said something like 'Who cares?' They're still cleaning up after that one, sir. They had to change the upholstery on all the seats. We're talking big bucks for just the upholstery, forget about the lawsuits."

Clifford saw he would get nowhere with the conductor, so he stepped around him and continued forward, to the next car, toward the locomotive. Maybe the engineer would listen. The engineer had to listen. It was either that or—Clifford felt the blaster under his belt, felt the Finnish gun from Mom-n-Pop's in his shoulder holster—it was either that or a hijacking. A murderer, then a hijacker. What next? He hoped he wouldn't be a hardened criminal by the time all this was over. A hardened criminal would not be a good influence as a parent.

48

Several cars up, another conductor blocked his way. This one was quite tall and broad and had feathers. Clifford said he needed to speak to the engineer. The conductor said that that was out of the question. Clifford went to step around him, but the conductor put a five-taloned, purple-pink claw politely but officially on Clifford's chest and stopped him. Clifford took a deep breath and prepared for the use of force. For blood and bits of entrails splattered on windows, etc. He reached for the blaster—but the conductor asked him for his ticket.

"Ticket?" Clifford said.

"I'm punching tickets," the feathered conductor explained, making a great effort to be patient. There were always a few people who didn't have their tickets out and held things up.

"I don't have a ticket," Clifford said.

"You don't have a ticket."

"No. I got here by taking some pills."

The conductor regarded him with a dour yellow eye, then finally cleared his throat and said, "In that case, sir, you'll have to pay double fare."

"Double fare?"

"Those are the rules. You boarded without a ticket."

"Is it a lot?"

"Fifty kroner."

"How much is that," Clifford asked with a sinking in his stomach, "in dollars?" Sometimes he had the feeling that everyone had their hands out. Gouging, shamelessly gouging, because tomorrow money might no longer be worth anything. It made him angry. Why was he on the receiving end of this all the time? Especially since he was bringing home less now instead of more, damn his boss and damn Mr. Hillsworth-Fenwick.

"No dollars," said the conductor in a voice now so pointedly weary, it was rude, "whatever *they* are. Kroner. Fifty kroner, please."

"I don't have any kroner," Clifford said, setting his jaw, "whatever *they* are." He was tempted to add something about stupid foreign currency, but thought better of it. It wouldn't have been dignified. It wouldn't have made much sense, anyway, because dollars could turn out to be twice as stupid as kroner. And they probably were, considering what the Fed was doing these days.

"Fifty kroner," said the conductor, whose single eye grew flatter, more opaque, and yellower with disdain, distaste, and disgust, "or we throw you off the train."

49

The old heave-ho was administered by a third conductor.
This one was a string bean—literally. But although his
string-bean weight didn't amount to much, he was
evidently skilled in some advanced extraterrestrial form
of martial arts, because he had no difficulty flipping
Clifford a couple of times and tossing him out—from a
door between the cars—into the void inchoate, before
Clifford could even think of doing anything aggressive
with the weapons he had on him. This time, when
Clifford vanished, it wasn't with a pop or a foop, because
he was in hard vacuum and therefore displacing no air.
(And to the occasional radio wave or neutrino, it made
no essential difference whether Clifford Koussevitzky
was there or not.) Was his vanishing a coincidence?
It certainly seemed to be a cause-and-effect thing.
Because another second or two of wheeling head over
heels in deep space without a helmet would have made
Clifford—no question—meat for Dis, a frozen corpse all
ruptured inside from the visceral pressures of his body,
the air in the lungs, the blood in the veins: 760 mm's
worth of mercury or, if you prefer, 14.7 pounds per
square inch. And if the vanishing was a cause-and-effect
thing, then perhaps his pineal gland was somehow
hooked up to one of the more volitional sectors of his
central nervous system. Unless, of course, physics and

biology had nothing to do with it and Clifford was merely dreaming all this. In a dream you couldn't be killed, because the dream had to go on from scene to scene until you woke up. So perhaps he was actually back at the commuter parking lot, or being transported now by wailing ambulance to the hospital. But more likely, to Franklin State, where they provided all kinds of state-of-the-art shock treatments to twitching, drooling druggies. What a way to end up, after he had been so reliable and responsible all these years, paying his taxes and keeping his Audi in good repair and writing a new song every day at the office even if that meant staying late.

String beans surrounded him. Talking string beans, gesturing animatedly. Could this be the home world of that third conductor on the space train? Clifford had better treat them with respect: they were probably all karate experts. He showed them pictures of Josh, of Trish. High-school photographs, the most recent he had. Not very good likenesses. High-school yearbook photographs tended to be either deadpans or sickly smiles. The string beans shook their string-bean heads: Sorry, haven't seen them.

As the setting sun shot garish streaks of indigo across the sky and the air grew cold, an elderly string bean escorted him to a shed. This was to be Clifford's place. There was no bedding, no plumbing. Clifford made himself as comfortable as he could on the hard ground. He shivered through the night, unaccustomed as he was to low temperatures. With the greenhouse effect back home, you started putting on sweaters and rubbing your hands together when the mercury fell into the eighties. Amazing, how human beings adapted. In the early morning, unable to go back to sleep because of the shivering, he counted the bullets in his pockets, lined them up on the ground in columns and rows. All together, an even hundred.

A week later, the string beans assembled, approached, and after much hospitable, ceremonial bowing put a young string bean in his shed, obviously a maiden female meant to be his wife. The young string-bean bride lost no time in letting her husband know, through simple, unmistakable gestures (but he was picking up a few words, too), that they were supposed to copulate. These string beans were straightforward people. No blushing or beating around the bush for them. Clifford was not sure that copulation was anatomically possible, but even if it was, he was a married man now, and God knows what you could contract from intercourse with an alien string bean. What if, assuming he made it home in one piece, he infected Marsha later? An off-world venereal disease would take a lot of explaining. Besides, his libido was currently at an all-time low, perhaps because of those numerous pink birth-control pills giving him the wrong hormone. Or because of the murder, his first murder. At night sometimes, when he closed his eyes, he still saw the bleeding body of Captain Jack Zodiac.

The string-bean maiden, finding her husband unwilling or unable, or both, whistled, and a clump of string beans rushed in, pinned him down, pulled off his pants, and forced into him—this part is extremely unpleasant—more than a dozen suppositories, which looked and felt like peach pits and contained God knows what chemicals. To serve as an aphrodisiac, obviously. But the question was, how would they affect his human system, which was probably worlds different from the string-bean system and which, in addition, had already been filled with a veritable witches' brew of designer drugs? What would happen when chemical met chemical in his bloodstream?

A mist passed before his eyes, and he found himself dandling a baby on his knee. A flashback? No: this could not be Trish or Josh. The child was extremely thin, thinner than a rail, and green. Even when they had the flu, his kids had never been that green. Or that thin. Sitting opposite him was his string-bean wife, twiddling her thumbs and looking pleased. Her figure was a tiny bit fuller, and her face seemed to have a few wrinkles. The baby was his, then? Theirs? He had not been aware of any passage of time. Did this make him, now, my God, a bigamist? A pair of older string beans came in: his in-laws. They produced happy noises, proud noises, over the cooing baby. Clifford looked carefully at the baby, trying to find a resemblance. Well, yes, maybe. Slovak eyes and nose. Aunt Milena would turn over in her grave. Marrying a Jew and converting had been bad enough. And Marsha, dear Marsha, what was she doing now?

Clifford told them that it had been nice but he had to go. Really. He had to reach mall zombieland and rescue his daughter before the pale-brown pill wore off. Yes, let us continue to worry about the pale-brown pill wearing off. Let us not even think about the possibility of synergy. Synergy is so unpredictable. Like bullets ricocheting off moving prisms and trompe l'oeil statues of the god of chance. Let us pretend that he took one pill and not five as the police closed in at the Franklin train station, and that the peach-pit love-potion suppositories had been nothing but a ridiculous, embarrassing dream. He got up to go, placing the baby delicately on the hard ground, but his string-bean father-in-law barred his way and said in a stern voice that leaving was not possible. Clifford had a family to support. Clifford, for one thing, might supply this shed with a few amenities, such as bedding or plumbing, or even a heating system, because the nights, as he well knew, were cold on this planet. "It's time," said the father-in-law, as straightforward as any string bean, "that you got a job, my boy, and started providing."

And, in and out of mists, Clifford must have done this, because he saw several young string beans in the shed, and they were all his. Every one of them. Slovak features. The shed not only had a bed and a rug now but also an extension—a combination playroom and laundry room—and a fenced-in yard with a small circular bathing pool. At the door was a mat that said COME ON IN in the string-bean tongue. Clifford even dreamt now in string bean. His only tie with the past was his guns, and on Sundays he would spend an hour or two dusting and oiling them. The children were not allowed to play with the bullets. "Why do you carry all that stuff around with you?" asked his wife. "It's heavy and bulky." What could he tell her? That he had to be prepared, to keep the blaster and the pistol on his person even when he went to the bathroom, because at any time he might disappear with a pop or a foop and find himself in another world, attacked by bug-eyed, fire-breathing, phlegmy horrors? If he told her that, she would have him committed one-two-three. And how could you blame her? There was a good chance that he was already committed, in Franklin State, and at this very moment twitching and drooling in a ward for those poor bastards whose brains had been irreversibly fried or scrambled by the treacherous pills of Captain Jack Zodiac and his ilk.

By coincidence—but maybe it wasn't coincidence— the next day, as Clifford was sitting on the john, he was whisked by the Davis Effect to a world where he was immediately attacked by bug-eyed, fire-breathing, phlegmy horrors. He used the blaster for a minute straight, filling the air with cinders and a revoltingly sweet stink. It was only after the horrors beat a disorderly retreat—apparently they were not accustomed to victims having blasters—that he was able to pull up his pants and utter a curse. No time, for Chrissake, even to wipe himself. And the place didn't look like it had toilet paper. Basalt crags, ravines, craters. Not a scrap of vegetation anywhere. Not even lichens or moss. A shame there was no moss. Moss was soft. In a pinch, a person could wipe himself with a clump of moss. On the other hand, extraterrestrial moss might be like poison ivy, or worse, and then where would you be? Probably in the space-cadet handbook, paragraph 4: Avoid having exobiota come into contact with the private parts.

After walking for hours across this barren and jagged landscape, he was so faint with hunger and thirst that he stopped fretting about his soiled underwear and increasingly sore anus. "Am I going to starve to death?" he thought. "Or will my pineal gland, at the last minute, pull me out of this one?" But his pineal gland wasn't called upon to do any pulling just yet, because in the next dismal canyon he traversed, he came upon a tavern. The wood shingle said TAVERN IN THE CANYON. Hoping this wasn't a mirage, Clifford went in and ordered a beer and a cheeseburger.

"That'll be fifty pice," said the bartender, who seemed quite human. The man had a handlebar mustache and, on his left bicep, a tattoo of a rose and dagger with the inscription OMNIA VINCIT AMOR.

"You're from Earth," said Clifford.

The bartender smiled. "You're probably asking yourself: What's an Earthling doing way the hell out here in the MLQ213 galaxy, on the other side of the Great Attractor? Yes, sir, this isn't Toronto, and that's a fact. The natives, what's left of them, you wouldn't believe the way they hold their grapefruit spoons in the morning. It takes a bit of getting used to. My name's Sam, Sam Taylor." And he held out a hairy hand.

"Clifford Koussevitzky," said Clifford, shaking the hand. "But I'm changing it to Katz. I converted."

"I have nothing against Jews," said Sam. "My sister married a Jew. Nice people. Clean. You eat a lot of gefilte fish, with horseradish?"

"Not yet."

"The only thing I don't care for is that jelly it comes with. I don't like my food to wiggle."

"So what *are* you doing here?" Clifford asked.

"Space cadets," said Sam, slowly pouring a St. Pauli Girl into a mug for Clifford. "They bop in and out on this planet all the time. You wouldn't believe how many. I do a good business. I'm even thinking of opening another tavern, in the other hemisphere. But things on Earth must be going to hell in a handbasket. All these kids tripping out."

"We're at war with Russia."

"No kidding."

"And the garbage collectors have been on strike now for more than three months."

"Jesus."

The cheeseburger, hands down, was the best cheeseburger Clifford had ever had. Thick, savory, and dripping juices. The platter was smothered with golden French fries. He was so ravenous, he practically made like a vacuum cleaner. Thwoop. And the beer was divine. It blew the mist out of his head; it steadied his hands; it made him hopeful again. Perhaps the years spent with the string beans had amounted only to minutes in mall zombieland and he still had a chance. Why not?

"Fifty pice," Sam said.

"Do you have toilet paper here?" Clifford asked.

The bartender pointed to the men's room. Yes, things were definitely looking up. Finally the gods were smiling on this persistent father. When Clifford returned from the men's room, he felt such relief, he purred inside.

Sam, however, was no longer smiling. He held out his hand, palm up, the fingers stiff and horizontal. In his eyes was a hard look, on the way to becoming a glare. "No extra charge for the toilet paper, Mr. Kouss," he said, tight-lipped.

"You wouldn't believe," said Clifford, "what a blessing toilet paper can be."

"I don't like deadbeats," said Sam.

"I had to go unwiped a whole day. Amazing, how we take some things for granted."

"One cheeseburger and one beer. That's fifty, five-oh, pice. Cash, please. We don't take credit cards. I don't want to hear any more about the toilet paper."

Clifford sighed and reached for his wallet. This was getting monotonous. He knew what was going to happen, but said anyway, "How much will that be in dollars?"

"Dollars?" said Sam, twisting his mouth. "Very funny." An image: an armored truck, and uniformed guards bringing one heavy sack of bills after the other into the tavern, while Sam stands there shaking his head. Millions, billions, trillions of dollars, all worthless. Good only for wallpaper, or for wiping yourself in a pinch. So it had finally happened, the monetary plunge to zero. Probably while Clifford was off raising string beans. There would be panic back home, mobs frothing at the mouth.

"I don't have any pice," Clifford said.

"I didn't think you did," growled the bartender, and pointed at Clifford's belt, pointed at the blaster.

"Pay with that?" Clifford asked.

"What else do you have?"

"But that's my defense against the perils of space. The moment I arrived on this planet, for example, I was attacked by—"

"I know," said Sam. "Bug-eyed, fire-breathing, phlegmy horrors. They're all over the place. And multiplying. Which is why I can use that blaster. It's a good one, better than what the space cadets from Earth usually have on them."

Clifford pictured a line of confused kids stranded in this craggy basalt wilderness and faint with hunger. Naturally, not one of them would have pice. There was probably a whole roomful of blasters in the back, piled high. And then the space cadets would leave the Tavern in the Canyon and find themselves, blasterless, at the mercy of the monsters, who had not a merciful bone in their monstrous bodies. Could Josh have been here? Clifford showed the bartender his son's photograph. A flutter of anxiety.

"No, doesn't ring a bell," Sam finally said after scrutinizing the photograph at arm's length. "Sorry."

Clifford put the photograph back in his pocket and the blaster on the counter. "Well, anyway, that was a good cheeseburger," he said.

"Thanks," said Sam. "Drop in again."

But when Clifford's hand was on the doorknob, he heard the bartender say, "Hold it"—in exactly the way people said "Hold it," deep and steady, when they pointed a gun at you. Clifford turned and saw, sure enough, that Sam had the blaster leveled at him, and that the bartender's eyes were red with murderous intent. Not the same person.

"I don't understand," said Clifford.

"This blaster," explained Sam Taylor with a voice of ice, "belongs to Captain Jack Zodiac. I'd recognize it anywhere, even without the monogram on the butt. You see, I know the captain. Know him well. We were on the *Smuggler's Dream* together, seven years. Fought the Frymp, rescued damsels in distress—"

"And probably charged them an arm and two legs for the service," Clifford said. He was getting tired of these self-righteous, bloodsucking entrepreneurs. Sure, there was no free lunch. He could accept that. He knew better than to argue with the first or second law of thermodynamics. But this grasping for mammon over the bodies of others, especially when those others were innocent and underage, it infuriated him.

"There is only one way you could have got this blaster," said the bartender, his finger tightening on the trigger. The OMNIA VINCIT AMOR on his left bicep rippled like a neon sign advertising condoms.

Clifford dodged the purple beam with surprising nimbleness (he had picked up a few quick-on-your-feet skills, apparently, from his string-bean father-in-law) and dove at the bartender. But the souped-up pineal gland wasn't taking any chances (the old saw about discretion and valor), because with a loud foop it dropped him smack in the middle of a Frymp stronghold/nest on the other side of the Universe. The Frymp warriors, in black leather, cut him to ribbons with their lasers. Their reflexes were the best, hands down, in all of time and space. A Frymp warrior was so fast, he could slice off your nose and sew it back on upside down before you got your gun halfway out of its holster. Really. Clifford awoke on his back, in a hospital. A man with a clipboard was standing over him and smiling. Behind the man, a unisex nurse. They helped him sit up and gave him a Coke to drink. "This proves," Clifford thought, "that I'm not in Franklin State after all, strapped to some cot and twitching and drooling." Unless, of course, he was in Franklin State and dreaming now that he was dead.

He spent a few weeks (or so he estimated) in Dis. He dropped in on his mother-in-law, who seemed to be losing interest not only in her daughter and Clifford but, incredibly, in things Jewish. When he asked her about the kosher problem and if the Jehovah's Witnesses were still bothering her, she waved a tired hand and changed the subject. But perhaps death did that to you after a while. Mr. Feldman he found running a novelty shop on Fifty-third Street: a dingy place with hardly any customers. But Mr. Feldman didn't seem to mind; he sat behind a cluttered counter in a shadowy corner, as peaceful and regal as if he were on a veranda overlooking rolling green fields and, in the distance, a bay filled with the sailboats of international bankers. "My regards to the Nagels," he said.

Everywhere he went, Clifford showed people the pictures of Trish and Josh, but—thank heaven—no one recognized them. One man, in a laundromat, nodded and said that the picture of Trish reminded him of his daughter. "She became a mall zombie," he said with a sigh, and added: "But, you know, they all look alike." Clifford also visited his former wife's sister, but she was not good company: she had the television on the whole time, was watching cartoons, and would answer him only in monosyllables.

No sign, anywhere, of Captain Jack Zodiac. The captain would not be carrying his blaster now, and Clifford still had the Finnish gun; it sat comfortably in his shoulder holster and made no telltale bulge. But the captain might sneak up behind him and hit him over the head with a two-by-four that had an ugly nail sticking out of it like a witch's fang. Clifford began looking over his shoulder so frequently, he developed a stiff neck.

He returned to the world of the living by using the black-token method, successfully dodged some machine-gun fire in the subway station, but then one of the soldiers threw a grenade at him, and Clifford didn't have time to put any meaningful distance between himself and the grenade, so he found himself again on his back in the hospital, with the man with the clipboard, George, who made jokes that amused no one. Clifford tried again. This time he got off at a different stop, where fortunately there were no soldiers, only a few dozen foul-smelling, clammy homeless who had to be stepped over on the way out. He called Marsha from a pay phone. The line was busy. He went to Mr. Nagel for advice. The exorcist-warlock wasn't home. His wife told Clifford that Ben was at a funeral in Pennsylvania: an old college chum.

"Osborn sends his regards," Clifford said.

"Oh, how is he doing?" asked Maureen Nagel.

"Fine."

"Would you like to stay for lunch? Tuna fish."

"No thanks. I have to be off." Off to save his daughter? But it looked like the pale-brown pill was a dud, after all. Seven hundred and fifty million dollars for nothing. A murder, for nothing. Because he had been killed twice now, lasered to ribbons, grenaded to jam, and not a peep out of the pineal gland. Probably he had spent too much time with the string-bean people, those mist-inducing peach pits in his rectum. Too much time building circular bathing pools for alien children—his own, God help him—on the other side of the Great Attractor. And meanwhile the drug or drugs had all worn off, and Trish was still undelivered from her eternity of drifting in and out of malls, shopping without stopping, looking without buying, going from store window to store window with vacant eyes and not a thought of home.

50

Clifford was wrong. Oh, was he wrong. The combination of the underground-ultraexperimental pill, which was the brown of a chicken's brown egg, and the four miscellaneous space pills, each packing an unknown punch of its own, and the several dozen birth-control pills of his wife's, no matter what their shelf life, plus the string-bean peach-pit suppositories, a real wild card there, not to mention the radioactive, doctored St. Pauli Girl served him by Sam Taylor in the Tavern in the Canyon (for Sam Taylor was a notorious master of synergistic concoctions and had learned a thing or two, you bet, about poisoning from Captain Jack Zodiac during his days aboard the *Smuggler's Dream*) was really only beginning, only beginning, only beginning to percolate in Clifford's unsuspecting bloodstream.

To percolate, to cook, to simmer. And trigger, finally, a greenhouse effect no less dire, warped, and mutagenic than the one that was claiming the third planet from the sun, our own. An internal greenhouse effect, this, of the cerebral cortex, spawning monsters that would have made Bob Petruzzo's lawn blanch, whimper with fright, and retreat with its tail between its zoysia legs.

51

From A to Z, then.

A. On his way to the bus stop (he would take the Five or the Seventeen home), there was a four-way shootout between some dirtbag crackfiends, a limousine-ful of slick gangsters, a division of confused Soviet paratroopers, and the usual commuters trying to avoid Interstate 28, because Interstate 28, even without the goddam ridiculous construction, was bumper-to-bumper now around the clock, no exaggeration. The commuters won. Their weaponry, as always, was more state-of-the-art than anyone else's, and what they lacked in skill, training, and experience they more than made up for in ferocity. The most fanatic Third-World commando was no match for a man or woman who had been seething three hours to get from Exit 12 to Exit 12A and then left the expressway only to find the same shit on the side roads.

Was it last summer?—a mother of four, wielding only a Samsonite briefcase, killed twelve foreign junkies, all armed with assault rifles, near the overpass at the Holiday Inn in Compton. The junkies had allegedly made some offensive macho-sexist gesture as they stood leaning on the railing by the road during their lunch break. The mother of four became so steamed, the rain of bullets as she attacked didn't stop her. Didn't even slow her down when they hit her. Nor did the twenty-foot concrete wall. She scaled it in her high heels, too, bleeding buckets, holding the briefcase in her teeth, as some of the other commuters cheered and honked in their cars. Such is the power of adrenaline. The Samsonite people paid her medical bills, featured her in their ads for months, and made her a vice president when she was done with all her reconstructive surgery.

After the shootout, the police came to write up a report, and unfortunately one of them recognized Clifford and arrested him on the spot. Suspicion of murder. Clifford's picture had been taken by flash camera before he popped out at the Franklin train-station parking lot over the highly incriminating corpse of Captain Jack Zodiac, a known figure in the community, particularly among the schoolchildren. Clifford, allowed one phone call at the police station, called Marsha. The line was busy. Then, as he waited, looking at some curiously unobscene graffiti scratched on the dirty yellow wall beside the phone, YOUR SISTER HAS ZITS and LET'S NOT PAY OUR TAXES HA HA, Clifford fooped.

B. And found himself surrounded not by string beans this time (which would have been awkward, since he had, after all, abandoned a family there) but what resembled peas and carrots. He looked up at the sky and saw an eerily glowing disk—an accretion disk—beside the sun. This meant a companion neutron star or possibly a black hole and therefore frequent bursts of very hard X rays, which perhaps accounted for the peas and carrots.

"Do you speak English?" he asked them.

They danced around him. A cannibal dance? But you could hardly call them cannibals in this instance, since he was neither pea nor carrot, not even remotely.

His Finnish gun and hundred bullets, worst luck, were back in that police station around the corner from the Nagels. Exhibit A.

Perhaps he should just serve his time. Life in prison might not be that bad. A little peace and quiet. An unchanging routine. Would Marsha visit?

The peas and carrots kept dancing. Were they worshiping him?

He could catch up on his reading, in prison. When was the last time he had curled up with a good book? His existence was so hectic.

He felt extremely weak. The X rays, no doubt. How much longer did he have? He groped in his pocket, picked through the loose change, looking for black tokens. None left.

The trip to Dis now would be one-way.

But apparently not, because when everything faded and he came to on his back in the hospital and George stepped forward, for the third time now, with his clipboard and a smile, damn if Clifford didn't foop.

C. Into what had to be mall zombieland. A thousand soulless Trishes drifting. At last! "Captain Jack Zodiac," he cried, "I take it back, you did deliver after all, God bless you!" He immediately began to question everyone there. "Do you know Trish Koussevitzky? Here's her picture. It's not a very good likeness, but you know what high-school yearbook photos are like. She has a scar on her left knee, from when she fell off her bicycle at the age of eight. It was my fault. I insisted on removing those stupid training wheels. How she cried! She didn't cry much, my girl, but when she did, it went right through your heart, like a knife. I ran to her. A ragged cut, on gravel and dirt, an ugly cut, though there wasn't much blood. Tears running down her cheeks, one after the other. Poor blubbering Trish. It isn't easy, I can tell you, it isn't easy being a father."

He looked into the distance and saw mall zombies floating in the mist like big cottony flakes of snow, the kind of snow that swirls in slow motion, in all directions, and never lands. It was like being inside a Santa-and-reindeer paperweight.

"Have you met my daughter?" he asked one girl, who could have been Trish's twin. He swam after her, waved to catch her eye. Could it be Trish herself? "Excuse me," he said, and put his hand on her shoulder, then they both sort of materialized (half materialized) into a mall in Bombay. Turbans, saris, dots on foreheads.

The girl made for the bead bags. It was certainly possible that Trish wouldn't recognize her father. Why, she had hardly recognized him in that last year she lived at home. She would look right through him when he told her about the Surgeon General's latest report on alcoholism and suicide among suburban white youth.

Then they were in Manchuria, at a perfume counter. He took the girl's head in both his hands and forced her to look at him. "Are you Trish or aren't you?" But even if she was, the reunion was abruptly ended. The mall zombie didn't melt or segue away. No, Clifford was the one who departed. Foop.

D. It was like being on a roller coaster. You hold out your hand for the ice-cream cone Aunt Milena offers you, but—sorry—whisk—no time—you're clutching empty air as the car careens teeth-grindingly around a bend and takes you to a garage-Ford-dealership-type place where a lot of red devils are hammering on metal and chewing tobacco. The stink of gasoline is overpowering, but not to worry, in another second—whisk—you're in the countryside where Bossy the Cow is tinkling her bell and lowing bucolically and the Evening Star (that's Venus) appears in silent splendor in the east. Though this, too, is only for a second. On you go—whisk—to the next frame, and the next. The thing about roller coasters is not that they shoot up and down and around, or that they alternate between good and bad and fear and relief; the thing about roller coasters is that they don't stop.

Clifford wasn't thrilled to find himself back with the peas and carrots.

He wanted his daughter, damn it, not a bunch of dancing orange and green parboiled vegetables.

He was getting fed up being the butt of pointless cosmic jokes.

He fooped by sheer force of will.

Fooping by sheer force of will is next to impossible, but it helps if your pineal gland has already been twisted out of shape and is swollen to maybe three times its normal size through repeated psychopharmacological abuse. Anger and despair in themselves won't do the trick. Otherwise we would all be fooping, wouldn't we?

E. *Complete darkness.*

CLIFFORD: Where in the hell am I now? I can't see anything.

VOICE: Dad?

CLIFFORD: Who's that?

VOICE: Dad?

CLIFFORD: Will somebody turn on the lights, please? Or am I blind now? I wouldn't be surprised. Nothing would surprise me.

VOICE: You're in a dungeon, Dad. There are no lights. How did you get here?

CLIFFORD: Is that . . . Josh?

JOSH: It's me, Dad.

CLIFFORD: What are you doing here? A dungeon, you said?

JOSH: They threw us in here.

CLIFFORD: They? Us? What's going on? What happened?

JOSH *says nothing, sighs*.

CLIFFORD: It's like pulling teeth, to get anything out of you. You always were that way. Brick wall. No communication. I wasn't a good father, I guess. Too impatient. If I had it to do over, I'd work on being more patient. On taking more time. Listening better.

JOSH: You're all right, Dad.

CLIFFORD: Why are you here, Josh? Where is this?

JOSH: I don't know exactly. We took a pill . . .

CLIFFORD: Ah. From Captain Jack Zodiac, by any chance? But of course it was Captain Jack Zodiac. Who else? I see it all. Curse him.

JOSH: The captain's all right.

CLIFFORD: No, he's not. He's a villain. An evil money-grubbing vampire. Trust me, I know what I'm talking about. *Was* a villain, I should say. No more preying on young boys for him. I don't regret what I did. What did the bastard charge you?

JOSH *says nothing, sighs*.

CLIFFORD: What kind of pill was it?

JOSH *shrugs, but no one can see his shrug in the dark*.

CLIFFORD: Was it a brown pill?

JOSH: Yellow, with red spots.

CLIFFORD: Ah.

Half a minute of silence.

* * *

JOSH: Bobby died.

CLIFFORD: Bobby who?

JOSH: Bergholz.

CLIFFORD: Maury's son? Around the corner from us? When did this happen?

JOSH: I don't know. You lose track of time here.

CLIFFORD: You mean, he was in the dungeon with you? You took pills together?

JOSH *nods, but no one can see his nod.*

CLIFFORD: And the pills put you into a dungeon?

JOSH: No, Dad, it was the lawyers. Seph Glowp. Phex Plowg.

CLIFFORD: What?

JOSH: We wanted to fight the dragon bears of Moon Two. But when we wouldn't sign the waiver . . .

CLIFFORD: You're losing me.

JOSH: It doesn't matter.

Another long pause.

CLIFFORD: So there's a corpse with us here? I'd hate to step on him . . .

JOSH: He's not here now. The body goes back.

CLIFFORD: Oh.

JOSH: Dad, can you get me out of here? I haven't had anything to eat or drink in days. My tongue feels like a cactus.

CLIFFORD: Of course, of course. I'll do my best. The only problem is, I keep fooping.

JOSH: What's that?

CLIFFORD: It's unpredictable.

JOSH: Dad, are you . . . are you spacing, too?

CLIFFORD *clears his throat with embarrassment.*

JOSH: Wow. I never heard of anybody's dad spacing.

CLIFFORD *begins to say something but instead foops*.
JOSH: Dad? Dad?

F. In a nebula five billion light-years from Earth—
and each light-year is six trillion miles, roughly, so if
we're talking miles, we're talking a lot of zeros after the
number three, more than will fit comfortably on a line in
a book—too big a distance, in other words, to wrap your
mind around, unless you're peculiar—Clifford Koussevitzky tumbles head over heels through the void
inchoate. If his eyes were good enough, telescopic
enough, and if he could stop his tumbling and look
Earthward, he would see a cloud-covered, rust-colored
planet. Our planet. It has no oxygen yet, no life, just
rocks and rain, and sulfurous fumes fizzing up with a
hiss. It will take the photons bouncing off this Earth five
billion years to travel the abovementioned zeros' worth
of miles to reach the eyes of Clifford Koussevitzky as he
tries to scream in the absence of air, which doesn't work,
in a nebula so removed from any civilization that no one
has ever named or numbered it. The Universe, Clifford
thinks—or perhaps he is not thinking at the moment,
which is understandable, so we will have to think for
him—is not a hospitable place.

G. Jeannette Koussevitzky, his former wife and the
mother (no mother, she) of his children, yowlped with
surprise. Which was not surprising. A man appeared,
blue in the face and pop-eyed, in her shower.

Jim, Jeannette's companion, lover, and fellow assassin in the name of the dolphins and orcas of the North
Pacific, hearing her yowlp, ran into the bathroom bran-
dishing a Holcomb 7K.

"It's my ex," Jeannette gasped.

"Wait," Clifford gasped, throwing up his wet hands.

But Jim, jumpy because the police had been on their trail for weeks now after Topeka, had already squeezed the trigger—too late, sorry—and three cadmium-cased needle bullets put a hole in Clifford's forehead, a hole in his chest, and a hole in his abdomen.

The tub, shower curtain, walls, and even the ceiling were covered with gore. Bits of lung and liver sticking to everything.

Jeannette, whose nerves ordinarily were as steady as a plinth, had to take two Quiets, and at supper that evening she didn't have much of an appetite.

Not two minutes in Dis, Clifford was dispatched by Captain Jack Zodiac, who this time was indeed waiting for him. It happened so quickly, Clifford got only a glimpse of the captain's creased, maniacally grinning face before darkness fell and bore him to Dis 2, where, in a war, over a couple of beers, he struck up an interesting conversation with one Jiménez Quindío Vichada "Dusty" Colón, the former Colombian cocaine kingpin.

"You must be always careful," Dusty Colón said, puffing on a cigar. "Eyes in the back of the head, always."

"He has lots of experience," Clifford sighed. "He's an old spacesalt, has seen all kinds of action. And I imagine he's the type who holds a grudge."

"Sure. He was doing a good business."

"Is that all anyone ever cares about, money?"

Dusty Colón finished his beer and smiled a broad Mayan brick-orange smile. "What do you have, amigo, if you don't have money?"

"Yes, I suppose you're right."

H. In Dis 5—what was he doing in Dis 5?—he seemed to be sitting at the same bar, though the light was too dim to be sure. He was drinking beer with Captain Jack Zodiac. The place was filled with Russian soldiers and kids between the ages of two and twelve—the sandbox years. There was also a group of tough, self-satisfied Hispanic types in bandannas, leather jackets, and pimpy nose rings.

"—bygones," said the captain.

"Excuse me?" asked Clifford, leaning forward and cupping his ear, because of the din.

"I said," said the captain, "let's let bygones be bygones."

"I'll drink to that."

They had been drinking for some time. Lost count, how many beers. One good thing about Dis 5, the inflation hadn't reached here yet. You could buy four beers with a twenty-dollar bill, and get change. Another good thing about being deceased was that you didn't need to keep running to the head and staring for long minutes at an ugly urinal. Bernie Rifkin would like this place.

The beer, on the other hand, wasn't good. Tasteless, flat, not even cold. Scratch that thought about Bernie Rifkin. Bernie was particular about his beer.

The captain was growing sentimental. "I had a full life," he said. "The only thing I regret is not taking my revenge on that bank."

"Death to banks," said Clifford, raising his bottle.

"Amen."

They drank.

"Did I ever tell you about the time—" the captain began.

"Excuse me," said Clifford, feeling a foop coming on.

I. He was walking on railroad tracks. Woods to either side. This could be near Franklin, for all he knew, the scene of the crime. But it could be anywhere. He walked and thought that tracks had only two directions: going and coming. There was something limited, mechanical, about railroad travel. Point A to Point B. Point B to Point A. Time tables; schedules; tickets punched click-click. And the collisions were fixed and unimaginatively head-on, when train C, going from Point A to Point B, clickety-clack, met train D, which was going (you guessed it) from Point B to Point A, because a switch shorted somewhere along the line or a signalman was looking at a woman, undressing her mentally, at just the wrong moment.

Clifford walked for an hour, two hours, along the ties. He began to feel very lonely.

J. A place in the sun: literally. Was it our own—was it Sol?—or some other star? Did it matter? He was vaporized, pfft, before he felt it, and back to Dis, with a sunburn. Another bad joke. He went to the corner pharmacy to buy ointment. There he met, what a coincidence, small world, Leslie Karen Giambucci from Apalachicola, Florida.

"Leslie! Remember me? Class of '12?"

"Kouss! Son of a gun!"

"You work here?"

"Well, I have to do something," she said. "It's either this or stare at old wallpaper all day. The wallpaper here is really depressing, don't you think? Faded roses, faded ivy."

"So how are you doing?"

"Fine, and you?"

Clifford sighed, shook his head. "Things are a little too hectic lately."

"I know what you mean. But, my God, where'd you get that burn?"

"Don't ask."

* * *

K. A planet inhabited by people who went around on stilts. Red hair, and noses like can openers. The inhabitants paid no attention to him. They were at war. With pirates. The pirates also on stilts, also with red hair and can-opener noses. You could tell who the pirates were by the traditional black eye patches they wore, and because they held cutlasses in their bared teeth. The hand-to-hand combat very convincing. The people on this planet, it turned out, died when they came into contact with the ground. Hence the stilts. Perhaps the soil was badly polluted. Although it didn't seem to harm Clifford. During the battle, people fell from their stilts, both pirates and nonpirates. They died in a matter of seconds, writhing. Tragic. Clifford never found out what the bone of contention was.

L. A planet with no air, only ice and craters, so back to Dis. When would this be over?

M. Reverend Bennison gasped. The reverend thin as a rail. AIDS? He returned Clifford's censuring frown: Mr. Koussevitzky a space cadet? What was the world coming to?

N. The void inchoate. Back to Dis. How much longer?

O. Things were definitely speeding up. Perhaps that meant they were now accelerating to a conclusion, a sort of grand finale. Clifford hoped he wouldn't blow up at the end. But he felt, in his bones, that he would. The pressure building, building. Time to say a last prayer?

* * *

P. Q. R. S. T. Whew!

U. On lush green grass. Good. But the sky was all wrong, not a sky at all, more like the inside of a giant animal, ribs vaulting up and organs pulsing red and purple-brown. What kind of place was this? A bad smell. Death. Zombies in the distance. No, not zombies. Bobbing up and down. The heads like wads of bubble gum, much chewed. Except paler than bubble gum, chalky. Were they singing?

V. Peas and carrots again. Why did these peas and carrots, under an accretion disk, piss him off so much? It was not their fault. But please, no more peas and carrots.

W. On a mountaintop. A gentle breeze. A sunset. The only problem: litter. Styrofoam and false teeth everywhere. Disgusting, when even mountaintops were trashed.

X. Space again, the last frontier.

Y. Sliding down one of those wormhole chutes from a singularity, twanging on a cosmic string, floating thirteen-dimensionally in a sea of quarks and leptons, spiraling spiraling through a seahorse valley of infinite regress and perhaps insidious intent, where things are generally so loose and unlabeled, you don't have to worry about where the subject is and where the predicate. Clifford, even though he's of the Mosaic faith now, crosses himself.

Z. A long dark road. A sign that read: SIMULATION 97 TRIPLE PRIME, FRAME J. An office building filled with computers and cables. Clifford had a cold feeling in his stomach. The cold feeling said that the ride, finally, was over. Entering, he saw a man at one of the consoles. The man looked up, turned around. The man was quite lifelike but made entirely of metal and plastic.

52

"What's this? Another explorer. Hello, hello," said the man, getting up and holding out his hand, which Clifford took. "From the triple or quadruple prime, no doubt."

"Clifford Katz," said Clifford, shaking the hand. The metal and plastic were curiously warm. "I'm from Wood-haven. It's a community about two hours east of the city. Used to be, that is, before the traffic got completely crazy."

"How quaint. An introduction. Pleased to meet you, I'm sure, Clifford Katz," said the mechanical man. "And now my name. What shall we call me? Not something with a lot of numbers. That would be trite, trite." Still holding Clifford's hand, he looked up, as if for inspiration, chewed on his lower lip, wrinkled his metal-and-plastic brow. "Something from Classical mythology?" he murmured to himself. "No, no, overdone."

"That's all right, you don't need to—" Clifford began, but the man waved that away.

"Just give me a minute," he said. "This should be peanuts for me. I'm really very creative. It's part of my job, you know, thinking up things. I think up whole worlds, you know. A name should be nothing."

He hmmed, nodded, gave a quick embarrassed smile, then scowled in concentration.

Clifford looked around. Monitors, rows of them.

Panels of blinking lights. Red, yellow, green, blue. It reminded him of Christmas. Christmas would be the one thing he would miss, as an ex-Catholic Katz. A slight pang inside, bittersweet. A fuzzy memory of Trish opening her presents, bent over, flushed cheeks, hair falling down. Photographs couldn't do it justice.

But a curious office building, this. More like a warehouse. All these computers and only one person.

And what was being simulated here?

"Zed," said the robot. "Call me Zed." His eyes sparkled. "Appropriate, no? Simple. Unpretentious. With just enough algebraic resonance. And for those who like a little symbolism, it points, rather neatly, I think, to the fact that for you, in this scene, I am the end of the line."

"Scene?" asked Clifford.

"All the world's a stage, my friend," said Zed. "That's Shakespeare. We include Shakespeare in all our runs."

"Runs?"

"Shakespeare, in my opinion, Clifford, has got into the blood of human history. Leave out the bard, and the frame goes flat. Flat. Every time. Interesting, isn't it?"

"The frame goes flat?"

Zed smiled, tsk-tsked, and put a comradely metal-and-plastic arm around Clifford. "But here I'm boring you with shoptalk, and you're at the brink, as it were, of your denouement. Selfish of me. Unhospitable. A million pardons. One gets that way from working alone so much. Solitude. Only you and the screen and the program, for centuries on end. Sometimes I sing opera, just to hear the sound of my voice. Verdi. Puccini. Our supervisor hardly ever drops in. I don't complain. Other fish to fry, I'm sure, other fish to fry."

And he led Clifford to one of the monitors.

"What is this?" asked Clifford, uneasy.

Zed leaned over a keyboard, tapped a few keys, and the screen brightened. A city. A very familiar city, and yet very different. Incredibly clean. As if a gray scum had been removed from everything. Several gray scums. The colors were so rich—even the color of the concrete and the color of the asphalt, and of the cornices and pigeons and water towers—that you felt you were in a kind of Disney heaven. Even the garbage looked good.

"It's self-explanatory, on a gut level," murmured Zed.

The picture changed, then that picture changed, then that one, too, all at the pace of an expert TV commercial, packing in loads of information with impressive economy and professional pizzazz. The story was told, the truth revealed, in seconds.

"Occasionally," Zed was saying, as Clifford watched spaceships taking off, stations being built, robots building robots, then close-ups of bytes and chips and DNA, "an explorer makes his way here—damned if I can figure out how—but occasionally it happens."

Automated factories in space. Self-correcting, self-programming. Drawing energy from the sun. Machines being fruitful and multiplying. Evolving. Filling space, the whole solar system. Darwinian competition among them. War, ultraweapons, Earth burnt to a crisp. A few human enclaves underground: storing water, the complete works of Shakespeare, and back issues of *The Wall Street Journal*.

"I show them this," said Zed, "and then I erase them."

An exodus of most of the machines to parts unknown. Deep space. Cosmic destiny. The one robot species left: digging the charred soil, burying the last bodies, cataloguing artifacts, reconstructing the past by computer. Simulation. Extrapolation from tooth fillings and belt buckles.

"Erase them?" asked Clifford.

"Oh, it's voluntary, ninety-nine percent of the time," said the metal-and-plastic man. "They don't want to go on, when they learn the truth."

A paean to the glories of simulation. Enormous molecules mapped without anyone having to dirty a test tube or put a piece of chalk to a blackboard. The trajectory of a flea on a spaniel's flapping ear, done with different frequencies of flap, different wind speeds, different air pressures, and different age of spaniel. A meteor (follow the dotted line) among seven erratic moons and a planet sporting 112 rings. The Big Bang played back in slow motion, and stopped at ten to the minus eighty-three seconds so we can go out for a quick sandwich and a beer.

Because logic is logic the universe over, and it makes no difference, my friend, whether something happens here or there, in outer space or in a Duluth dog pound. Or inside a computer.

"I want to go on," said Clifford. The truth was shocking, it took his breath away, yes, but it didn't bother him that much, somehow, not in his heart of hearts. Perhaps he had never really thought life was real to begin with.

The robot historians now build computer centers, throw everything they have into the alphanumeric hopper to get the necessary output, which is the present. A sad present.

Before you know it, the gaps are filled in, the chain of cause and effect completed, every blessed link of it. Mission accomplished. The human race from A to Z, may it rest in peace. A moment of silence, bow your heads. A bound book, a closed book. Put in on the shelf with the others.

Meanwhile, in the various computer centers, n Earths have been created, n alternate realities, and our historians, who enjoyed the game of parameters—take this factor out, put that one back in, here, yes, or double it, or turn it upside down, or maybe upside down and backward—the old game, in other words, of Let's See What Happens When We Do This—our historians keep playing.

"I'm not interested in being erased," said Clifford, whose hands felt very cold. "I'd like to bring my family together."

"You have a family."

"A son, a daughter, a wife."

"And a cat and a dog? Don't tell me. And a parakeet and a goldfish in a bowl?"

Zed sounded—no one's perfect—condescending. His plastic eyebrows were raised sardonically. His metal lips were pursed.

Clifford ignored this. "We never went in for pets much. Trish had a cat, Annie, when she was ten. For two weeks. It was hit by a car. Also, my wife, my first wife, was against pet food. On principle. She would say, 'Why kill horses to feed dogs?' She had a point."

"Erasure," said Zed, "is quite painless, Clifford. Peaceful. Not like being hit by a car, believe me. No blood, no unpleasant crunching of bones. Imagine a large magnet being passed over you."

Our computer historians have all the time in the world. Well, that's an exaggeration. They have another five hundred million years, conservatively speaking, before the sun uses up its hydrogen and turns to heavier stuff, thereby beginning the more interesting process of going nova. Five hundred million years. No need to hurry.

So the game, the experiment, continues. Our biological ancestors, computerized, are put through all kinds of paces. Some funny and some farfetched—we indulge in a chuckle now and then—but every run, every run is educational.

The problem with reality, you see, is that it comes in only one package.

The hero kills the villain, or the villain kills the hero, or they kill each other, and one has to go on from there. No retakes, no replays. What happens, happens, period.

In a simulation, periods do not exist. Throw out the commas, too, if you want. All is possible.

If a law of nature cramps your style, change that law of nature. Why not? The only constraints are esthetic.

And from each run, no matter how fantastic, no matter how wild and bizarre and silly, we learn something, as I said, about our biological ancestors. We take notes. We add to the body of knowledge.

These human beings—you get to see them in new situations. Take an Earth, for example, that has recursive hereafters in ladder formation. Or where a nuclear strike, say, is less of a problem than a garbage strike.

Or where adolescent boys can teleport to other galaxies by popping pills made in Manila and sold on a street corner by kindly old Captain Jack Zodiac.

53

"Any last words?" asked Zed, smiling like the host of a television game show as he touched another key.

"So I'm just a character," said Clifford, "in a program in a machine, like a Mario brother?"

"Correct," said Zed.

"And that city"—it was on the screen again—"is the real city?"

"A photograph, digitalized. Taken three to four hundred thousand years ago."

"The real world . . . was it a lot different from mine?"

"Different, not different," sighed the metal-and-plastic man, rolling his eyes, showing impatience and perhaps a touch, now, of boredom. "I really don't want to get into a discussion, Clifford. Don't take this personally, but you're not, well, that intelligent. I mean, talking to you at any length, and heaven knows I like to talk, is not going to do a lot for me in either the enlightenment or the entertainment department. I'm sorry, but there it is."

Clifford pictured a programmer programming his, Clifford's, brain, pictured an IQ meter with a label that said FRAME J, and a couple of equations on a blackboard, with limit symbols and less-than-or-equal-to signs. Zed was probably right. You couldn't expect a Mario brother to be a mental giant.

So this was why Clifford, although he had applied himself, never did that well in school. B's and C's, not A's. The eightieth percentile, never the ninetieth.

This was why he had had so much trouble, in the sixth grade, with fractions. Always confusing the denominator with the numerator. Or was it the numerator with the denominator? Koussevitzky, what's one and a half divided by three-eighths?

Four, Mrs. Bellamy.

Well, at last. Class, a round of applause for the blockhead.

"Last words, last words?" Zed prompted, fingers over the keyboard. He probably wanted to get back to his world simulating. The break was over.

"I'd rather not be erased," said Clifford.

54

"Those are not particularly memorable last words," said Zed under his breath, tapping a key.

Clifford closed his eyes, put his hands at his sides, thought of Trish, Marsha, Aunt Milena.

"And I hope I didn't offend you"—another tap, another key—"with my remark about your intelligence."

"That's all right," said Clifford, eyes closed, as if he were at the dentist's, in the drilling chair, waiting for the hum, the whine, the buzz. "Songwriters don't have to be intelligent. In fact, it's probably a liability."

Into thy hands I commend my spirit.

"You're a songwriter?" The clicking of the keys stopped. "You write songs? You don't say. Really? Fancy that. Well, I had no idea I was talking to a . . . fellow creator."

Clifford opened his eyes and saw, in the eyes of the robot, the gleam of new interest.

"Perhaps," continued Zed, with a little ceremonious bow signifying fellowship, "you could sing one of your songs for me, before you go. If you don't mind."

"I'm not much of a singer," Clifford told him. He was always telling people that. No voice. And it was true. "Anyway, I don't have my guitar."

Zed turned to the keyboard, and after a flurry of clicks a gorgeous Gibson popped out of the air and fell

243

into Clifford's hands. Blond wood, ivory inlays. Top of the line.

Clifford tried the strings: in perfect tune.

"You have godlike power," he said.

"It's relative, it's relative," said Zed.

When Clifford turned the Gibson around, he saw emblazoned on the back, in curlicued letters of gold:

CLIFFORD KATZ, SONGWRITER.

55

What followed was not terribly intelligent. It was more on the level of Bugs Bunny and Elmer Fudd than Stephen Crane or Leo Tolstoy. But, what the hell, it worked. Clifford chose "Brother Dolphin," and when he got to the lines

> I'll carry you,
> Yes, I'll carry you,
> We'll all carry you,
> Out of the doom of extinction,

he broke off at "doom," raised his eyebrows and puckered his lips in surprise, then cleared his throat and said, in the most convincingly truthful voice he could muster—and the adrenaline did help: "Oh, look, Zed, there's another explorer." And pointed. "There, behind you."

Zed turned around to see—and Clifford took the gorgeous Gibson by the neck (this is murder number two, they get easier) and in a big sweep brought the guitar down, wham, on the programmer's metal-and-plastic head. Using both arms and putting his whole body into it. On impact, Clifford's feet were lifted from the ground, just as in cartoons or a video game. He sang "of extinction" as he swung, and guitar came into contact with head on *extinc*, and the *extinc* turned into a shrill string-bean karate shriek, a sound so unnerving, it is better left undescribed.

In the hall, echoes of a jangled twang, lasting for five, ten, fifteen seconds.

On the floor, Zed. Around him, pieces of wood. Guitar strings still vibrating slightly and sproinged beyond all possible use.

In the top and center of Zed's cranial case, a dent. Not a big dent, but evidently big enough.

And thus it might be said that Clifford Koussevitzky—second cousin to Sergey Koussevitzky's grandson, Harry, who works for an important men's clothing chain in Seattle—achieved his most significant musical success not on the upbeat, after all, but on the downbeat.

56

He looked high and low for a computer manual. Found one finally in a drawer, with a few booklets, which were filled with rows and columns of numbers plus weird, impressive symbols he had never seen before. Instruction booklets. Software, programs. Not his cup of tea. More like poison. This computer stuff always made him feel retarded, mush-brained, hopelessly undeveloped. As if everyone else could tie their shoes and he still couldn't.

He sighed. He sighed again. He took all this literature to a desk and spent an hour trying to make head or tail of it. No luck. He couldn't. He sighed, rubbed his eyes, loosened his collar, took off his jacket, and went at it again. Another hour, two hours, three. Until the numbers and the symbols started blurring and dancing and sticking out their tongues at him.

"I can't do this," he said.

But there was no one to commiserate or give encouragement or shake a head no or nod yes. Head-dented Zed lay facedown, motionless. No comment from him. No chatter. No advice.

Clifford made a tour of the place; looked in all the drawers; found more booklets, some printouts; piled everything on the desk. He sighed and tried again. Gave up, took a walk, came back, tried again.

He wasn't that intelligent. With his Mario-brother brain, how could he hope to do this? It was impossible. And this computer stuff was probably some kind of robot superscience anyway, which even a Harvard Princeton Ph.D. professor in mathematics with thick glasses and bushy hair couldn't handle, let alone a run-of-the-mill songwriter who was only trying to get his family together.

Was he looking at the books upside down? He tried turning them. It made no difference, absolutely none.

Hopeless, hopeless. He gave up. He said, "I give up," and banged his poor cartoon head on the desk, which caused some of the incomprehensible, undecipherable printouts to flutter and slip to the floor with a sigh.

He sighed. He tried again.

He tried pressing keys on one of the keyboards and watching the screen above it to see what happened. Nothing happened. The computer beeped at one point, and there was an error message. Clifford had no idea— not the remotest—not the foggiest—what the message meant. The words said no more to him than did the numbers and the symbols, and the numbers and the symbols said nothing.

Careful with the keyboard, Clifford. You might create something by accident. Something unpleasant if not dangerous. You might even erase yourself. Do be careful.

He went back to the books and the printouts.

Days went by. Weeks. No progress. It was hopeless, impossible, with his Frame-J IQ. His limited B-brain. Never an A-brain. Sorry, but there it is.

Throw in the towel, you poor bastard.

He gritted his teeth, thought of Trish, Josh, Marsha, and for the nth time forced his eyes to take in the numbers and the symbols one by one, as if he were reading words on a page and not computer gobbledy-gook.

He had terrible headaches.

He tried the keyboard again. He gave up and went back to the books and the printouts. He gave up and tried the keyboard again. Was cautious, holding his breath; was reckless, desperate, furious, and practically hit the keys with his fists. Did hit the keys with his fists.

Cautious, reckless, fingers, fists, it made no difference. No difference.

A month passed. A year passed. By now he had memorized whole sections of the booklets. But they still made no sense to him. None. More teeth gritting. More time passing.

But he had all the time in the world, didn't he? Another five hundred million years—wasn't it?—before the sun used up its hydrogen and turned to heavier stuff.

It took Clifford a thousand years.

A one with three zeros after it.

A thousand years to read the software and figure out the operational system, and get the hang of multivariable concatenation and heuristic parameter play, which is the backbone of any kind of world simulating, at least for subtransfinite phenomena in this particular corner of the Greater Continuum.

It took him another hundred years to learn the ropes of the Double and Triple Primes.

He made a Gibson.

Then he put on his jacket, straightened his tie, cracked his knuckles, flexed his fingers, smiled, and got to work.

57

Oh yeah.
You gotta be
My silver lining.

These sure are rough times,
Scrapin' nickels and dimes,
The dollar it don't go far.
But with you at my side,
Baby, I can ride
To the moon in my getaway car.

Can't see the day
Through this damn ozone haze,
The sun it don't wanna shine,
But when you're near,
Baby, even landfill air
Smells like a forest of pine.

I see your bright face
After the rain.
I hear your sweet song
After the thunder.
I feel your soft love
After the storm
Of my pain.

Oh yeah.
You gotta be
My silver lining.

We got moral decline,
All kinds of crime,
People they don't seem to care.
But when you smile,
Baby, the bad guys go to jail
And they all get the 'lectric chair.

Society's ills,
Poppin' polka-dot pills,
And everyone fadin' with AIDS.
But when you take my hand,
Baby, I'm a thousand-piece band
In a Fourth-of-July parade.

  I see your bright face
  After the rain.
  I hear your sweet song
  After the thunder.
  I feel your soft love
  After the storm
  Of my pain.
  Oh yeah.
  You gotta be
  My silver lining.

58

The Kaplan family at the table. To Clifford's left and right, his son and daughter; opposite him, his wife.

It is Christmas Eve. An enormous Christmas tree, all lit up, near the fireplace. Under it, quaint Lionel trains going choo-choo around hundreds of colorfully wrapped presents. The fir branches are filled, snow-heavy, with twinkling Stars of Bethlehem, glittering David Menorahs, and those lovely cut-crystal tesseracts that turn themselves inside out slowly as you watch.

As Clifford says the blessing over the matzo, his family bend their heads solemnly. "*Ne rushay hono ta budet smerditi*," he intones. "*Ne rushay hono ta budet smerditi.*" They cross themselves.

He is the rabbi, in his spare time, of the Beth Witch Congregation around the corner. Goes there on foot, on *Shabbos*. Never uses the car, on *Shabbos*. Never. He is so echt-Jewish, his mother-in-law swells with pride, in the frame of her picture on the mantelpiece. "Such a son-in-law," Emma Feldman sometimes tells visitors, from her frame. "He is even more Jewish than me, can you imagine."

The car, since we've mentioned the car: a Maserati sedan, sedate but powerful. When Clifford opens it up on the highway, it can attain a speed of two hundred mph in five seconds, without straining. Marsha sometimes tells him she would feel a little more comfortable at a lower speed, but it gives him such a good feeling—he replies with a smile—to zoom down that straight, wide, smooth, unbroken, empty ribbon of road toward the city.

Maybe once every fifteen or twenty minutes, on his way to work, he passes a car.

They honk at each other and wave. Howdy, neighbor.

The Maserati, on the weekends, is fire-engine red, because that's when Josh uses it on his chaperoned dates, but during the week the car is a more peaceful and domestic pale-brown, the brown, almost, of a chicken's brown egg.

On the Fourth of July, of course, it's red, white, and blue.

Clifford Kaplan, incidentally, is also commander of the local veterans' lodge in Woodhaven. Decorated innumerable times for single-handedly storming innumerable Commie machine-gun nests in the last war, in Ticonderoga. He doesn't talk about his medals, doesn't show his scars. If only we had more like him.

As the Kaplan family eats, birds are twittering on the branches outside. Wonderful dinner music, compliments of Mother Nature, while the sun sets. They are all bluebirds, by the way. A cool breeze comes through the open window. Clear, clean, scented air. Delicious.

A rumble in the distance, like thunder. It is thunder.

"Thunder," remarks Josh.

"Yes," says Clifford. "Looks like we'll have a little rain tonight. The garden can use it."

In the garden in the back, big tomatoes, cucumbers, squash, string beans. No peas and carrots. Clifford never did like peas and carrots. Well, to each his own.

On the vegetables, in his mind's eye, he can see raindrops collecting.

As it grows dark, the crickets start, the music of a summer night, even though it's Christmas Eve.

A gust of air brings in the refreshing, exciting, always slightly spicy smell of coming rain. The curtains billow.

"Trisha," says Marsha, Mrs. Kaplan, "close the window a little, will you?"

"Sure, Mom," says Trisha. Puts down her napkin, gets up, and closes the window a few inches but not all the way, because this family loves fresh air.

"Thank you, dear," says Marsha with a sweet smile.

Clifford nods with approval. He is very pleased to see his children so solicitous of his wife, who is eight months pregnant now, with twins, yet hasn't lost her lovely figure.

She's carrying one boy, one girl.

Comfortable, convenient symmetry. The boy will have a big brother, the girl a big sister. They'll go to the 4-H Club together someday, hand in hand.

Trisha and Josh have turned out all right, Clifford muses. After that worrisome slump last year, Josh is exercising at the gym, has a paper route, and is getting straight A's. And Trisha is really into civics. Student government. President of her class. Clifford is very proud. Proud of both kids. Thank God he won't have any problem with the tuition, when they go to college, Trisha next year, Josh the year after. Princeton or Harvard. No, after his last hit, "Come with Me to Eden," at the top of the charts for forty-seven weeks, a platinum platter, and then that incredibly generous raise from Mr. Drucker, and the unexpected promotion to senior executive songwriter, a tenured position with parachutes, Clifford won't have any problem with the tuition.

He's earning so much now, he doesn't like to tell people how much; it's embarrassing.

They would make a fuss, too, over his philanthropy, if they ever found out. The halfway houses he has set up, in the city, for the homeless. All done anonymously. How he hates people making speeches about him and giving him awards and clapping genteelly, with raised chins, over fine china and snow-white linen at banquets. A person is supposed to help his fellow man. That's a commandment, not a thing to be patted on the back for and written up in the Sunday magazine.

Dinner is over. It's time now to light the twelve holy tapers and open the presents. A knock at the door. Philip Hirsch dropping in to wish them all a Merry Christmas and Good Hanukkah. He's brought some presents, too. A blowgun for every member of the family. Folk-genuine, of course, with Tasaday carvings that symbolize all sorts of fascinating things from the Dawn of Civilization.

Clifford lifts a hand, shakes his head ruefully. Sorry. As valuable as this gift obviously is, still, blowguns are weapons, and he doesn't allow weapons in his home. He delivers a short sermon on the subject, a sermonette, about how the mere presence of a weapon can tempt a man to the sin of violence. A perfectly peaceable man who wouldn't hurt a fly, give him a Finnish pistol, for example, the kind that doesn't make a bulge in your breast pocket, and the next thing you know, he has shed the blood of a fellow creature and besmirched his soul irrevocably and for all eternity.

"Power corrupts," admonishes Clifford Kaplan, and everyone lowers his head, moved and mortified, especially Philip, who meant no harm.

"Forgive me," stammers Philip, and blushes. "I

wasn't thinking." He holds the four blowguns awkwardly, then leaves.

Clifford wonders what Marsha ever saw in the man. A pleasant-enough type, but limited in intelligence. Rivals at school. But Marsha chose Clifford, not Philip, for the prom. And surrendered her maidenhead to him that night. The rest is history.

The patter of rain.

Clifford lights the twelve holy tapers, chants the Te Deum Hatikvah, a lovely, haunting melody, and distributes the presents. For Marsha, a telescope. She is thrilled. "You wonderful man," she says. "You respect my mind." For Trisha, a complete set of Hobbes, leather-bound. "Great, Dad," she says. "I can use this at school." For Josh, the hottest new video game, Zed. "Wow, thanks, Dad," he says, hardly able to sit, he is so excited. Everyone on the block loves the antics of that solipsistic chatterbox robot, and it's educational. "All work and no play," says Clifford to his son, giving him a light punch in the shoulder. "You've spent enough time with your nose in the books."

"I'm turning in," says Trisha. "It's been a long day, and tomorrow we have that fund-raiser."

Clifford kisses her on the forehead.

It *has* been a long day.

The rain on the lawn outside sounds so peaceful. A chorus of whispers. Its message is friendship. Contentment. The earth.

"You know, my dear," he tells his daughter, looking into her blue eyes, "you're going to be twenty-one next week. It's time you started dating. I'm sure many young men, that Howard Clayton, for example, would find you attractive."

"Oh Dad," Trisha says, making an exasperated face. Then laughs and runs upstairs.

Marsha, clearing the table in her Jewish shawl, asks him if he wouldn't mind going to the drugstore for her. She needs a refill of her prescription for those special vitamins-and-minerals she's been taking for her cramps when the twins kick.

"I think I'll walk," says Clifford, because the drugstore isn't far.

"But, dear, it's raining."

"It'll feel good." He likes the rain in his face, in his full, thick hair. Cold rain. Man and Nature. Invigorating. We should all spend more time out of doors. Good for the body and good for the soul. Clifford Kaplan, among his other duties, vocational and avocational, is a scout leader. Has taken troops on long hikes through the thousands of acres of undeveloped, unspoiled land to the east. Essex County. Government parkland. Streams, hills, woods, fields.

Let the kids have a chance to see the occasional deer or fox or bear.

Alone in the rain, he walks down Washington Street and communes with his thoughts.

Passes the house of Bernie Petruzzo, an accountant who works for Burk Brothers. Always jogging, a fitness freak, Bernie. And a teetotaler. On the boring side, maybe, but an exemplary father and husband. And you couldn't ask for a nicer neighbor. The shirt off his back.

Clifford and Bernie see eye to eye on a lot of things. They vote the same. It doesn't matter that Bernie, being Italian, is a Catholic. Catholicism is a perfectly fine religion. So what if they roll in the aisles, froth at the mouth, and speak in tongues? That's their way of reaching God.

Who's to say their way is worse than anyone else's? Clifford looks up at the sky, at the dark-green clouds, low, moving with the wind, full of rain. He is thankful. It is good to be alive.

Another block, and there's the drugstore. The lights are on, even though it's Christmas Eve. The cheerful rust-red sign says ZODIAC PHARMACY.

He opens the door, the old-fashioned bell rings, and the white-headed pharmacist, Captain Jack, waves to him from the back.

"Be with you in a minute, Mr. Kaplan!"

Clifford is always amazed, when he looks at the shelves here, how many different kinds of pills there are. Pills of every size and color. For a hundred and one ailments. And the shapes, too, vary. Some are spheres, some tablets, some miniature footballs or dirigibles.

Of course, Clifford himself has never taken a pill. Never had to. Has not been sick, knock on wood, *cayneh-horah,* a day in his life.

"So how are you doing, Mr. Kaplan?" says Captain Jack, coming up, wiping his hands on his white smock. His crow's-feet crinkle. A friend of the family for years. "Merry Christmas and Good Hanukkah."

"Same to you, Mr. Zodiac. Marsha needs some more of those vitamins-and-minerals for the twins kicking."

The old man nods, goes behind the counter, rummages, whistling tonelessly, through his files and bottles. "Prescription number 97-J, yes," he mutters to himself. Then: "H'm." He comes out from behind a file cabinet with a bottle in his hand and squints at Clifford. A frown-squint.

"Anything wrong?" asks Clifford.

"No, no," says Captain Jack. "It's just that the number of refills on the prescription isn't clear. Looks like a 5, could be a 2. Could be anything. I'll have to call the doctor and check. Won't take a minute." He goes to the phone on the counter and starts dialing.

"On Christmas Eve?"

"I'm calling the doctor at home," says the pharmacist, dialing.

This makes Clifford uncomfortable. The doctor, too, has a family, and very likely at this moment is sitting by his Christmas tree with them, with his wife and children, opening presents. And then the phone will ring, disrupting that happy family ceremony, all because the number of refills on Mrs. Kaplan's prescription wasn't clear enough.

"Look," says Clifford hurriedly, "this'll be the first refill for my wife. You have a record of that, don't you?"

The pharmacist, holding the phone, looks at him quizzically.

"I mean," Clifford goes on, "you could refill her prescription now, without bothering the doctor, and call him later, after Christmas, and in the worst case, if the number is a 1, no harm is done, because my wife will have had only one refill. It seems a shame to bother the doctor on Christmas Eve."

Silence. The sound of rain on the window.

Captain Jack, waiting for Dr. Taylor to pick up the phone at the other end, shakes his head at Clifford, an unaccustomed sternness in his creased, weather-beaten face. "No, no, I can't do that," he tells Clifford, with a look that says, "And shame on you, Mr. Kaplan, tsk-tsk, for suggesting it."

It truly takes only a minute; Dr. Taylor doesn't mind a bit; he asks the captain to convey the Taylors' season's greetings to the Kaplans; and the prescription is refilled, baby-blue pills, an even hundred, in one of those new plastic cylinders.

The price is rung up at the cash register. Thirty-five cents, tax included.

Clifford gives the pharmacist a dollar.

"You don't have anything smaller, do you, Mr. Kaplan?" asks Captain Jack.

Clifford fishes two quarters out of his pocket, receives fifteen cents in change, a dime and a nickel, plus a receipt, stamped paid-in-full, for the insurance company.

"Thank you," he says, taking the package. "And I'm sorry about . . . well, asking you to bend the rules like that. I should have known better."

Captain Jack nods. "We pharmacists must always be careful, Mr. Kaplan. Meticulous. Must check every detail, twice, even three times. I often check something three times. Why? Because we deal with drugs, Mr. Kaplan. And the human organism is, as I'm sure you know, a very delicate proposition. All kinds of precise balances in it. An extra 5 cc of a medicine could be a serious if not, God forbid, a fatal overdose. Yes, we pharmacists have a tremendous responsibility. A tremendous responsibility. Our profession, Mr. Kaplan, demands that we cross every *t* and dot every *i*. Letting nothing slip by. A pharmacist cannot play fast and loose, even for one moment, with the instructions it is his duty to convey from physician or drug company to the customer."

"It is a comfort," says Clifford, "to know that my family can depend upon one who is so reliable and proper."

"Thank you," replies the pharmacist. "And remember: for Mrs. Kaplan, three times a day, one pill after every meal, with a full glass of water."

They shake hands. Kindred souls.

"Good night," says Clifford.

"And good night to you, Mr. Kaplan," says Captain Jack Zodiac.

ABOUT THE AUTHOR

MICHAEL KANDEL works as an editor in New York City. He lives on Long Island, rides the Long Island Rail Road, and has a lawn.

From the original creator of Dr. Tachyon
comes the very first solo Wild Cards novel!

*An alien virus from the planet Takis has forever transformed humanity.
There are three kinds of human now: the Aces, gifted with superhuman
abilities; the Jokers, cursed with bizarre physical and mental disfigure-
ment; and the Nats, never affected by the Wild Cards plague.*

Wild Cards X: Double Solitaire
by Melinda Snodgrass

Now, the seed planted by the people of Takis comes home to take root.
Blaise, Dr. Tachyon's psychotic grandson, has fled Earth and the chaos
he created to begin a new endeavor: the conquest of Takis itself. The
only person that can stop him is Dr. Tachyon, trapped in a body not his
own!

Be sure to read Double Solitaire and all the other books in the Wild Cards series: